ALLIANCE RISING

ALLIANCE RISING

THE STAR GUILD SAGA™ BOOK THREE

BRANDON ELLIS

LMBPN Publishing
PMB 196, 2540 South Maryland Pkwy
Las Vegas, NV 89109

First US edition, July 2020
Version 1.02, July 2020
ebook ISBN: 978-1-64971-069-7
Paperback ISBN: 978-1-64971-070-3

THE ALLIANCE RISING TEAM

Thanks to our Beta Team:

Kelly O'Donnell, Allen Collins, Larry Omans, Rachel Beckford

Thanks to our JIT Team:

Veronica Stephan-Miller
Dave Hicks
Kerry Mortimer
Peter Manis
Paul Westman
Lori Hendricks

If I've missed anyone, please let me know!

Editor
SkyHunter Editing Team

PROLOGUE

SKYE

This planet may be worse than a long, excruciating death, thought Skye.

Skye Vortek, the Space Templars' Grand Master, breathed heavily and leaned against a boulder. He glared at the sunset looming over the line of volcanoes in the distance. Black smoke lifted into a cloud above the tallest peak, polluting a portion of the golden sky.

At the base of the volcano range stood a large city. Flying craft zipped in and out of the metropolis. Tall buildings almost reached the mountain tops, though a statue of this planet's king, Anu, topped them all.

A vast forest of charred, wilted trees stood rooted between Skye and the capital. He brought his wrist to his mouth, his lips nearly touching the gold band communicator. "Sabra, of all places, my training is here?" He peeked around the boulder.

She chuckled. "The monks sent you there. Don't blame this on me, Skye."

"I'm glad you find this comical."

"You've been there for four days, and you complain now?"

"It's not a complaint. I'm observing my misgivings."

"Nice try."

He glanced around the boulder again. Sweat dripped from his forehead, wetting his shirt as if he'd been tossed in a shower.

Planet Nibiru was hot and home to the Anunnaki, the very people that had enslaved his race for thousands of years. It was a practice they no longer held except by the king's rogue son, Enlil. The Nibiru council frowned on Enlil's slave race undertaking. They were slowly dismantling the practice with help from the Space Templars.

Skye shifted his gaze to his boots. The midsoles, toes, and sides were caked in what looked like red chalk. The same soot covered his jumpsuit's legs. He touched his belt and pressed a button. "My body temp regulator hasn't been working for days."

"Part of the training, I'm guessing," said Sabra.

"I figured."

Skye waved his hand over the communicator. "Maps and coordinates." A holographic image lifted, displaying his location, coordinates, and a topographical twenty-kilometer view all around. A pinned point, along with coordinate numbers, blinked two klicks north.

He tipped his head to the side, shrugging. "I called you a little early. You're supposed to give me my next coordinates..." He flicked another glance over his shoulder and around the boulder. "When I reach the pinned point, another two kilometers northeast."

"You just couldn't wait, could you?"

He grinned. "I could wait. I just chose not to."

"Free will. Ain't it a bitch?"

Skye shrugged, smiling. "It's a blessing. Now, do your job."

"All right, all right." She paused. "I'm pulling them up now." She inhaled sharply. "Look at this. Say hi to my dad for me."

He furrowed his brow. "Excuse me?"

"You see the city right in front of you?"

"It's not exactly right in front of me, but yes, it's a good hike. Why?"

A growl echoed in the distance.

"Was that a bonswin I heard?"

"He's been tracking me for an entire day. He's a gentle giant." Skye looked at his forearm. A bloody gash streaked across his skin, a fresh wound. "Well, not so gentle, but I guess if I got to know him, I could calm him."

"Skye, I know you with animals. Finish your training and cuddle with him after, okay?"

"Yes, ma'am. What are the coordinates?"

An animal's sniffs carried across the wind, and heavy feet pounded on the hard ground behind him. The bonswin crept closer, smelling Skye's scent.

New coordinates blinked on the map, highlighting a building in the city. "Zoom in," said Skye. The map rotated, shifting from Skye's current location to a bird's-eye view of the massive structures littering the expansive city. "Anka City, capital of Nibiru."

"Don't get too comfortable there."

"I could never get comfortable on a planet like this. It's ugly."

"Don't tell my father. He'd rip your throat out."

"Noted." Something dripped on his shoulder, then oozed down his arm. Saliva. Skye slowly looked up to see the bonswin standing on top of the giant boulder Skye leaned against. The creature glared at him, baring sharp teeth. It resembled a grizzly bear on steroids with fangs the size of a sabretooth tiger's.

"Gotta go, Sabra." He slowly swiped his hand over his communicator to turn it off. The holographic map sucked into the device and blinked away. He dipped his head at the beautiful bonswin. "Hey, buddy."

It roared and jumped with its claws extended. Skye blew outward and raised his arms, his palms facing the animal. His emotions rushed through him and out his hands, his mind and heart partnering with the energy around the colossal bear.

The connection took like it always did, and he threw his hands in a windmill motion. The bonswin's eyes widened, and its mouth shut. It hit the ground five meters away and tumbled down a slight decline. Rocks cascaded and fell toward the sliding bonswin, slapping and thumping at the creature's furry back.

Skye turned and dashed in the opposite direction, jumping over scorched rocks and black, spindly brush. He dipped his head and gave a silent thank you to the Sight, without which he'd have been dead countless times before. He hurried through the forest, his legs pumping in unison with his arms, passing trees that let off streams of smoke, burnt from a recent fire.

Twenty minutes later, bustling past charred plant life, he jumped over a thin, bubbling tar creek, and exited the forest. Skye's boots hit the concrete at the edge of the city. He rested at the base of a round, rock building, his chest heaving in and out. He brought up his map to find his training's last location, Anka City's capital building—King Anu's home. Hopefully, the guy expected him.

He slid down the building and rested on his rear, swallowing hard. "I can't stand this planet. It's not only ugly. It's hot." He wiped the perspiration off his face with the back of his hand. It did nothing but add more sweat.

He let out a gush of air, recalling his training on this planet, and glad that it ended soon. He had landed on the outskirts of another town, his entry into this world granted by the Nibiru council and King Anu. They would have shot him down if he'd come in unidentified.

Upon landing, VISION QUEST had blinked on his holopad, sent by the monks. He knew vision quests well. Four days with no food, four days with no water. Four days without protection other than the Sight. All the while moving from pinned coordinates on the map to pinned coordinates.

On Nibiru, he had defended himself against deadly sliths, boa-constrictor-sized poisonous millipedes, a pack of wild monsus—a half-hog, half-wolf creature the size of a rhinoceros—and a bonswin.

The sweltering heat bothered him the most. If the Sight hadn't given him the extra energy he needed, death from heatstroke, exhaustion, or dehydration would have grabbed him by day three.

By day four, his meditations led him to the ancients, the long-dead Space Templars Grand Masters. They gave him a message. "You've found the next Grand Master, and with your replacement comes a gift." A thought packet entered his mind and opened with a phrase, "On the other side of fear exists freedom. You are now free."

His heart lightened. "I fear less?" he asked. "I didn't know I had an ounce of it left in me."

"We have lifted the rest from your heart. Death will no longer worry you. You have evolved."

"That's why I'm here?"

"Is there any greater reason? Your gift to the galaxy is to show others that daily gratitude eases an individual's suffering. You will learn more of this on your quest."

Coming back to the present, he stood with his back against the dome building. He dug into his pocket, glad he still had the small, silver coin-like device. He shook it, and it expanded to three times its size. "A ten-day visa. I'm damn grateful today is my last day on this planet."

He walked around the building and onto a sidewalk, a hover vehicle flying overhead. A ten-foot-tall Anunnaki woman jumped when Skye came into view, her hands coming to her chest. He held up the silver coin-shaped visa. "Sorry, ma'am. I'm here legally under King Anu's permission." The woman nodded and walked away from him as if slime came out of his pores.

He held the visa high as he walked from sidewalk to sidewalk, passing Anunnaki businessmen and women. He walked by markets filled with bots selling everything from food to tech. When he rounded a corner, kids his height and build were playing hoverball games on an empty side street.

He didn't see a tree, plant, or weed in sight. Everything in the city was covered with streets, buildings, palaces, and energy stations. The city planners had obviously crossed off any recommendations of adding any semblance of nature.

He took the high steps up tall, wide stairs leading to the capital building lobby. He held up the visa to a panel next to the door. The door whooshed to the side, and he walked in.

Boots clicked on the lobby floor, as busy workers walked by, ignoring him. He made his way to the reception area. He had to reach high to show his visa to a bot hovering behind the desk. The bot scanned it and beeped. "Sir, you may enter the elevator marked fourteen, and head to King Anu's office. He's excited to meet the Space Templars' Grand Master. Welcome to the capital building."

"Thank you."

Across from him were a dozen elevators, none marked fourteen. He scanned the lobby and spotted a lone elevator with fourteen stamped on the doors. He made his way over and stepped inside. He pressed his visa against a panel.

"Going up," said the elevator.

Minutes later, he stepped into a foyer. A Nibiruian marble floor sparkled at his feet, and palace-like columns stood from floor to ceiling. A fire roared in a fireplace across the room. On a grand, ornate table in the middle of the room sat two glasses of mead, one empty, one full. A couch was on one side of the table, and a chair with a man asleep in the other.

Skye covered his nose with his hand. A stench like dead roadkill wafted its way to his nostrils. "King Anu?" Skye bowed, clamping his nostrils shut with his thumb and index finger. There was no response, so he walked closer.

The king had lanky hair and a red beard that covered his face like the fur on a bonswin. He wore a long, purple robe as if he'd just gotten out of a bath. A red smear ran across his forehead, perhaps something the king recently had tattooed.

Skye's lips downturned the closer he came. The ancients had said that fear had left him, and perhaps that's why his adrenaline didn't spike. He reached the King and observed his blue lips, pale face, and closed eyes.

Skye pressed a finger on Anu's neck, checking for a pulse. "No pulse." He dropped his hand to his side. Shaking his head, he glared at a round bullet hole smack in the middle of King Anu's forehead. There was a dry streak of blood from the bullet hole down the ridge of his nose.

"Murdered." He'd died days ago, if not longer. Skye stepped back and lifted his wrist band communicator to his mouth. "Sabra?"

"Yes, Skye?"

"Who's the next in line as the king of Nibiru after your father? Is it your brother Enlil or your brother Enki?"

"Sadly, Enlil is the oldest. He's the next in line."

"Are you seated?"

"No."

"You may need to take a seat, my friend. I have grim news."

1

ALI

Lowell, Michigan—Earth

SEPTEMBER 1946

Ali awoke in her parents' wheat field. The night before buzzed in her mind, and a headache streaked across her eyes. She cringed.

The morning dew stuck to her pajamas as she rolled to the side before pushing to a standing position, her head pounding. She held Sol, Sword of Light, in her hand. Only the Chosen Ones could wield the sword and apparently, life had thrown that in her lap.

She turned in a circle, squinting. She observed a few farms bordering her mom's and dad's farm. Facing her house, she noted the damage on the roof, a sore thumb she created. She'd accidentally shot a plasma bolt through her ceiling, and consequently, through the roof.

The wind buffeted the wheat surrounding her and died down a moment later as if its temper had quickly raised before calming. Similar to the ebbs and flows of anger which consumed her last night when Skye Vortek paid her a visit.

He had snuck into her bedroom, his movements jostling her awake because, at three in the morning, she abruptly opened her eyes.

Eventually, she got to the meat of his visit. Someone had murdered King Anu. "Enlil was the next in line and has taken over the throne on planet Nibiru. Against Sabra's and Enki's wishes, he plans to bring Anu's entire fleet to Earth."

Skye had asked Ali to accept the sword, and her father to accept his Space Templars' pendant, something he'd worn while living on Starbase Matrona.

Ali accepted the sword. Would her father do the same with the pendant? She rolled her eyes and took a step in her father's field. He would.

She took another step forward and almost stumbled from the electrifying pain around her eyes. She managed to stay on her feet and headed toward her parents' home.

Staggering through the shrubbery separating the field from the backyard, Enlil came to mind. *Enlil, you're a piece of work.* She spat on the grass as she made her way to the back door. *You're as evil as evil gets.*

The guy twisted her gut worse than being in the same room as Sleuth and her tech friend, Hank. Enlil reminded her of a child who never got his way. In response, he'd never learned to chill out, or to accept that he couldn't control everything in life, especially other races. He didn't care about right or wrong. He cared about himself, his wants, and his riches.

"A classic, spoiled prick." She wanted to throw more words out, but her mom could be listening.

She grabbed the railing and walked up the stairs to the back porch. Her legs were wobbly, and her headache was getting worse. "Did I sleep in a bad position?"

She eyed the sword. Her intuition told her exactly what occurred. The powerful weapon zapped her energy last night, along with her emotional outburst as she screamed at the night sky. How she hadn't roused all of the neighborhood farms, she didn't know.

She sat at the top stair and lay Sol on a porch step below her. She thought for a while, wishing Daf had followed her to Earth, and maybe William, the doctor she'd met while looking for survivors on Eos.

She grinned. He'd be a handsome boyfriend. She shook her head, then flopped her forehead in her palm. "Don't move your head, Ali," she told herself. She massaged her temple, the headache like a vice grip.

She missed Daf above all. Apparently, Daf had a family back home. The inhabitants of Starbase Matrona now lived on planet Aurora, the Space Templars' stronghold, so Daf lived there too.

She smiled, remembering Daf saving her butt several times when the Anunnaki attacked her ebb mining team on planet Eos. Daf had accompanied her in the Bawn prison cell inside Mount Gabriel, too. She snorted when she recalled Daf hobbling to Din Garum, the city in the mountain.

Ali came back to the present and snatched the sword off the step. She walked weak-kneed onto the porch, swung the house's back door wide, and let it bang shut behind her.

Dizziness took over, and she dropped Sol. Her legs buckled, and she followed Sol to the floor, grasping for the table. She missed and caught the chair, pulling it down with her with a loud crash in the dining room.

She went to get up, but the headache grew and kept her down. "Water. I need water." She smacked her lips together and crawled to the kitchen.

She made her way to the sink and pulled herself up to the linoleum countertop. Leaning over the ceramic hudee-ringed Kohler, she turned on the cast-iron tap.

She pursed her lips and sucked. The water flowed into her like oxygen flowing into someone suffocating to death and brought her to life.

She slapped the faucet off and rested her butt on the black and white checkerboard floor. Mysteriously, perhaps from what seemed like a liter of water she consumed, her headache disappeared. She looked up and gasped, her hand splayed against her chest. "You."

Skye stood between the kitchen and the living room. "If you

learned the art of the Sight, Sol wouldn't suck the life out of you when you get emotional."

She threw a dismissive hand. "I don't even want to know what the Sight is. And I didn't have this problem before."

"You didn't hate as much as hate consumes your heart now."

"I want him dead."

"Many want Enlil dead, but has death come upon him? No. The difference between those people and Enlil is that Enlil doesn't focus on death. He focuses on power and taking what he wants. Do you see the difference?"

Ali dropped her head. She didn't want a Space Templar teaching, especially now. "No, and I don't care. Why are you here? For my dad now?"

He nodded. "With your theatrics last night, you gave us your answer. Thanks for sticking with us. I now wait for your father's answer."

"I can already tell you it's a yes."

"But your mother."

"He'll take her into consideration more than anything, but he's a man of the people, wanting to save every damn person he meets. It's a curse, really."

Skye smiled. "I can relate."

"I'm sure you can."

They stared at each other for an uncomfortable minute. Ali wanted to throw anger bombs at him for insisting on getting her father involved, but the more she stared, the more this man's compassion saturated her.

She calmed, and the moment she did, Skye caught the change and reached forward, fingers extended. "Need help up?"

She pushed his hand away. "I'm not an old maid." She stood and faced Skye. They stared at each other. Ali interrupted the silence. "So, what's new?"

He shrugged and shook his head. "I'm not one for small talk."

"I've noticed."

Skye bowed. "Okay, then. Let your father know I'll be around." He walked out the door.

Ali shook her head. Perhaps Space Templars' customs differed from Earth's. Here you knocked. You didn't sneak into people's houses. Here you didn't walk around someone's home like you owned it. If she mentioned this to Skye, she'd get an entire spiritual view of life, how no one owned anything, and that all were connected, blah, blah. She'd keep her musings to herself.

Ali picked up the kitchen chair she'd knocked over and sat. Yesterday morning she thought today would be the day she'd look for a job. Not the case anymore. A threat named Enlil came this way.

Barely anyone on Earth knew that a galactic storm brewed, an armada wanting to kill countless men, women, and children. She imagined ships hovering over cities and leveling buildings. "Guild damn war." She hated the idea like a poisoned apple, but she'd be in the middle of the coming onslaught, doing her best to stop Enlil.

The stairs creaked. From the sounds of it, her mom Helen headed downstairs. A turn around the corner and she'd see Ali and the sword. Ali grabbed Sol, and it vibrated. She went to hide it somewhere out of view. The edges flamed purple plasma.

"No, Sol. Stop." She relaxed her grip, which usually worked. Today it didn't, and the flame grew brighter. "Sol? What are you doing?"

Her mom entered the kitchen and came to a halt with a start. "Ali, what are you holding?"

Ali turned, Sol in hand and eyed her mother. The flame died down. "What's in your hand?"

Ali's shoulders drooped, and she stared at her feet. She said softly, "I have another mission, mom. And so does dad."

2

———————

EDEN

With the weight of humanity's imminent death off her shoulders, the Space Templars still found a way to kick Eden's ass.

Eden Gaines crouched, her bare feet digging into round pebbles. The small rocks pushed deep into her soles, and an ache traveled up her calves.

"Why am I doing this?" she asked.

"You be less pain now?"

Soft ocean waves gently crashed on the rocky shore. The sun rose above the sea in the distance, its light on the side of the monk's face, who sat cross-legged across from her. His thin orange robe flowed in the wind. Of Balinese descent, he spoke with a thick, but understandable accent. Bald, he appeared no more than twenty-five, but rumor had it he and the rest of the monks training her aged slowly.

The monk touched his heart. "Feel, Eden. Feel. Now, answer question I just ask. You be in less pain now?"

Eden thought for a moment. The pressure points in her soles gave off less pain than when she first went into a crouch, and the kink in her neck from a near death-defying fall out of a tree subsided.

Today's training had been difficult, yet today had just begun. "Yes, the pain is gone. How?"

He slowly dipped his head. "Our Space Templars' technology be grand, yah. But if no healing technology around, you have body technology to heal." He extended his hand toward her feet. "You see? All pressure points lead somewhere to healing in body, yes."

"You're saying my body can heal itself?"

"Only if you know how. Not if you don't know how. Body be self-healing organism if you know how to control cells, yah. To get out of body's way, to fast from food when necessary. If you know how fascia tissue work, you understand body like doctor. If you know brain, intestine connection, yes, you then master part of healing."

For the last several months, Eden had trained in the art of the Sight on her race's home planet—Earth. She liked it here, though she couldn't leave this portion of the Bali island while on this planet. They'd given her strict orders. In fact, seeing anyone else but the monks was a hell no.

"You go lay in ocean. I go, then be back. Heal more, okay?"

She stood and waded into the water, the waves rushing around her legs. Taking a few more steps, she fell into the sea, her head going under.

She pushed through the surface, whipping her hair out of her eyes. Sea salt stuck to her lips, the water cascading off her body. She submerged again and pushed away from the shore; her legs no longer able to touch the bottom. She closed her eyes and floated, the touch of the sea calming her. She wrinkled her brow. "I'm training to be the next Grand Master." She didn't know if luck weaseled its way into her life or a curse. Regardless, she'd make Skye Vortek proud.

There was a crash, and an explosion splattered water in the air. A large ripple struck the side of Eden's face. She lurched away after another explosion, water splashing.

"Hello?" She kicked her legs and swam toward the shore. More waves crashed and slapped her across the face. She spit out saltwater, the taste sticking to her tongue. "Does anyone know what's happening here? Hello?"

The monks didn't have names, so she couldn't call out to the one who had left moments ago. He couldn't have gone far, so where the Guild did he go?

She reached the shore as another explosion went off, this one big. Water washed over her like a whale shooting water out of its spout. She jumped back, crouching on the rocks that helped heal her, their pressure an afterthought. She surveyed the jungle on the rolling hills in front of her as she reached for her boots and pulled them on.

Laughter reverberated off the trees, carried farther and louder by the sea. Three monks stepped through the bush, pushing away fronds and ducking under the coconut trees' feather-shaped leaves.

Their Balinese faces curled into a smile, and one man held a remote of some type. A monk lifted it high as he approached Eden. "Space Templars' technology." He giggled. "For purposes of training, you see."

Eden's nostrils flared. "Why?"

A monk halted in front of her and placed his palm on her chest. "Your heart be beating super quick, yah. You see, one day, Sight be automatic. But to be automatic, you practice at all times, right? Yes."

Eden crossed her arms, eyeing the same monk who sat across from her on the beach less than ten minutes prior. "You told me to relax and to heal in the water. So I did."

"Relax, no. Heal, yes, but did practice Sight? No. Keep practice every day, every moment, and you be more aware."

Eden placed her hands on her hips and took a big breath. She nodded. "Okay, practice every day, every damn second."

They turned to walk away. One of them spoke over his shoulder. "Training isn't over. It's never over."

Eden closed her eyes, breathing in the life force that she harnessed easier each time she pulled it in, the Sight. A wind, different from the breeze outside, tickled her chin. She opened her eyes, lifted her hand in a flash, and caught a rock ready to split her jaw open.

"Good," yelled a monk, his arm extended from throwing. "More." He picked up another rock.

Eden rushed at the culprit. "You could have killed me." Here, training never ceased, and it never ceased to amaze her. These little monks had more energy than toddlers.

"But me know I wouldn't kill. You start Sight. Well done." He let the rock fall from his fingers and went into a defensive stance as she approached. She threw a punch. He ducked and lunged, wrapping his arms around her waist and tackling her.

She rolled on the rocks, grasping his robe, and throwing him. She screamed, sending energy through her arms and out her hands and pushed him meters away.

He landed on his feet and dusted himself off, then bowed. "Excellent. More."

Her shoulders tingled with pins and needles as the Sight warned her of something. She twisted and landed a kick on a rushing monk. He fell and rolled to his feet.

She turned to ward off another monk. His foot met her cheek, and she stumbled. A punch rocked her stomach, and she yelped. She staggered backward in the opposite direction of the ocean and toward the edge of the jungle.

Eden ran and pushed away large, tear-shaped leaves. One student against three Sight Masters required a different strategy. Out in the open had its limitations. The jungle had plenty of places to hide and plenty of places to ambush.

She hurried up a hill, grasping roots and pulling herself until she reached the top. Panting, she spun around. Birds singing and leaves rustling came to her ears, but nothing more.

She extended her Sight, like an octopus weaving its tentacles around trees and reached as far as she could. Nothing. No humans. "Where are the monks?"

A commotion came from behind her, and she twisted her stance, her arms up and hands in fists. No one stood behind her, yet she could make out words coming from somewhere.

She pursed her lips, walking cautiously forward through a patch of grass, her boots crunching the green blades down. She made it to a line of trees that were swaying in the breeze. She pushed away the feathery leaves and halted. The voices were louder.

She tilted her head to the side. About five meters away, a light flickered through a cave opening. She glanced around, her eyes darting left and right. There were still no monks. She closed her eyes and let her consciousness expand into the cave, a red tint covering everything she observed. It was the way of the Sight, the sacred color that brought more focus.

Water droplets dripped off the cave walls, and the ground was empty of foot or shoe prints. The light continued to flicker, and voices mumbled as if in conversation.

She stepped inside the cave. Light danced off the cave walls, high-lighting two human shadows. One was taller and wider than the other.

She crept forward, her footsteps silent—the way the Sight taught her— knees bent slightly, creating less force at every footfall. She placed a heel on the ground and rolled the rest of her foot down slowly, outside first.

She continued this movement until she rounded a corner. Then she stopped and her mouth gaped open. There stood Enlil and, of all people, her mother.

3

SHAE

Lowell, Michigan

Shae bolted to a sitting position, his breaths heavy and fast. He looked around, blinking wildly. "Where am I?"

Sunlight filtered through a bedroom window, slipping between half-closed flowery curtains. Perspiration dotted his body and soaked the bedsheets. He touched his chest, feeling his heart beating rapidly.

He let out a deep breath. The dream was vivid in his mind, a horrendous event that occurred on Starbase Matrona not too long ago. He had shot his friend in the chest. Blood splattered against a closed infirmary office door, and the man had dropped lifelessly to the floor.

Captain Stanley Jenkins. Shae rubbed his eyes and focused on the flowers sitting on a table at the base of his windowsill. Damn nightmares.

Many nights, Captain Stanley Jenkins haunted Shae's dreams. The man's last words echoed in every nightmare Jenkins appeared in, penetrating Shae's skull, like starfighter cannon cutting through an Anunnaki transport. "The entire human race rests upon your shoulders, and you're going to let us fall into extinction because you have some stupid oath to follow? You'll be the downfall of our race, Shae. Just think about what you're doing."

When Stan had gone for his gun, Shae pulled the trigger and ended twenty years of friendship. He'd taken a Star Guild captain's life, a captain he considered his brother.

Shae yawned. "How good is a friend who'd sell out his own race to better his own life?"

No matter how many times Shae told himself that, the dreams didn't relent. As days turned into weeks, and weeks turned into months, new dreams drummed themselves into his sleep. All violent. All memories from his time on Starbase Matrona as the fleet admiral for Star Guild. He and his race had fought for their freedom, eventually taking it back from the Anunnaki.

Humans won. Ali won. He won.

Yet the dreams scared him. He didn't want his memories to change him, to tear his heart out. He feared he'd turn into a monster, and that Helen and Ali wouldn't be safe with him in their lives. The thought constantly fleeced his mind. What if he had a nightmare of Payson Cole, the elite soldier trained to protect the Prime Director, Zim Noki? When Shae pulled the trigger, would he open his eyes with a real gun in hand, and Helen on the floor, dead?

"Helen?" He twisted to look at her. She wasn't there. He pushed out of bed in a start, his eyes wide. Had he thrown her out the window while he slept? Had he killed her and buried her in the backyard? What did he do?

"Helen?" he yelled her name, grasping his hair and pulling. He paced. "Helen?" He halted and went to his knees. "What have I done?"

Shae lurched back as Payson popped into his mind, another recollection blasting into the forefront. The man's hands were wrapped around Shae's throat and Payson seething. "I see now that it's not only Stan who needed to die. You, as well, Fleet Admiral Shae Lutz, need to die."

Someone touched Shae's back, and he flailed his arm, striking someone's leg. Helen gasped and jumped away.

Shae stood, his face slack. "Oh my Guild, I'm so sorry, Helen. I'm so sorry." She put her hands up to tell Shae it was okay. He wrapped his arms around her, apologizing more.

"It's okay, love. Did you have another unpleasant dream?" Helen asked.

"Yes."

"You have to get this fixed."

"It'll go away…eventually."

"Can you see Doctor Walsh? I can set up an appointment for tomorrow. He's an excellent doctor."

For the last two months, ever since Shae and Ali returned, he'd been on somewhat of a honeymoon phase with his wife. They were like a young couple again, not able to keep their hands off of each other. They fooled around in bed and smooched around every corner they could find.

He didn't want it to stop, and these nightmares were stopping things. He could see Helen pulling back more with each passing episode, but these episodes were worse than she knew.

A week ago, he fell off his moving tractor. An Anunnaki starfighter came in view, passing through the Michigan clouds and strafing the wheat field. Dirt clods blasted upward, scattering soil and pieces of wheat in every direction.

When he came to, he was face down in the field. He'd jumped to his feet and seen the tractor head toward the barn. Chasing it down, he caught up, was able to successfully press the brake just meters before it put a tractor-sized hole in the barn wall.

No starfighter came. There was no strafe run and no pock marks in his wheat field. He'd imagined the entire thing. It was as though it had replayed in his head from the war he and the Space Templars had recently ended.

Helen patted his back. "Let's get some food in you before you decide if a doctor is what you want. I, for one, am for it."

The house's back door slammed. Helen stiffened and Shae went for his holstered gun. He didn't find a gun or holster.

"Who's that?" asked Helen.

Shae relaxed, letting out an exhale. "It has to be Ali. Otherwise, your brother."

"Probably one or the other. It better not be my brother trying to steal a Pall Mall. You know he's thinking of taking that position in Florida, and it's making him nervous."

"Let him take it."

"We're floundering, Shae. We need him until we can make enough money to hire additional hands."

"We'll make do."

"We have only a few months of money stashed away. That's all we got left." She reached for the Pall Mall packet on her dresser.

"That smoking of yours is hard on my lungs."

"It's in my lungs, not yours."

"I sniff it just the same."

"Not really the same, but I'm slowing down."

She had taken up smoking after Ali went missing. It calmed her system, and four cigarettes a day was better than lonely Bueller McGavin, their neighbor, who smoked a pack a day.

A month and a half ago, Helen told Shae about the World War and how it changed her smoking habit for a brief time. After the United States' involvement in the dawn of the 1940s, she smoked a dozen on a good day, twenty on a bad one.

Now that World War II had ended, a war Shae had been studying as of late, she'd culled her cigarette usage to almost nil. He couldn't wait for the nil part.

"I'll look for something to cook up, all right?" said Helen.

"Thank you."

Helen smiled, looking him up and down. The side of her lip twitched as if she saw something she didn't like.

"I'll see Doctor Walsh tomorrow."

She winked. "Good boy." She exited the room and walked down the stairs.

He went to his waterfall dresser. An oversized rounded mirror was attached to the wall above it. He pulled a drawer open and stared in the mirror, leaning in. He grabbed folded shorts while keeping his eyes on his pupils. Helen had just seen something in him, something terrible. Maybe his eyes, the gateway to the soul, had blackened? Hardened? Death, killing, and combat ate at him daily, and his spirit was fading away like a dying storm. Perhaps she had seen a glimpse of his drowning soul.

He wagged his head like a wet dog, then calmed, took in a deep breath, and cleared his throat. "Straighten up, Fleet Admiral." He pointed a finger at himself in the mirror. "You're better than this. Be a man." He let out an annoyed exhale and shoved on his shorts. He pulled a white, short sleeve shirt out of a drawer and slipped it on.

He took a step toward the doorway and paused. There, past the door, a note sat on the floor. He picked it up and read the beautiful cursive writing.

"No." His heart sank to his knees, and he looked absently through a hallway window that faced the front yard. "No, no. You're not doing this to me." He flared his nostrils and crumpled the note in his hand. He pushed it in his pocket, gritting his teeth. "I'm not leaving my family."

He pounded down the stairs, hurrying toward his rifle rack. Taking a right at the bottom of the stairs would take him to the living room, kitchen, and dining room, and to the left, Ali's room, a bathroom, and his study.

He took a left and balled his hands in fists. He twisted the doorknob to his study, the chill from the cold brass moving through his palm. Pushing the door open, he rounded the wide and thick desk he bought from the Sears, Roebuck Catalogue. It nearly matched the design for the desk he had in his admiral quarters on Starship *Brigantia*, though this one wood, the desk on the starship made from ebb.

He snagged his Remington off the mounted rifle rack, skipping his Winchester and Stevens Bolt Action. He hurried down the hall for the front door. On the note, Skye had written that Shae would know exactly where the Grand Master would be waiting and to meet him there.

In his mind's eye, he saw the Space Templar on the front lawn, and that's where he'd point the gun. One thing was straight, Shae wasn't going back into action.

Shae passed the stairs, speaking through clenched teeth and under his breath, "I'm my family's fleet admiral now. Not the Space Templars."

4

EDEN

Amed, Bali

"Mom, really? You, of all people?"

Her mom lurched away in a start. "Eden?" She glanced at the tall man beside her and then back at Eden. "I can explain."

Enlil stood, his bushy beard lifting in a smile as his eyes penetrated Eden like a dagger through her heart. His muscular arms, chiseled chest, and mountainous shoulders shook when he chuckled. His voice lowered, and he slapped his hands together. "Yes, Sonya Gaines, please explain to your daughter…everything."

Eden's eyelids grew heavier at the sight of them together. Her chest weakened and felt like it was caving in on itself. Her arms drooped as if fifty-pound weights were attached, and a flash of rage raced through her, sending a burst of sweat out her pores.

"Eden, I can explain." Her mom's raggedy hair hadn't changed since Eden had last seen her when she was a young teen. Though blond, and not matching Eden's dark brown, Sonya's long locks stuck to each other and twisted in braids on its own accord.

Her mom's clothes reminded Eden of the homeless men and women she'd seen on the sidewalks in Starbase Matrona. Ripped in a few places, the backside darkened from sleeping on the black ebb concrete. Her jeans were torn at the knees, and there were dirt and grease stains up and down her pant legs.

"How did you two get here?" said Eden.

Enlil rested his hand on a double-barreled gun holstered at his hip. "Why don't you tell her what we were talking about, Sonya?" His smirk broadened.

Eden turned. "Monks, where are you?" She took a step back and twisted her back foot. She bent her knees, going into a defensive stance, ready to jump the bastard if he pulled out his blaster. Be aware, Eden, she told herself.

Her mother's eyes narrowed, as they always did when about to flay Eden with words worse than bullets. "I hear you're training to be the Grand Master for these Space Templar people?" She shook her head with a knowing look that Eden would lose the promotion and fail Skye.

Eden kept her eyes on Enlil, just in case, but spoke to her mother. "You don't know me, mom. You never gave me a chance to show you anything, other than being your favorite drug retriever."

Her mom rested her palms on her hips. "And you weren't even good at that."

"How did you get here?" Eden glanced at her mom before shifting her gaze to Enlil, his hand remaining on his weapon. Any movement and she'd use the Sight to throw the gun and Enlil against the wall. She should do it now, but she needed answers from her mom to lessen the weight growing in her heart. The answers would weigh her down, nonetheless.

"Well, your mom and I have become close." Enlil winked and laughed. "No, not that kind of close. Just friends. You see, she's helped me understand more about this new potential Grand Master. You know, you. That's something I value. Know thy enemy better than thy friend resonates deeply within me, and anyone associated with the Space Templars are my enemy. Since your mom is now my good buddy, anyone associated with the Space Templars are her enemy as well. Isn't that right, Sonya?"

"You better believe it." She scowled at her daughter. "It doesn't surprise me that you joined forces with the ones I hate the most."

Enlil laughed. "Your mom hates them more than I."

Sonya nodded, her eyes flitting between Eden and Enlil. "Just let her become the Grand Master. If we kill her now, then the Space Templars stay strong under Skye Vortek's leadership. Allow her to become the Grand Master, and she'll screw up the Space Templars like she screws up everything."

Eden physically flinched at the low blow. She shouldn't expect anything less from a mom who had abused her from birth to her teenage years. "You didn't answer my question. How did you get here?"

Her mom snickered. "How else? We flew."

"Bali is a protected Space Templar bastion. No one gets in and out without the Masters' approval. You wouldn't have been given permission."

Enlil raised an eyebrow. "Are you sure?"

Eden's jaw tightened. "There's no way in hell the monks would let you pass."

Enlil waved his hand in the air like a maestro. "Then how are we here?" He dropped it, his lips flattening. "Good, you didn't shift your gaze and kept my gun hand in sight. You're learning well. She might be a good Grand Master, after all."

Sonya closed her eyes as she shook her head. "My daughter a good Grand Master? Not a chance. Give her the reins to this knighthood, and we'll watch her burn it to the ground."

Enlil lifted his hand off his holster and clapped. "So it's settled. We let her kill the Space Templars from within. We'll consider this a game. I give her six months to dismantle them. What do you give her, Sonya?"

"Six months? You're far too kind. I give her four." She held up four fingers, thrusting them toward Eden.

Pebbles underfoot shifted, and a monk walked into the cave. For a moment, calm spiraled down Eden's spine. She turned to see the monk who trained her this morning, the one that set her up. Go into the water, he said. She did, and the monks detonated explosives only meters from her before she fled and found herself in this cave. Did he set her up to run inside this cave too? From the look in his eyes, he had.

He stepped closer, his robe flowing though no wind exited or entered the cave. Extending his hand, palm up, he blew. A force hit her and took her off her feet, slamming her to the ground.

She stood, breathing quickly, and her heart rate peaking. "What are you doing?"

"I'm not doing. You're doing," said the monk, taking slow, cautious steps, like a wild cat ready to pounce on its prey.

"You train me and then attempt to kill me?"

He shook his head, his face expressionless. "No attempt. Death, for you, is a necessity. Your dying is the point of training, yes."

She curled her hand in a fist. Did Skye set her up too? Why did they want her dead? Screw it, she wasn't dying today, at least not without a fight. "Then I fight to the death. Prepare to die in the process...all of you." She clenched her teeth, positioning herself in a way she could see both the monk and Enlil out of the corner of her eyes.

The monk slowly cocked his head to the side. He sized her up, moving his hands in front of him as if he held an invisible ball. "The hardest aspect of defeat is facing yourself, the hardest element of success is looking in the mirror. It's the way of the ego. Let the ego die."

His voice didn't carry a hint of an accent. The Space Templars and these Masters lied just like the Anunnaki. How had she missed that?

"Eden," said her mother. "We'll let you defeat your Space Templars on your own terms, all right? We won't kill you today, ego or not. Okay, honey?"

"Mom, you're not—"

Eden turned and went rigid. Her mom and Enlil changed. Her eyes darted between them, seeing herself, her eyes, her nose, her outfit, her toned body on both Enlil and her mother. Her heart palpated. "What's happening?"

The monk moved closer. "How long will you carry your mom inside your head, inside your heart? How long will you hate Enlil and carry him on your back? The entire journey as the leader of the Space Templars? Do you think that's the way of the light? Do you think the light gives life or kills it? Do you think it forgives or grows anger? Do you think it holds harm inside itself, allowing it to thrash around in its body until it has nothing left but spit and vinegar? Or do you think it shares what is harming it with those who can help release the pressure?" He extended his other hand, palm up. "These are choices."

He blew, and she leaned into the force. She rocked back and maintained balance.

"Good," said the monk.

Her mom's voice roared, "Don't pay attention to the monk. When you do, you forget where you came from. Your roots, Eden. Your family." She ran toward Eden, balled up her fist and threw a haymaker.

Eden relaxed her arms, foregoing the Sight. "Mom, I won't fight you." She bowed her head and looked at the floor. "I no longer give you my power."

5

———

ENLIL

Nibiru

Nibiru's heat subsided as Enlil walked down the stairs, sweat dotting every millimeter of his body. He held a holopad in his hands, and stared at a still image of his brother, Enki, standing in King Anu's, their father's, home.

In the still, Enki held a gun, and King Anu sat on a chair, his arms extended as if welcoming his son back after a long stint away.

Enlil finally leveled out into an enormous chamber, his heart pumping fast. Dampness clung to the walls and air down here, the smell stale as if needing a blast of fresh air.

For the first time Enlil could remember, he felt nervous. He didn't want to kill Enki, but if he did, it would have to be on his own terms—out of anger for attempting to slight him for keeping Nibiru's atmosphere alive. Enlil didn't want to have to execute his brother because he killed their father. That was too easy. Plus, he still didn't know if his brother had killed Anu. One broken vid didn't wholly prove Enki pulled the trigger. Yet as the hours went by, the still vid showed more. On that day, the hour his father had been murdered, the security cams went black. Piece by piece, Enlil's tech team had dragged back the darkness.

Enlil eyed a guard who sat at a desk several meters away from a jail cell. He stood at once when he saw Enlil stride into view. The man was rigid, and like a dutiful soldier, kept his eyes on the wall and not on Enlil. He saluted. "Welcome, King Enlil."

Enlil looked the man up and down. "You can sit." He faced the cell. "Open the door."

The guard pressed a button on the desk and with a clink, the door slid to the side. There sat all of eleven-foot three-inch Enki, his back against the wall, and a smile donning his face. "Brother."

Next to him, and just as tall, stood Senator Gronis. Enlil hadn't jailed the Senator. The man obviously came down on his own accord to visit Enki. "What are you doing here, Gronis?"

"I'm attempting to get answers." Gronis' eyes held compassion and kindness that rivaled Enki's, something Enlil wanted to spit acid at and stamp out.

"Ask for my permission next time. You need to leave."

Gronis stroked his graying beard, the thick wrinkles around his eyes reminding him of his father's aged face. "Your father would listen to my council. You don't. I fear you're taking us to a place that may harm us all."

"I'm the King now. I'm not like my father. I make decisions that keep our planet and our people alive and have done so while under Dad's rule. Piece by piece, you harmed my slave operations while Dad was alive, convincing him I was wrong. No longer will the council override a king." He pointed toward the staircase he'd just arrived from. "Now, I said leave."

Gronis bowed. "Yes, my king." He walked out of the cell, then turned to face Enlil. "The council won't support your decision to invade. I hope you understand."

Enlil's lips flattened. "The military is under my power, so your support doesn't mean much in the overall picture. I suggest you support my decisions if you want to remain in the council and get paid like a councilman. I know you enjoy those riches, and I can take them away with a snap of my fingers."

"Yes, my king." Gronis bowed again and walked toward the stairs.

"Brother." Enlil turned to Enki, his lips flat. "I'm entering, so do nothing stupid." He lifted his coat to reveal a holstered blaster.

"You're always welcome for a chat. You know that." Enki stood.

Enlil flicked a glance over his shoulder at the guard. "Keep the door open. If my brother pulls any funny stuff and I can't shoot him, you have my permission to take him out."

The guard dipped his head and shifted in his chair, pulling out his weapon.

Enlil nodded. "Good. Now keep an eye out for anything." Enlil stepped inside the cell. A bench with a thin mattress occupied one wall, and a toilet sat against another. The walls were black, and a single light hung from the ceiling, illuminating the cell. He eyed his brother. Stripped of his Space Templar garb, Enki wore a white one-piece outfit, more like a sheet with a hole for his head to pop through. They shared the same thick, curly red beard, their eyes both steely blue, and one was just as muscular as the other.

Enki sat on the bench and pointed to the opposite end. "Sit, Brother. It's wonderful to see you."

Enlil shook his head. "I'm fine standing." He held up the holopad, a holographic image floating in front of it. "You know why you're here. And you don't have to be."

Enki tilted his head. "What do you mean, I don't have to be?"

"I'm not stupid, Brother. You let my people capture you."

"How so?"

"Two days after you killed father, you stayed on Nibiru in the home Dad purchased for you. You're a trained Space Templar, and you didn't put up a fight."

"That doesn't make me guilty. I wanted to stay on my home planet for a week or two. I haven't been here for decades."

"Why did you let them take you?"

"To show our people your cruelty, even to your own family."

"You're holding a gun on the day Dad died, and you're in the same damn room as him." Rage boiled through Enlil, and he leaned against a wall, his knees going weak. He couldn't believe the one person he loved most in life had died by his brother's hands. "Never would I think about killing him. Why would you do such a thing? He's our father. Our king."

Enki looked down at his cupped hands. "I never said I pulled the trigger."

"You never said you didn't. Now I have to show our people that this crap doesn't go on under my rule."

"They know you've wanted to kill me for as long they can remember. It won't show anything."

"That doesn't make you innocent, and me wanting to end your life was only words, brother. I never wanted to kill you. But now I must unless you confess your innocence. I'm willing to listen."

Enki kept his mouth closed.

"Are you innocent or guilty?"

"I'm guilty in your eyes no matter what I respond with. You'll kill me to prove a point to our people, just like I'll let you kill me to prove my point. And it will be their own choices weighing on their chests to see the tyrant you are or to ignore your ways altogether."

"You've attempted, and have succeeded many times I might add, to halt my operations from the get-go. You continue to do so to this day. For me to stay my knife from your throat for so long proves I don't want your blood on my hands, and it proves to our people that I have their best interests at heart. I keep them alive by keeping our atmosphere alive." He clapped his hands together. "On Eos, you won. On Opus, you're winning. On—"

"And that's just a fraction of what I've stopped. You have no right to enslave any Being in the galaxy. After you execute me, the Space Templars will continue to stop your psychotic mission."

"You're killing your own race. Can't you see that? Ending slave world by slave world, you chip away at this world's life."

"We have other ways—"

Enlil made a fist and punched the wall. "We've gone over this. The last time we used our own people to mine, they revolted. We have no tech to repair our atmosphere, we have no tech to keep us alive if we live without the atmospheric gold on our planet. We already know what bots get us when they mine, and that's not good enough."

Enki rubbed his face. "If you're worried about longevity, take it internally like I do."

"That doesn't clear up the problem with the atmosphere. No matter how many times we've used our tech to fix the planet, the planet spits it back at us. White powder gold is the only thing it doesn't spit back."

"This is a dying planet. It needs to go to its next phase of evolution. The longer we stay here, the more dangerous Nibiru becomes. The more we keep the atmosphere alive, the angrier this planet gets. Move the Anunnaki to another hospitable planet free of other races. There are plenty around."

"This is our home." Enlil sighed and shook his head. "You don't change. You claim to be the champion of the people, and here you are, trying to end Anunnaki life." He threw his hands out. "You ended our father's life."

"I never claimed to be the champion of anything or anyone. I do what I believe is right, not just for my people, but for every people."

Enlil pointed to the holopad. "Why did you kill Father?"

Enki shook his head and threw a dismissive hand. "Don't bother me with that question."

"Then why did you have a gun in his presence?"

Enki shifted on the bench. "I have a gun everywhere I go."

"Then why wasn't it holstered?"

Enki folded his arms at his chest. "It doesn't matter. Our father is dead, and I'm glad to be next."

Enlil let out an exasperated breath. He eyed the floor, slowly shaking his head. "I just want to know the truth. It's not like you to lie. There's a deeper reason you killed Dad. You don't do things out of spite or anger. I loved Dad. We didn't see eye to eye, but he meant the universe to me. I don't want to be king this early in my life, brother, but you forced it on me. Is that why you did it? To force something so hideous, so confining? I can't do my own work, that of enslaving other worlds, if I'm ruling over all Nibiru, can I?"

Enki didn't speak.

"That's all the answer I needed." Enlil pursed his lips and walked out of the cell. He looked at the guard. "Close the cell and watch him with a sharp eye until execution day. He's a sly one, my brother."

The door slammed shut, and Enlil walked up the stairs, eyeing the holopad. Another still shot came through of Enki taking a step toward their father, gun still in hand.

6

———

SHAE

Lowell, Michigan

Shae took another step down the hallway and stopped. He thought of checking to see if he'd loaded his Remington. Who was he kidding? He wouldn't shoot Skye. Scare him, yes.

Passing the staircase that led upstairs, Shae's eyes swept across the kitchen and to the dining room. There sat Ali and Helen at their new Burl walnut dining table he found in a Montgomery Ward catalog.

"Mom, I know. I know." Ali hugged Helen.

He lay the Remington on the mahogany table near the front door and hurried to his daughter and wife. He rested his hand on Helen's back. "What's wrong, love?" He heard and felt the crumpled note in his shorts when he bent down, a note from Skye asking him to leave his family and join another war. A fire erupted in his belly at the thought, and he bit his lips to keep it inside.

Ali rested her hand on the hilt of a sword that sat on the dining table. "Your Space Templars pendant is here too. It's on my bed, thanks to our buddy, Skye."

"Oh, dear," said Helen, pulling away from the embrace. She wrapped her arm around Shae's. "I don't want to lose you two again. Never, ever again."

"You won't," he assured her, digging into his pocket and pulling out the note. His hand tingled, and Skye lying on the front yard flashed to his mind. He dropped the letter, and the image disappeared. "He's on our property, isn't he?"

Ali bit her bottom lip, her eyebrows widening. "I told him you'd probably accept. I apologize. I don't know why that slipped out of my mouth."

"Not this time." He kissed Helen on top of her head, her hair soft against his lips. He walked to the front door as he jabbed an index finger at Ali. "Don't talk for me ever again, young lady."

He held in the rage that was welling and his tongue from slinging more anger toward his daughter. His always-help personality wasn't her fault. His need to save others had created a precedent his daughter and wife could easily see. With his rifle in one hand, he curled his fingers around the front doorknob with the other. He slowly opened the door, telling himself to be strong and to say no.

Swinging the door wide, he pushed the screen door open. It squeaked like a screaming mouse. *I have to fix that tomorrow.* He took slow steps down the front porch, exhaling.

Skye lay on his back in the front yard, rhododendron bushes in a large patch behind him. Bees dithered about, jumping from colorful flower to colorful flower, appearing as if they couldn't make up their minds. Right now, Shae could relate.

Skye's hands cradled his neck as he watched the clouds. He wore a chestnut color robe that matched his overlong hair. His knees were up, bare feet planted on the grass, boots by his side. "You know, your planet is gorgeous. I haven't been to every planet, just a smidge. When Space Templars took an analysis of the galaxy using a wide range of holocomps, they identified Earth as the most beautiful planet. But beauty is in the eyes of the beholder, right?" He sat up, wrapping his arms around his knees. His blue eyes beamed when he smiled. "Did you know there's more life teeming on this planet than on any other world in the galaxy?"

The man's voice, his tone, and his aura calmed Shae. Shae didn't want to be at peace. He tried to tell Skye off and tell him to never come back. "Aurora is just as beautiful. You should go back and enjoy it for a while."

"Almost as beautiful. You have everything here. All the seasons. As many climates as there are continents, and more. Aurora is tropical, nothing more, nothing less. You fly from one side of Aurora and land at a similar-looking locale on the other. The variety there isn't widespread like Earth. On Aurora, the northern hemisphere and southern hemisphere are habitable. We can't live near or on the equator unless you want to be fried human." He laughed at his own, terrible joke.

Shae tilted his head and crossed his arms, his rifle pointing upward in one hand. "What do you want, Skye?"

"Earth needs you and your daughter."

"Good, because we're already here. You can leave now."

"I'm afraid it's not that simple."

"Plenty is simple on this world."

"Ali didn't tell you?"

Shae shook his head. The screen door opened and, on the porch, stood Helen and Ali. "What was Ali supposed to tell me?"

"Shae," Skye patted the grass next to him, "please sit. There's a lot to explain."

Shae stood his ground. "Give me the quick version."

"Quick?" Skye dipped his head. "I can do that. The king of Nibiru, home planet to the Anunnaki, has been murdered."

Shae pushed out his lower lip and thumbed over his shoulder. "What does that have to do with Ali and me?"

"Enlil, next in line to the throne, has taken his position. Among the many changes he incorporated, he's ordered a sweeping change in policy. No longer is Earth off-limits. No longer will Earth continue without mass slavery if Enlil has anything to say about it, and the challenge is, he has all the say. He's taking his dead father King Anu's, elite fleet and getting ready to invade the very planet you stand on. The only thing that stands in his way is his brother, Enki. If Enlil can get Enki out of the picture, he has full reign and fewer Enki sympathizers in his way, and fewer issues to tackle before invading Earth."

"Those people aren't so dense as to allow one man to make all the decisions."

"They're more patriarchal than the worst governments on your planet. What the king says, the people march to. King Anu was lenient and allowed much say in the council. Enlil shut up the council as fast as he could. The only other person who wields any semblance of power is Enki. As Enlil's brother and now next in line to become king, he can slow things down, even hold them up for a time."

"With Sabra on Enki's side, it's two against one."

"Again, it's patriarchal. She holds no power. Enlil took Enki prisoner and plans a public execution."

Shae's heart plummeted, and a knot formed in his throat. "That wasn't on the note. You just said you needed me to command Starship *Ascension* again."

"Yes, that's what we need."

Shae turned to face Ali. "You knew about this? About the coming armada? About Enki?"

"I learned last night. Believe me, I'm not happy about it. This will be the last of it, Dad. I won't let Enlil take our home, my mom, or you." Her face reddened. "Enlil won't survive. I'll make sure of it."

Skye cleared his throat, and Shae twisted around.

"Shae, we towed *Ascension*, *Tranquil*, and *Swift*. We parked your starships on the far side of the moon, next to our Space Templars' base. Take the pendant and defend Earth."

Shae glanced over his shoulder at Helen. Though tears streaked her eyes, she held her chin high. She dabbed a handkerchief on her cheek and walked inside the house. Ali followed her mother, letting go of the screen door. It slammed shut. Shae let out an exasperated breath and stared off at a few white ash trees. Their green leaves were blowing in the breeze, the soft wind holding a rare summer morning chill.

"If you don't help, many will die," said Skye.

Shae took his time replying. He shifted his focus again, staring at a neighbor's farm and then his. "You know, they use the word pal here a lot. I don't know if that's like the rest of the United States, but pal means friend or enemy. I'll hear a thank you, pal, or a don't take a step further, pal."

Skye nodded. "Which pal am I?"

"You know what pal you are, which pisses me off. You're the good pal. Earth, and all its people, regardless of whether I've met them or not, are my good pals as well."

"You're a rare breed, Shae. It took me years training as a Space Templar to get to an understanding that comes naturally to you. You're as good as they get. When I was your age, I would have considered most I'd known the bad pal."

"At my age?" Skye couldn't be over forty years old and looked only twenty-five. "How old are you?"

"It doesn't matter, does it?"

"I guess not."

"So, what's your answer?"

"I have to do this, don't I?" He twisted his torso and stared at Helen, who gazed through the screen door at him. She gave him a nod, and for the first time, he could tell she knew this was all too real. He hadn't been lying about Starbase Matrona and Star Guild. In her mind, he indeed flew starfighters and met blue-furred, ten-foot-tall Sirians with cat-like features.

"You don't have to do anything. But this is your planet, your home. The fight is coming to you. As far as I can tell, you wouldn't stand by. You'd do everything in your power to save the world. Just like I'll do everything in my power to save the galaxy. Even if you want a way out, your heart is true, it's solid gold. You'll die for humanity in the name of freedom, just like I would."

"I have a family. I don't want to do this anymore. My fighting days are over."

"Space Templars are here for the weak, for those who can't defend themselves. For as long as war exists, there will be Templars fighting for people's freedom, keeping them a safe distance away from constant fear and war. Even though you're not a sworn Space Templar, you're more Templar than me. That's why even though you may decline our offer to help humanity, your soul won't. You'll join us to keep your pals safe."

Shae cleared his throat. "That's some speech, Skye." He gave his house a side glance, as he heard the screen door again. He watched Ali and Helen walk down the steps.

Helen's chin trembled as she reached Shae. She extended her hand toward Skye in greeting. "As long as you have a way my husband and I can communicate, every day, then I'll speak for my husband..." her voice cracked, holding in a sob, "...and tell you for the sake of Earth and all her people, he'll take the job."

7

ALI

Lowell, Michigan

Where West Main and North Hudson Street met, Ali took a left and peddled toward Grand River. Granz Bakery, her destination, stood a few blocks away.

Two and a half days ago, and at around three-thirty in the morning, she and Skye talked. She agreed to help the Space Templars. On the same day, Skye and her father shared words too. Her dad agreed to join the Space Templars' cause as well, to save humanity…again.

Am I safe anywhere in the galaxy? Hell, the real question was whether humans were safe anywhere in the galaxy.

It had been nothing but crickets since then. No Skye. No Anunnaki armada. No Space Templars' ships coming to pick them up or brief them, or show them maps, or talk strategy.

A boy in a striped knit shirt with shorts and a hat took a step on the street. He held a lollipop in his hand, his eyes set on the sidewalk on the other side of the road. Ali rang the bell on her Schwinn bike, and the boy jumped back. She eyed the kid. "Pay attention. No more rushing across the street without looking, all right?"

The boy nodded, then ran across the street without looking anyway. She'd seen that same boy dash across other streets without a care in the world before. One of these days, he'd be on the terrible end of rotten luck. And she was supposed to protect these people? This wouldn't be easy.

She turned into a small parking lot and stood her bike under the Granz Bakery sign. Chryslers, Buicks, Mercurys, and types and models she couldn't care less about lined the lot. She walked to the glass entrance door and saw a crowd of people, all wearing their best church garb.

Mid-afternoon Sunday, and the after-church usuals strolled the store. Wives bought baked goods, getting ready for their habitual Sunday night family get-togethers, and the men and children snagged their favorite cookie or cinnamon buns.

She pushed open the door and looked at a car coming up the drive. Its tinted windows caught her eyes—it was something she rarely, if ever, saw in this town. It's long slick build, four doors, and wide front end bounced up and down when it stopped between two white lines in front of the curb.

She wrinkled her brow, waiting for the occupants to exit the car, though, after thirty seconds or so, none did. "Odd," she said and stepped inside.

"Hey Red," said a young man, Bobby Dawson, grandson to Granz Dawson, owner of the establishment.

Ali waved, not giving him a second glance. He liked her and grinned from ear to ear every time she arrived, and she hated that nickname. Did he ever ask if she enjoyed being called Red? No. Strike one, two, and three. No matter how handsome, the kid didn't have a shot. What was she, ten years his senior?

In front of the cashiers and the few bakers, stood glass cases full of bread, cakes, pastries, and anything else bread-like for a customer's palate. Ali rounded a row of shelves in the middle of the shop and turned to look out the long windows that pointed at the parking lot.

The tinted-window-mystery-car remained in its spot. She couldn't tell if someone had opened the car door and made their way inside, but she figured not. A few people in the bakery noticed the car and gave it furtive glances here and there.

Ali crouched, grabbing at a loaf of red rice bread, her favorite. It was expensive since the rice came special delivery from across the sea.

A hand gripped her wrist. Ali wrenched away and hopped to the right like a rabbit. Looking at the person crouched next to her, she went to stand and froze. Ali's bottom jaw dropped as she stared at a black-haired beauty squatting next to her. The woman had brown eyes and a heart-shaped face, tan skin, and a medium-sized, textbook nose. She wore a plaid, padded shoulder, nipped high waist top, and an A-line skirt that came down to her knees. A pink hat with a circular brim topped her crown, and a white handbag hung loosely on her arm.

"Daf?"

Daf smiled, her lips straightening a moment later. "Some hybrids followed you."

Ali shook her head, creasing her brow. "What?"

"Half-Anunnaki, half-human."

Ali went to stand. "Where?"

Daf held her down and opened her handbag. A blaster sat inside, nothing else. "Don't worry, I've got your back." She tipped her head to the side, motioning toward the windows facing the cars. "You see that car with tinted windows?"

"Yeah."

"They're waiting for you."

"Those are the hybrids?"

"Yep."

Ali stared into Daf's eyes. She couldn't help but smile. "I hate to say it, but I missed you."

Daf grinned back. "I missed you too."

"What are you doing here? To save me from the people in the car?" Ali looked around, keeping her voice hushed. A few customers gave her a look or two, probably wondering why two ladies crouched in conversation.

"I'm here to help you."

"Help me fight the Anunnaki armada?"

"Not really, but if an Anunnaki attacks you, consider them mine." She curled her lips in an almost evil grin.

"You're different."

"I've been training with the Space Templars. I'm one of them now."

Ali looked her up and down, noticing her toned legs and buff arms. If it weren't for the padded shoulders, she'd probably see muscle protruding through her upper sleeves. "You're fit."

She looked Ali up and down too. "What happened to you? You're a little plump in some places, skinny in others."

Earth was paradise and being with her parents and watching their love grow had been heaven. But she'd watched life instead of participating. She sat in bed most days, wondering what the hell kind of job to find that wouldn't feel like an ebb miner's daily grind.

"Well, how do we get out of here, Miss Space Templar?" asked Ali.

"Back door."

Ali turned to a back door with a sign, No Entry. With hybrids in the parking lot, No Entry didn't pertain to Ali and Daf.

"Let's go." Daf stood, holding Ali's upper arm. Daf pulled the blaster out of her purse and held it against her hip. She kicked the door open.

"Hey," yelled Bobby, rushing toward Ali as if he'd do anything to save the love of his life.

Daf turned and pointed her weapon at the young man. "We're walking through here, buddy. I don't think stopping us would be wise."

Bobby halted, hands up and his eyes practically bugging out of his head. He suddenly clutched his chest as his face turned red, and his breaths came too quickly. He bent over, hyperventilating.

So much for Mr. Hero. "Bye, Bobby." Ali shut the door as they stepped into a back room housing ovens, tables, flour, cooking utensils, and you name it. The smell of cooked bread wafted to Ali's nostrils, and her stomach growled. "You can let go now, Daf." Ali pushed Daf's hand off her arm.

"Sorry." Daf looked around. "This way." She curled around a table full of loose flour with a half mound of dough on top. "We've aligned

with your president, you know, the president of the United States."
Daf walked toward another door, picking up her pace.

"President Truman? As in, Harry S. Truman?"

"That's the one."

"They'll help us with the coming invasion?"

"You're catching on." Daf halted in front of the door, glaring at Ali
as if she were a lackey, the way Ali used to look at her.

A shock hit Ali's system like a gut punch. Had things changed that
quickly? Did Ali lose her bold, quick thinking? She'd become a brain-
less nitwit like Daf when they first met?

Daf stopped in front of the door. "Truman has it on record that
before the United States entered some big war, they sent you on an
archaeological investigation?"

Ali nodded. "More or less, yes."

"In the records, it states you can translate languages others can't
translate."

"I feel like I'm being interrogated. But the answer is yes. Why?"

"They found something in a place called Peru."

Ali's eyes widened. "What did they find?"

"Cuneiforms, several of them. They don't know what they say, and
the Space Templars don't know who wrote them. Essentially, they're
unable to translate the tablets. You, however, translated the tablets at
the Madkhal Tomb just before Enlil took you. These recently found
tablets have the same inscriptions, the same codes, or whatever the
hell they're called."

"The ruins of Madkhal."

"What?"

"It's not the Madkhal Tomb, it's the ruins of Madkhal."

Daf threw a dismissive hand. "Same, same."

"Not really." Ali shook her head and squeezed her eyes shut.
"Sorry, keep going." Her archaeological mind crept in, and her archeological ego too. Perhaps that's why she excelled at translating ancient
languages because getting it right trumped 'same, same.'

"You and I are joining Truman's archaeological team in Peru."

Ali's heart lightened. "An archeological dig?"

"It's already dug up."

"When do we go?"

"Now."

Ali crossed her arms. "We tell my mom and dad first. I'm not leaving until they see me off. Plus, I need Sol." She knew the Space Templars, and when urgency came, they went. Now meant right now.

"We already grabbed Sol for you."

"We?"

"You'll see."

Sirens blared in the distance. Bobby or someone else in the bakery had called the police, no doubt thinking Daf kidnapped Ali.

Daf grasped the doorknob and twisted her hand, opening the door. "Let's go."

Outside, and in an alleyway between a shop across the way and Granz Bakery, the tinted window car idled. A man, clearly a hybrid, large and bulky with a square jaw and a hefty beard, leaned against the car. He aimed a weapon at the now open door.

"Dammit." Daf lifted her blaster and pushed Ali out of the way.

The hybrid let loose, the gun discharging. The door frame blasted inward, blanketing Ali with chunks of cement, splinters of wood, and gray dust. Ali fell back. She saw out of the corner of her eye as Daf was thrown backward, her gun pointing at the man.

Daf landed on her back and slid across the tile flooring, pulling the trigger over and over. Purple plasma bolts shot from her weapon, whipping by at a fast pace.

The building rocked and shook a second time. More cement fell like a dust storm, graying Ali's vision.

8

EDEN

Amed, Bali

Eden's mom's fist came down on her. Eden stood, staring at her mom, an exact image of herself. Her mom's fist went through Eden like wind through a screen. Eden felt it, not the punch, but the breeze. Her mom and Enlil then shattered like broken glass. Pieces bounced off the rocks, and twinkled the many colors of an Earth rainbow, glittering, and vanishing moments later.

Eden let out a gush of air, her heart lumping in her throat. She dropped to her hands and knees, sobbing, squeezed her eyes shut and screamed. Tears dripped to the cavern floor.

A monk bent down next to her and rubbed her back. "Good, good. You faced your biggest demons."

Eden continued to cry, her stomach spasming as guttural sounds flew from her mouth out of her own control.

For several minutes, the monk comforted her, and when her cries and sobs lessened, she pushed to a standing position. Wiping the tears and slobber from her face, she nodded at the man. He grasped her in a hug, and she cried more. He gave her back two hard pats, jostling and startling her.

He stepped away and bowed. He motioned with his hand toward

the cave's opening. "All this training is for naught, and is for mere puppies, if you do not overcome your grandest fear—yourself." He cleared his throat and continued. "What did your mom do when you were young? Lots of things, terrible things, unhappy, unthinkable things." He pointed to a wall behind Eden. "Look."

Eden turned and stepped back to stare at a rocky wall. "What do you want me to see?"

"Watch."

The wall faded like a still pond rippling outward. A pixilated screen appeared, slowly moving into focus. A scene formed, and in that scene, Eden could see herself as a child standing inside her mother's apartment.

A ripped sofa butted against a wall. There was a table with three legs and a broken piece from a pallet that acted as a fourth. Cracked walls with stripped paper revealed gray ebb behind the couch.

Eden watched the scene. She looked about eight-years-old. She wore raggedy clothes, her hair disheveled, a common theme her classmates at school poked fun at.

Facing the kitchen, pots and pans filled the sink, and half-eaten food on plates and bowls sat on the counter. Her mom's boyfriends and drug-induced acquaintances looked at her to clean them because Guild knows her mom wouldn't.

"You know your father left because of you."

An energetic punch hit Eden in the heart, and in the vision on the wall before her, Eden's eight-year-old self spun around. There stood her mom, eyelids half closed, spittle on her lips. She wore a bra and underwear, nothing else. Her arms hung loosely at her sides, and her legs wobbled as if she'd slump to the floor as she'd done many times in the past.

And after hitting the floor, her mom would throw her arms to her stomach and wail in laughter. Other times she'd pass out. Eden liked the latter.

This time, Sonya remained on her feet, her face slack. "He wouldn't have left if you weren't born. He protected me. He thought I was beautiful." She took a heavy step forward, shoving her index finger in Eden's face. "You never tell me I'm beautiful. He gave me money to do things, to buy pretty things. I can't have that now." She let her hands rest on her hips, and they fell as if she couldn't hold them up for too long. "Do you know why I can't have them? Because you were born, and even after he left, I stayed to protect you, to buy you beautiful things. What're the thanks I get? None."

She slapped Eden across the face. Eight-year-old Eden fell to the floor and held her cheek. It quickly swelled and throbbed as her mom stomped into the kitchen, yelling, "Clean up this Guild'n mess, you leech."

Eden's lower lip protruded, and she wanted more than anything and everything to run to her daddy, someone she'd never met or remembered. She stood and walked through her mom's angry words. Invisible bullets shot from Sonya's mouth with every step Eden took into the kitchen.

The screen slowly pixilated, crumbling in on itself and displaying the cave wall again. Eden dropped her head, her chest heavy. "I don't know how to overcome my mom's rage, my mom's hate for me."

The monk placed his hand on her heart, closing his eyes and breathing inward. "It was too much for a child to bear. Few had that experience, the horrible moments you endured. But some have, and they have overcome." He heaved in another deep breath, and Eden's chest lightened her energy lifting.

Eden's lips curled upward, her eyes bright, and her tired, melancholy state dissipating. "Thank you."

The monk rubbed his hands together, then tipping his head toward the cavern's ceiling he blew outward as if letting Eden's energy out of himself. "It's my pleasure. The rest of your life must be released and healed by you, and you only. You'll not be a Grand Master until you can overcome yourself and the burdens you carry. Understand this, and you've completed the first phase of your training."

Footsteps echoed off the walls, and they both turned. "Skye?"

Skye halted, placing his hands together at his chest and bowing. "The one and only."

The monk narrowed his eyes. "What are you doing here? This training session doesn't end for another several months."

Skye's lips pressed tightly into a grimace. "Training's over."

The monk walked forward, crossing his arms. "That cannot be. Follow me."

Skye dipped his head to Eden and followed the monk to the cave's entrance. They talked in a low hush. The monk shook his head, and Skye shook his head more. After more shaking of heads, the monk nodded. He bowed to Eden. "I hope to see you again one day." He turned and left, disappearing around the rocky corner.

"What's going on?"

Skye scratched his head, looking out the cave, and then at Eden. "Right." He shifted his thumb to the side, pointing in the direction the monk left. "He thinks you have a lot to overcome and that you should stay and train, no matter what. As acting Grand Master, I have the final say. But do you feel you need to stay longer?"

"I don't have a clue. I've learned a lot, but I hold a lot of pain inside. Regardless, why is training over?"

"I misspoke, which I let the monk know. Your training isn't over. Here, on Bali, it's postponed."

"And?" Eden impatiently waited for Skye to get to the point.

"I'm sorry Eden, but I need you to take your seat on Starship *Swift*. The Anunnaki are coming. We need your presence and your leadership."

He explained Anu's death and the sweeping changes Enlil had thrown across the council, demanding they be accepted. As king, they were.

Eden sighed. "That guy just doesn't know when to quit."

"He's persistent. I give him that."

"I'm to lead *Swift* into battle, then?"

"Not exactly, although eventually. I need you for something else, first."

Sonya's voice entered Eden's mind. Yes, lead Eden. And screw everything up. Eden's eyebrows rose, and she coughed, shaking her head. She did her best to mask her mind's interruption. Her mom's voice rambled on, and Eden touched her chest, trying to stop the thoughts dogging her.

"Don't heed her advice, Eden. Heed mine." He walked closer. "You aren't in training to be the Grand Master to see if you are capable. You're in training because you are capable, and you will become the new leader. It's written in the stars. It's written in your heart. You must, however, find that writing."

Eden's brows drew close, her face tightening. "But you took away my captain ranking when I more than deserved it. Who's to say you won't take away my Grand Master position?"

"A lesson. You became a captain when you were ready to become captain. I took the leadership role away from you, and you got it back. That's more important than losing it, and you're looked at more highly because you learned and overcame that lesson."

"I need more training to become the Grand Master."

"Yes, you do. You'll have to do on-the-job training for the time being."

"All right, so when do we go to Starship *Swift* and my crew?" She smiled at the thought of seeing Jantu, the blue-furred cat-like Being again, and oddly, Nyx, the bad-ass Space Templar no one in their right might should ever mess with.

"Soon, and we go straight to the lion's head."

"Where's the lion's head?"

"Nibiru."

Eden gave Skye a double-take. "Excuse me?"

"Enlil's evil doesn't end with wanting to enslave humanity on Earth and decimate Earth's population. It thrives on his planet, as well. He shut up the council and locked Enki in prison."

Eden flared her nostrils. "So, we'll bust him out."

"Yes. He's scheduled for a public execution."

Eden gasped. "Enlil plans to kill his brother?"

"It's a power grab. He's doing so to instill fear into the public, and to show his people not to mess with him or disagree with his political leanings. If he kills Enki, he has all the power in the government. After that, the invasion of Earth begins."

"What about Sabra?"

"Unfortunately, it's a patriarchal society. Women have no place in government there."

Eden strode toward the cave's opening. "Then let's go."

"Before we free Enki, we'll have a brief chat with Enlil. All right?"

"We kill him."

"No, we chat first. It's diplomacy, Eden."

Eden stopped, a grin creeping on her face. "Oh, I'll have a chat with Enlil." She pulled up the Sight and eyed a wide, thick rock at the base of the cavern wall. She focused, and soil cascaded off the rock as it lifted into the air. She shifted the Sight's energy to another wall, and the rock blasted against it, breaking into a dozen pieces before falling to the ground. "I'll be nice and sweet."

9

SHAE

Helen paced the living room as Shae took a seat on the couch. The RCA TV set's volume was low, and Doodles Weaver performed on *Hourglass*, an American variety show.

"It's been two days, Shae. Do you think they defeated the scoundrels?" Helen held up a fist and shook it as if she were a commander in a Space Templar fleet Combat Information Center—a CIC room.

Shae wanted to laugh and weep at the same time. Staring at his wife, he realized more and more that the time they had together was priceless. Her beauty had ripened with age, and his attraction to her was stronger than when they first met.

She continued to pace. Shae watched her, admiring her strength, and her understanding that he had a higher calling. She'd again keep the farm going while he was away. But their money dwindled faster than he could farm his land.

"Do you think the Space Graplers beat the Ankies? Held them off before they came to Earth?" Helen paused, staring at Shae with a hopeful gleam in her eyes.

Shae laughed. "It's Space Templars and Anunnaki, not Ankies and

Graplers." He laughed more, doing his best to keep his spirits high. These were perhaps the last moments he'd ever see his wife again. Death lurked an Anunnaki gunship away.

She grinned, pointing at him, slightly bent forward. She held her other hand on her hip. "Are you poking fun?"

"Just enjoying your gams."

She pulled up her dress a little and twisted her thigh back and forth. "You snarky devil." She let go, her lips flattening as if something else came to mind. "Where's Ali?" She peeked out the living room window. "It's been hours."

"You'll gain weight with all of those cinnamon rolls, love."

She twisted around and hurried toward him. She jumped on the cushion and began tickling his stomach and sides. "I'll gain weight? Really? You're the one addicted to those silly things."

Shae giggled, pushing her hands away. "I know." He grabbed her and pulled her in, grasping her thigh. He kissed her then and wrapped his arms around her. A knock at the door and Helen and Shae paused. They slowly stood, eyeing each other. Ali didn't knock, and the neighbors rarely did because they never came over. Skye didn't knock either.

"Who's that?"

"Maybe the Space Templars?" said Helen, her hands coming to her mouth. "They've come."

"Maybe. And maybe not." Shae raced to the study and opened his desk drawer. Maybe an Anunnaki or some guys working for him had tracked Skye's movements and found Shae.

He pulled out his Smith and Wesson and loaded it. Walking to the front door, he kept his gun pointed low. He stood back from the door and to the side. "Who is it?"

"Harry S. Truman, Sir."

"Who?"

"The President of the United States."

Shae scrunched his eyes and shot Helen a look. She shook her head. No way would the President of the United States be at their door. Shae aimed his weapon. "I have my gun in hand. Slowly open the door, showing your hands first, or I shoot."

A pause. "Understood. My personal White House police agent, Les Coffelt, will open the door. He'll be wearing a blue police coat and a blue cap with a DC Metropolitan Department badge. Behind him will be two secret service agents, both in blue suits. I'll be in the rear. When you identify these men, and you see that I didn't lie about their appearance, I ask you to please stay your weapon the entire duration I'm here. If I'm lying, pull the trigger. Les will show his hands first."

Shae nodded. "Fair enough. Open the door slowly."

The doorknob turned, and the door crept open. Bare hands came through the opening, and a man with a blue cap and a blue coat, an obvious policeman, stepped inside. Shae lowered his gun, though he kept his finger near the trigger just in case. Two blue suits followed, and one secret service agent nodded at Shae's gun. "The President cannot step inside with you wielding a weapon, sir."

"Then he can talk through the door for all I care. I have a family to protect, and at this time in my life, I can't take chances, even if I thought Jesus was on the other side."

"For Christ sakes, let me inside. This is Admiral Shae Lutz of the United States Navy. He won't shoot me. He's just protecting his family."

The secret service agent glanced at Truman. "I'm sorry, Mr. President, but—"

"Shae, I'm stepping inside. Don't shoot, or you'll have worse things than a dead president on your hands." Truman wedged his way between the secret service agents, who clearly felt uncomfortable at the breach in protection.

Helen inhaled sharply, her hand over her lips. "It's the President, Shae."

"I can see that love." Shae set the Smith and Wesson on the stairs.

Truman extended his hand, grasping Shae's. The man was dressed as if he'd been invited to meet the king and queen of England. He wore a gray suit, double-breasted cut, a tie with tight geometric patterns in red and deep blues. Shae noticed a bulky, thick wedding ring on his left hand. The secret service agents and Les stood still, their hands crossed over their stomachs.

"Can I take a seat?" asked the President. "I have some things I'd like to discuss." He turned, glancing at Helen, and let out a soft chuckle. "You appear to have seen a ghost."

She dropped her hand from her mouth and hurried toward Truman. "I'm sorry. Can I get you some tea or coffee?"

He stood straighter. "Thank you, ma'am. But I prefer an old-fashioned."

Helen looked at Shae.

Shae drew back. "I'm sorry, Mr. President, but I'm a bit old-fashioned myself. What may that be?"

A smile creased Truman's face. "A bourbon."

"Right away." Helen hurried into the kitchen.

Shae extended his hand to the couch. "This way."

Truman took a seat, shifting a bit. Likely, the cushions weren't White House grade. Shae sat at the edge of a rocking chair in the corner of the living room. He settled his elbows on his knees as he leaned forward. Helen walked into the room, a shot of bourbon in her hand and set it on the coffee table, a drip spilling over the edge.

Truman picked it up and took a drink, letting out a satisfied breath an instant later. "Thank you."

"My pleasure." She gathered the empty glass and shuffled back to the kitchen and coming out again as quickly, a cigarette in one hand, lighter in the other. She leaned against the wall at the edge to the entryway of the living room, lifting the cigarette to her lips. Shae shook his head, and she scowled, lighting it anyway. She took a drag and blew, smoke filtering past her teeth and out her mouth.

"I need your help, Admiral."

Shae glanced at Truman and leaned back. "That seems to be the theme lately."

"We know about the Space Templars. We've met with their Grand Master, Skye Vortek, and some king from a small race called the Bawn." He scrunched his nose as if trying to remember something. "I believe his name is King Bilrak. Along with them, a woman named

Nyx of the Space Templars and a blue colored furry cat-looking thing, tall as all get out."

"What do you need from me, Mr. President?"

"One, I wanted to meet you in person." He sat straighter. "Did you know they have these colored, large movie-like screens, and they record everything?"

"Yes, sir."

His lips downturned when he realized Shae knew all too well about vidscreens. "Well, they showed me a recording of the battle our radio frequencies detected in space above Earth not too long ago. You led that battle, and you won. From the government documents I've read, you were a battle-tested admiral in the United States Navy too. And I assume an even more battle-tested fleet admiral in Star Guild." He hesitated. "Is that right? Star Guild's the name?"

"It is."

"Two, I wanted you to lead our forces against the coming evil headed our way. We've seen what they can do, and what the Space Templars can do. We aim to defend our home, just as you aim to defend your home and your family."

"With all due respect, Mr. President, neither the United States nor the rest of the world has the firepower or the technology to fight the Anunnaki. Leave the fight to the Space Templars and me."

"We're training on our moon."

Shae pointed to the ceiling. "You mean, the moon orbiting Earth?" He didn't know if moon meant a top-secret base or a combat simulation room somewhere in the United States, or the actual moon itself.

"Yes, the one up in the sky. That moon. We've been training for the last month, thanks to the Space Templars. They're training a mass contingency of our Army, Navy, and Air Force. We'll be ready when the enemy strikes, or close to ready, but I need someone like you to lead our men."

Shae lowered his chin to his chest, eyeing Truman. "Does Skye Vortek know this? I'm supposed to be leading the Space Templars." Although if he remembered correctly, Skye hadn't specified who he'd be leading.

"Les, can you give us that vidcom device Skye gave us? Apparently, your wonderful wife over there wanted a way for you two to communicate every day. Well, we have that way."

Les walked into the living room and fished inside his back pocket. He pulled out two rectangular devices no bigger than a playing card, and only slightly thicker. "Here you go, Mr. President."

Truman grabbed the vidcoms. "Thank you, Les."

Les made his way to the front door, standing with his hands folded at his waist. Helen took another puff off her cigarette. Truman set the vidcoms on the coffee table. It rang, giving off a nice Bing Crosby jingle. Truman pursed his lips and picked it up. He jerked back, and the vidcom went flying to the floor when a holographic display extended several millimeters off the com.

Shae wanted to laugh but held it in. He gathered the vidcom off the floor. Skye's face greeted him. "By now, you're wondering if what your president is saying is true. And, yes, he's speaking the truth. You should help train and lead them." He dipped his head like he always did. "I'll see you soon." The vidcom blinked off, the hologram sucking back into the device.

"I assume the other one works," said Shae.

Truman shrugged. "I assume."

He took his eyes off Truman and went to his wife. She had tears again, and he couldn't imagine the hellstorm and emotional earthquake she was going through. "We have a way to communicate."

She took another drag, then bustled through the living room. She set the cigarette in the coffee table ashtray, then went to Shae and took his hand. "Then it's settled. They found a way we can communicate. A deal's a deal."

Shae lowered his eyes. "This was your deal. You decided for me."

"No, I didn't. You decided. I only spoke for you."

She was right. He couldn't let humanity live and die under the thumb of Anunnaki rulership, not as long as he lived. He'd stand and fight, just like his daughter.

Truman stood and ran his hands down his suit. "I'm sorry, Admiral, but to make an already longer day shorter, we have to go."

Shae stood and extended his hand. "Well, thank you for stopping by, Mr. President."

Truman looked at Helen and then Shae, making strong eye contact with the admiral. "Fleet Admiral, I didn't just come here to say hi or introduce myself. I came here to take you with me."

"Take me where?"

"We now have Space Templars' technology for a short time."

Shae looked at the vidcom in his hand. "Yes, I see that."

"They're also letting us borrow several of their craft. We're going to the moon."

Shae's eyes widened. "When exactly?"

Truman glanced at Helen. "I'm sorry, ma'am, but you'll have to say goodbye to your husband today."

ENLIL

Nibiru

Enlil sat in his father's home, a cup of mead in his hand. He stared at the fire dancing in the fireplace. He chewed, though he had nothing in his mouth. He stopped, realizing that crunching on anger and swallowing it down didn't fill his stomach.

"You look shell-shocked, son."

Enlil shifted his eyes and glared at King Anu sitting on his favorite chair with a jovial smile on his bearded face. Although smaller than Enlil, he'd never mess with his father on account he'd whip Enlil like a scrawny pup. "It's Enki. I don't understand him, and it angers me. How could someone of our race be so against us?"

Anu leaned forward. "If your mother was alive, she'd teach you two to get along and see things from a higher perspective. Can you do that with your brother?"

Enlil glanced at the floor, the Nibiruian granite shining from the daily cleaning it received from the bots. "I don't want to kill him."

"Then don't."

He narrowed his eyes, blowing wind past his lips. "His ways would ruin our race, and even though he's blood, I can't have him killing our people by changing the council's mind with his trivial ideas. He thinks that we need to change, to leave Nibiru, and—" He threw his hands in the air, cutting himself off.

"Maybe we should leave. Maybe our planet has had enough of us."

Enlil shot his father an angry look. "No. She loves us."

"Perhaps, but we'll never know. We haven't been kind to her."

"We are now."

"It might be too late."

Enlil emphatically shook his head. "I don't know." He bounced his head up and down, a thought coming to mind. "Earth."

"Why Earth?" Anu leaned back, resting his head on the headrest. "There are plenty of uninhabited planets in the galaxy."

"Earth is close to our system. It's the fastest route to any planet we know that caters to life. Life thrives there. It's the most beautiful planet I've seen. After we invade, after we decimate the population and enslave the survivors, we could live there."

"But, humans, son. Humans belong there. Not us."

"They don't have to belong there. We set nothing in stone."

"You know you wouldn't leave Nibiru or take our people to any other planet. You love it here. That's where you and your brother differ."

"I think clearly for my race. He doesn't."

"Or perhaps he has his race and other races in mind. I believe he thinks we're all one, working together, making the galaxy better."

"That's where he's wrong. If we didn't dominate on so many levels, the Graxic, the Reptilians, the you-name-its, would dominate us. You and I keep the Anunnaki alive. I fear what will happen if I die. I fear Enki would step up as king and dismantle what you created—our military strength, our leaders, and our way of life."

"The galaxy is changing. As history shows repeatedly, those who were in power in the past aren't anymore. Ebbs and flows, son. Ebbs and flows."

"Are you saying the Graxic and the Reptilians will lose power?"

"It's the way of history."

"Will we?"

"I don't want to have to repeat myself, son."

Enlil bit the inside of his cheek. "Did Enki kill you?"

Anu stared at him for a few moments then faded, slowly vanishing. All that remained of his father was the chair he died upon.

Enlil threw the cup against the far wall, smashing it into pieces. The mead splattered on the floor and dripped from the wall. Ever since his father died, he had hallucinated conversations with him. It never went his way, and he never felt calm afterward.

He rapped his knuckles on his head. "Why did you do it, brother? Why did you kill our father?" He still didn't have proof. He hated Enki, but not enough to kill him. He wanted the holovid of Enki to show his brother's innocence. Although killing him had littered Enlil's brain for years and years, they were passing thoughts, not based in reality.

But reality was a bitch. He stood and tapped on his shoulder com. "Kamina?"

"Yes, Enlil?"

"Move Enki's execution up four hours and let the public know." Maybe that will get Enki to talk and spill the truth.

"Yes, sir."

ALI

Lowell, Michigan

The smoke cleared. Ali lay on her side and turned, reaching for Daf. "Find cover."

Daf didn't. She stood and walked forward. Police sirens came closer, reminding Ali that someone called the cops not too long ago. They needed to hurry and get out of here.

Daf walked through the dust cloud and spit on the floor, her lips in a contorted, silent growl, her gun extended. More bolts expelled from Daf's blaster as she jumped through the hole in the wall. She landed athletically in the alley, her boots clicking on the black asphalt.

Ali picked herself off the floor and waved her hand to see more clearly through the dust. The man who took aim, the piece of ebb who blasted half the bakery wall to pieces, lay face down, blood pooling around him.

A car screamed forward, skidding, its tires spinning and smoking down the alleyway. Daf targeted the back of the car.

Ali rushed toward her and pushed Daf's arm down. "Bystanders."

The car rounded the corner and disappeared, the sound of its engine fading the farther it drove away. Directly across from the alleyway was a road where children stared at Daf and Ali from a side-walk, spellbound.

Sirens roared louder.

Daf hid the blaster in her handbag. "Good eye, Ali."

Ali swallowed hard, not wanting to imagine what might have happened if Daf held down that trigger. "Are humans safe anywhere in the galaxy?" asked Ali, voicing a thought she had less than an hour ago. She didn't need an answer, but Daf shook her head, anyway.

"Not really," Daf said. "But we're working on it."

Ali grinned, giving her a friendly kick. Nice and soft. "Look at you, Space Templar and all."

Daf eyed the kids, her lips straight as if calculating the potentially fatal accident had Ali not intervened and lowered her weapon. She dropped her gaze and drew in a calming breath. "And you, Ali, need to shut up." There was a sarcastic tease in her voice.

Ali giggled. "Nope, I won't shut up."

"Would I think otherwise?" She gently jabbed Ali with her elbow. "No one orders Ali around."

More sirens carried across the air. The police would be here any minute. A car entered the alleyway behind them, and Ali spun on her heels. A red Ford coupe, with a rounded hood, and a semi-domed roof. Ali grasped Daf's arm to pull her.

Daf stood her ground, pushing Ali's hand away. "This is a friendly." She took a step toward the car, throwing a disgusted hand outward. "CJ, I told you to park out back, right here. Because you didn't, we almost got ourselves killed." She pointed to the destroyed wall.

The car parked and a young, sturdy man in a fedora hat, wide-collared green shirt, high waisted pants, and two-toned, black and white shoes, opened the car door. He dipped his fedora. "Howdy, ladies." He winked and cracked a smile. "I've wanted to say that ever since I got here on this planet and watched your TV shows."

Daf glanced at Ali. "Get in."

Ali walked forward and nodded at the man. She opened the back door and slid in next to Daf.

"What am I, your chauffeur?" said CJ as he sat in the driver's seat.

He looked at Ali through the rear-view mirror, a half-grin popping on his lips.

Daf looked behind her through the back window. "Yep and the cops are coming. So press on the gas."

CJ turned, his eyes on Ali. "I'm CJ, Space Templar extraordinaire. I helped you all defeat the Anunnaki and save your—"

Daf slapped his hand. "Go, go."

CJ rolled his eyes. "It's not like we couldn't take them."

Daf shoved his shoulder. "They're cops. Not people you want to shoot, bang-bang, and walk away. They're the law here, and most of them are probably good people. Now drive."

CJ held his thumb up. "All right. I'll drive." He drove slowly out the back alley and turned in the opposite direction the hybrids had gone. He took a left down West Main as police cars passed by, screaming down the other side of the road.

Ali peered out the back window and saw the cops pull up to Granz, some cautiously getting out of their cars, pistols in hand. She faced the front. "We need to stop at my mom's house."

Daf shook her head, pursing her lips. "Sorry, sister. No can do."

"If hybrids are on this planet, then my mom and dad need protection."

"And I told you we, the Space Templars, were already there, grabbed your sword, and are making sure your mom and dad will be fine."

Ali squeezed Daf's wrist, her jaw clenched. "Take me to my Guild damn mom's. I need to say goodbye."

Daf's strong demeanor changed, her eyes softening. "I'm sorry, Ali. We can't. Your government's archaeology team needs to leave. We're heading to the airport. They took a special trip here just for you."

Ali pointed to her chest. "I'm the one doing them a favor. I'm the one who'll decode these tablets. I think they can wait an extra half an hour."

"For the sake of humanity, for the sake of your mom, don't argue and just trust me." Daf shifted in her seat, her face turning red. She glanced out the side window. "Plus, we have a tactical team stationed around your mom's neighborhood, and two people at your farm at all times. We have trespassing and trip sensors everywhere. Anyone comes within a kilometer radius of your mom, and we don't like their smell, we'll deal with them. Your mom will never know."

Ali huffed. They had the bases covered, she'd give them that. She shook her head, doing her best to settle the nerves blistering her stomach. Her dad would be fine. Her mom, she didn't know. "Are you sure?"

"Positive."

Ali bit her lower lip, squeezing her eyes shut. "Fine, proceed."

CJ looked over his shoulder. "Are you sure you two are good friends? The way Daf talked about you, Ali, it's as if you two have the greatest friendship in human history."

Ali gave Daf a happy pat on her cheek. "It's a love and hate relationship. We don't know what we'd do without each other." Since Ali had left planet Eos, she'd thought of Daf every day, figuring Daf had done the same.

"Sadly, Ali's right. But I'm glad she's who she is," said Daf. "I don't know what I'd have done had I not met her."

CJ made a face. "Okay, enough of the sappy talk." He turned down a street. Factory buildings, ugly and dilapidated, lined the road.

Ali eyed the area. 'This isn't an airport, or in the airport's direction. Where are we going?"

CJ turned into a factory parking lot and drove to the side, heading around to the rear of a building. The place looked vacant. Ali had never explored this area of the city, so she didn't know how long these buildings had been empty. Decades, maybe.

"I didn't say we were going to a city airport. We've created a makeshift airport of our own," said Daf.

Ali followed her eyes and leaned forward, lifting off the seat a bit. "An airplane."

She didn't know much about airplanes, other than they seemed a slow, bumpy ride to a destination. They were nothing like Space Templars or Star Guild technology.

This one had propellers, another strange apparatus used on a plane. Painted in Army green, it looked like it could hold fifty passengers, maybe more. It sat on a long stretch of concrete. Stairs went from the plane's door to the ground. But planes had to gain speed to take off. She eyed the short make-shift runway and wondered how the plane had landed, and if it needed more room to speed up and lift off.

CJ stopped next to two cement steps with a metal railing that led to a factory door. Next to them were two government-marked vehicles similar to their car. Ali mused that by chance, Daf and CJ, and probably other Space Templars posing as Earthlings, were given this car's make and model by the government. CJ turned off the engine and stepped out of the car, opening the door for Ali.

"Before we go inside, I need to explain something to you," Daf began. "Keep your eyes peeled for anything unusual. I don't know if the Anunnaki hybrids got to these government agents before us and are using us for information when we get to Peru."

Ali shrugged. "This is the government. How good can they be?"

"I'm hoping they want to save their people and their planet."

"But in saving it, what are they taking away from everyone?" She took CJ's hand and stepped out of the car. "Don't worry about me. I have a hard time trusting people as it is, and the government is not an exception. I've learned my lesson the long and hard way."

Five years ago, the Anunnaki took her from Earth, wiped her memory, and lied to her for years. Eventually, she discovered that the Starbase Matrona's governance had many hands dipped into the chest of gold-covered lies too, dipped in milk chocolate deceptions. Telling her to trust the government was like telling her to trust a snake ready to strike. Not a chance.

Daf scooted out of the car and walked toward the steps leading to the door. "They'll brief us inside. Then we head to Peru."

"We need weapons. Just in case," said Ali, following Daf.

CJ patted his shirt. "I'm all you need."

Ali shook her head. "We need more than just you."

"CJ can take down ten men, no problem. I can take down five. Plus, we're not allowed weapons."

"What do you mean we're not allowed weapons?"

She shrugged. "It's what the archaeologists demanded."

Ali stopped. "Sol?" She eyed the car. "Where's my sword? You said you had it. Why bring it if I can't use it?"

Daf stopped in front of the short staircase, her voice a whisper. "Yes, and it's in a certain carrying case. They won't know it's a sword, so don't let them in on it."

Ali held her hands up, chest high, palms out. "Yes, mother."

"Good." Daf's lips slowly curled into a smile at Ali's quick, verbal jab. "Skye had someone come with the archeology team to the factory building, but only to observe. He won't go on the trip to Peru with us. He's one of Skye's allies, apparently astute with incredible observation skills. He can smell a rat before a rat can smell itself."

"Who?"

"Some guy named Albert Einstein. No idea who he is. Maybe someone high in the military."

CJ walked around Daf and opened the factory building's door. "Our mission begins."

Ali winked at him. "So it does."

EDEN

Starship Swift

Eden ran her finger over the navigation console. It'd been months since she'd stepped inside and walked around Starship *Swift*. The ship's beauty still mesmerized her.

A day ago, Skye stole her from training, but for good reason. She'd do everything in her power to save Enki, and to stop the coming war. Skye had escorted her in a Space Templar transport to the far side of Earth's moon, where they docked with *Swift*.

"You done gawking at the ship? You act like you've never been inside her before, Captain."

Eden turned and caught a wink and a smile from Nyx. The blonde-haired, blue-eyed woman sat at the helm, and had for the last few hours, ever since they'd left Earth and headed toward the Solar System's middle planets. They'd jump to their final destination soon.

Eden shook her head, letting out a soft chuckle. "I could never get enough of *Swift*."

It was good to see Nyx. They rarely saw eye to eye, but ever since Eden became the captain, Nyx had fallen in line. Their arguments ceased, and Nyx helped more and didn't roll her eyes at Eden like she used to.

It had been Nyx who put Eden in the captain's seat after Skye had taken the position from her. Past Nyx's hard exterior, loyalty dwelled deep. Eden realized that even though Nyx gave her a hard time, she had rooted for Eden nonetheless.

Eden eyed the vidscreen, seeing the black expanse dotted with stars. "When are we ready to jump?"

"NMJ drives are charging. Give her more time." Nyx stood from her seat and took a step toward Eden. "I have a present for you."

Eden straightened her lips. "You do?"

Nyx motioned with a cock of her head toward Jantu. "You got it, buddy?"

Jantu reached under his station's desk and hugged a long and thin box to his chest. Red paper decorated with green trees, gold bells, and snowflakes was wrapped around the item, an obvious Earthling design.

Jantu handed it to Eden, his lips not moving, though his words entered her mind. "Nyx purchased the box and wrapping paper at a store called Macy's during her first excursion to Earth a month back. But inside isn't from Earth. It's a Space Templar—"

"Shut it, Jantu," came Nyx, her face like stone, an eyebrow lifted as if telling the blue-furred Sirian not to let Eden in on the surprise, or else.

Jantu bowed, then sat, legs crossed. He rested his elbows on his knees, chin on his intertwined fingers.

Eden unwrapped the gift to reveal a cherry-red stained wooden box. She opened the box and eyed a bow, no arrows. Her eyes widened, and her lips drew upward. The bow, silver and inlaid with black, gleamed from the bridge's ceiling lights. Eden glanced at Nyx, her mouth open. "Mine?"

Nyx gave her a nod. "I heard you were mastering the bow and arrow. I had Space Templar tech make this for you, though it's my design. Touch it and give it your energetic signature."

Eden curled her fingers around it, and the top and bottom end sucked in toward each other. A snap and Eden pulled her hand back in surprise. The bow was a quarter of its original size, the string somehow shrinking. "What the..."

"I have plenty of arrows in my quarters to give you, plus a magnetic holster belt to store them."

"A holster belt?"

"You'll see what I mean when I give it to you."

Eden's smile grew. "Thank you, Nyx."

"My pleasure."

Skye entered the bridge, his long robe flowing with every quick step he took. "Eden, I know we're jumping soon, but I need to show you something before we initiate NMJ drive operations." He stopped in front of Eden, eyeing the box and the bow inside. "Glad you got what you deserve. Congratulations." He gave Nyx a side glance. "Looks like you'll have some competition."

Nyx snorted. "I'm sure Eden is good, but not Nyx good."

"We'll see." He gestured where he'd just entered from. "Eden, can you accompany me to the brig?"

"Sure, why?"

"More training, something the monks wanted me to do for you."

She tossed a look at Nyx. "Run the bridge while I'm gone."

"Aye, Captain."

Eden set the bow on the captain's chair and followed Skye out and down several corridors to an elevator. They stepped onto the elevator platform without saying more than a word to each other the entire walk. Eden couldn't take her mind off of freeing Enki. She wanted to crush Enlil and his selfish plots. Skye, on the other hand, whistled a tune.

On the lowest deck, the elevator opened, and they made their way to a door guarded by several Space Templars. Skye swiped his hand in front of a control panel, and it slid open. Chairs, tables, and desks with guards and brig workers littered the room.

A guard strolled by, holopad in her hands. Skye gestured to her. "I'm here to see Ted Bays, otherwise known as Sleuth."

The guard stopped and gave a hand signal to a man at a desk by another door. She gave him a nod. A soft buzz, and the door that led deeper into the brig opened.

"Anything else, Grand Master?"

"No, thank you."

Eden tilted her head. "Sleuth?"

"Yes."

The guard at the desk motioned that Skye and Eden could proceed. Eden pinched the skin at her throat. "Why the hell is Sleuth on this ship?"

"Just in case we need him, and apparently, the monks think you need him even more right now."

None of this made sense, but she'd learned early on that even things made little sense with the Space Templars, they eventually would. They walked through a narrow corridor, the walls glowing a beautiful bluish-white hue. "*Swift*, why didn't you tell me about this?" Ever since Eden met Starship *Swift*, the craft never hid a thing from her. She'd kept Eden in the know, except today.

I'm sorry, Eden. I was under the assumption that you were privy to his presence.

Eden halted, her arm coming to Skye's shoulder. "Now, stop. Why am I meeting with him?"

"We're here." Skye motioned with his hand at a wall. The wall rippled, much like the cave wall she'd seen no more than a day ago. It slowly vanished, and in its place sat Sleuth, drinking red mead from a glass and watching a movie vid on a holodisplay. He leaned back in a comfortable seat, his feet up on a footrest. Strangely, Sleuth's balding hair wasn't so bald anymore, his pale skin not so pale, and he didn't wear glasses.

Eden continued to watch the piece of crap behind the thin screen. Sleuth couldn't see Eden and didn't have the powers of the Sight to sense her, so he remained lazy in his chair.

"Why does he look healthy?"

"A healthy diet and lack of stress can do that to a person."

Eden touched the top of her head, feeling her hair. "But his hair. He's growing it back?"

"Space Templars' technology. Nothing difficult. He'll have a full head of hair in two months." He reached forward and touched the screen separating them from Sleuth. The screen disappeared.

Sleuth dropped the mead, the glass shattering on the ground. He stood, wiping the red splatter off his lower pant legs. "You startled me." He gave a double-take, then paused. "Eden?"

The Space Templars' technology must have helped Sleuth's eyesight, something Star Guild and Starbase Matrona scientists claimed couldn't be reversed. Another obvious lie in a technologically advanced society. They had done well, dumbing-down Matrona citizens.

Eden gulped. "Close the screen."

Skye did, cutting Sleuth off from viewing them. The weasel wouldn't be able to hear Skye and Eden talk either. Sleuth shrugged nonchalantly and sat back down, more worried about his pants than the intrusion.

Eden faced Skye. "Why?"

"You're to train him, hence, part of your training."

Eden threw her hands out. "Train? What could I possibly teach that guy? He's a head full of ego and a traitor to boot." Her gut tightened, remembering her reaction when she found out Captain Diana Johnson was a traitor. Eden had almost pulled the trigger on the Star Guild captain before the captain could get a word in edgewise.

"He's a Space Templar asset. With all that we know about the Anunnaki holocomp systems, he knows more. That's his gift. All that he knows he keeps to himself, so we need you to turn him to our side. He could literally turn the tide of battle like he did last time. He's not only wanted, but he's also needed. If he works for us, fewer people die. It's that simple."

"Fine. Once we grab Enki, I can start charming Sleuth, but right now, I won't spend my time making this guy my friend. We'll be in Nibiru's system in what, a day's time? I have a ship to captain."

Skye crossed his arms, a twinkle in his eye. "Monk's orders, not mine."

"Screw monk's orders."

Skye's eyes widened, and he leaned forward, no doubt a little taken back by her response. "You're to train as our next Space Templar Grand Master. We never screw with monk's orders. All, and I mean all, the monks have been Grand Masters at one time or another."

Eden's mouth hung open. "What? They never told me that."

He smiled. "Yes. Now, get to training."

Eden held in a sigh, doing her best to take in this new test the monks threw her way. She'd made an oath with them when training started. Whatever came her way, she'd look at it as an opportunity, a lesson, a jump in her experiential intelligence, bringing to her a higher consciousness, the path of a Grand Master. She blew out spent air. "I'll do whatever needs to be done, even with Sleuth, a man who'll flip and flop as it suits him. The only side he's on is his own."

"Change that. Flip him to the helpers. To the light."

"I'll do my best."

"I hope you'd do that with everything."

"You know what I mean." Eden pressed on the screen. It dissipated, and she walked into the room. She sat on a chair across from Sleuth, who was still working on cleaning his pant leg.

Eden cleared her throat, glimpsing Skye over her shoulder before glancing back at Sleuth. "Hi, Sleuth." She fought against smiling, though she did anyway.

"So, the new captain has joined the Space Templars ranks again. I heard you've been training." He rubbed his eyes and yawned, making his way to a couch. He lay on it, intertwining his fingers behind his head and staring at the ceiling. "Are you here to fetch my order?"

Eden scrunched up her brow. "Order?"

"Yeah, I'm hungry. Out here, I never know if it's breakfast, lunch, or dinner time. But I'm hungry for lunch."

Eden stood, ready to exit the brig and get back to captaining the ship. Skye breathed in, eyeing Eden. Eden caught his distaste, and she sat back down. "Well, no, Sleuth, I won't get you lunch. I'm here to see if you can help us."

"To join you. Yes, you all want the smarts in my brain."

"We want you, the entire you."

"I helped you defeat the Anunnaki when they tried to invade Earth, and then boom, I'm thrown in the brig. An interesting game you guys play."

Her face reddened, and she kept her voice low, but sharp as an arrow. "You tried to kill the damn human race. They charged you with conspiracy to murder, along with wanting to commit genocide by helping Enlil's agenda. On Starbase Matrona, that'd be a death sentence in a millisecond. You're lucky you're still alive, Sleuth."

"Tit for tat." He threw his hand in the air as if none of it mattered.

Eden breathed deeply, quelling her anger. "What can we do to show you we want your help, that we want to be friends with you, and that we want you free of this cage you're in?"

"Your gun."

Eden paused, eyeing Sleuth, who continued to stare at the ceiling. "My gun?"

He shifted as if trying to get more comfortable. "I didn't stutter, lady. Yes, your gun."

"What will you do with my gun?" She touched the gun holstered by her hip.

"It shows me you trust me."

"You'll shoot me."

"And there's that."

"There's what?"

"You don't trust me, so why does any of this matter?" He threw his hand toward the exit. "You can leave now."

Eden stood and marched out of the room. She ran her hand over the jail cell's entryway, and the screen materialized, blocking her and Skye from Sleuth's view. She widened her stance. "He's a wasted asset."

"There's no waste in the Universe."

"Okay, understood. But he won't help us." She flicked her hand on the screen. It changed to a wall.

"Don't cut yourself short."

"I'm not cutting myself short. I'm stopping the inevitable. He won't help us."

"He will. And you'll be the one to get him to."

Eden glanced at the walls, the ceiling, anything to keep her eyes away from Skye's. Finally, she stared into his steely blues. To her, priority one was retrieving Enki, not fixing Sleuth. "Again, I understand that you want what's in Sleuth's mind. I don't think we'll get it. So, I'm focusing on what's most important—grabbing Enki and getting back to Earth to defend her."

"We'll be planet side on Nibiru tomorrow, and there you'll have plenty to keep your mind off of Sleuth. And I mean plenty."

"I figure my mind will be off of him in minutes, if not sooner."

"I'm afraid not." He turned and walked down the corridor toward the brig's main room. "We're bringing in another bed in your berthing quarters. You'll bunk with Sleuth."

Eden went after him. "What? You're joking, right?"

"Part of your training."

Eden stopped, bug-eyed, and watched Skye walk out of the brig. She shook her head and looked down. "Damn monks."

I 3

SHAE

Groom Lake, Nevada

The stifling heat radiated through Shae's body. The blistering temperature inside the warehouse sucked the water out of his pores and soaked his shirt. He touched the Space Templar pendant hanging from his neck. Oddly, it didn't soak up heat like everything else he wore.

He took off his denim coat, rolled it up, and held it in front of him at his waist. He wished he could drop the additional heat source, his coat, to the floor instead of holding it. He'd even contemplated taking off his shirt, pants, and underpants, but going in the buff wouldn't be appropriate, not that he had ever done such a thing or considered it before. Had this not been a gathering of top political types, high military brass, and the President of the United States himself, he would have arrived in shorts and a shirt.

He looked around for water, noting that several men in the warehouse seemed to be doing the same. Michigan never gave off this much heat, not even during its hottest summers.

The President dabbed his forehead with a handkerchief. "Sorry about this, Admiral. It's God-awful in here, and the Joint Chiefs of Staff are thinking of purchasing this land. The Air Force has dibs. Can

83

you imagine? Who'd want to train men here? They'd dehydrate to death."

"I agree." Shae eyed two Space Templar transports parked inside the colossal structure. The craft were tear-shaped, wide at the bow, pointed at the stern. Boosters were attached to each side of the ships, making them look bulkier.

Above the craft, long and wide lights hung in rows from the warehouse ceiling, giving off a monotonous buzz. The lights lit the entire place, shining brightly on each man who gazed at the ships before them. They gawked because the vessels did what Space Templar vessels do, and pulsed, changing from a shining silver steel sheen to a golden glow, repeatedly.

Yesterday, Shae left his wife for another military campaign. The last one had been an occupation in Haiti, this one a potential war. He'd been through these steps before, leaving Helen twenty years ago when shipped off to command the USS *Washington* battleship to lead the Cruiser Squadron of the Atlantic Fleet. He never made it to Haiti and had never returned to Michigan until recently.

Last night, he slept in a hotel in a town he couldn't care to remember. This morning, they took a long drive to a small airport where Truman's C-54 Skymaster plane, named *Sacred Cow*, waited. Shae recognized the plane's design immediately. He had studied the Second World War for countless hours. The primitive, four-engine aircraft held three-bladed, constant-speed, fully feathering propellers, a design a thousand years behind anything Star Guild and the Space Templars enjoyed in their own flying arsenal.

He had stepped on the plane with President Truman and the *Sacred Cow* took off. They landed hours later on a newly built landing strip next to the warehouse he now stood in. The warehouse sat next to a lake named Groom in broiling, blazing Nevada.

"We're headed to the moon," said a man, wearing an Air Force blue three-button coat with silver-colored buttons, matching trousers, and a service cap. Silver mirror-finish U.S. pins were on his lapels and epaulets on his shoulders. He shook his head as if he couldn't believe the words that came from his lips. Shae saw the man swallow hard, a worried physiological response.

Shae used his rolled-up coat to wipe the sweat dripping down his face. He eyed the airman. "Those ships right there," he nodded to the two crafts in front of him, "are an easy ride. Don't let them scare you. You'll be fine."

The man pushed out his lips and let out a stream of air. "Don't get me wrong, my friend. I'm far from scared." He looked away, trying to hide the fear in his eyes.

Truman stepped forward. "Everyone, listen up." He motioned to Shae. "This is Fleet Admiral Shae Lutz. He'll be training you, and letting you know the ins and outs of the flotilla we'll be facing. He's an expert. He's had experience fighting these things that are coming. Training starts the moment you land on the moon, because time is of the essence, people. We—"

The warehouse door opened loudly. In stepped a tall woman, two smaller men in Space Templars' fatigues flanking her. Their fatigues melded into the colors they walked by, Templar camouflage.

The tall woman's athletic strides and perfect cadence carried her like a ten-foot-tall queen. Her red hair bounced on her shoulders as she walked, reminding Shae of his daughter. She wore a white jumpsuit that displayed her hour-glass figure. "I'm sorry to barge in like this, Mr. President, but it's time we get going." The woman walked toward Shae and dipped her head.

Shae held in a smile, glad to see a fellow Being in the room other than himself with experience in craft a thousand years ahead of Earth's current technology. "Hello, Sabra."

She closed and opened her eyes like a purring cat when she walked by. "Hello, Shae."

The rest of the men in the warehouse stood agape, their eyes like saucers. They'd probably heard of the Anunnaki and had been briefed. They may have even seen pictures. But nothing was like the actual thing.

"Excellent," said Truman. He clapped his hands together. "Then I'll be off."

Shae cocked his head to the side. "You're leaving?"

Truman hesitated as if caught off guard. "Yes, Shae. The country can't run itself, can it?"

"Definitely not, sir."

Truman held out his hand for a shake. Shae took it kindly, dipping his head at the president.

"Good luck, Admiral."

"The same to you, Mr. President." Shae let go of Truman's hand. "But, Mr. President, before you leave."

Truman went to turn toward the exit, then stood straighter and faced Shae. "Yes?"

"Let the American people know." He shook his head. "Let me rephrase that, let the world know."

Truman nodded emphatically. "The world leaders are knowledgeable about the situation."

"Great, but we need other leaders to emerge, to understand what's about to happen to them."

"Like who?"

"Regular people."

Truman's head jerked back, surprised. "How do I go about doing that, Shae?" A few military men turned to watch their conversation.

"What I've learned when involved in a similar event was that those we call the average Joe and the average Jane, are the biggest heroes. They rise when we least expect it, and many times, they turn the tide of battle, of war. At times like these, we get the best and worst from people. The best always jump to the occasion, and they pull up many people we'd consider the worst—the overly panicked—bringing courage to those fearful lot. These invisible, unsung heroes will be ready, Mr. President, and they will surprise you."

Truman grinned, though Shae could see in the President's eyes that he disagreed.

"I'll do what I can."

Shae bowed like a Space Templar. "Get on the radio and get on the television. Let the world know, Mr. President."

Truman headed out the door, closing it quietly behind him. Shae spun on his heels and faced the men, catching Sabra and her Space Templar out of the corner of his eye stepping into one of the ships.

A few of the politicians and military men began speaking, although in a hush. They gave Shae side looks, either unimpressed by the way he spoke to the President or unhappy about Shae attempting to give Truman an order.

They had a point, but Shae guessed it was an old habit stuck in his bones from his days in Star Guild. He ran things there as fleet admiral, acting as more of a leader than Prime Director Zim Noki ever did. He had everyone's greater good in mind at all times, Zim didn't. The evil bastard soiled Shae's taste for leaders.

A politician in suit and tie and manicured hair wrinkled his nose at Shae, his eyes cold. He whispered into a military officer's ear. The officer nodded and puffed his lower lip out, as if in agreement.

Politicians. A fire hotter than the squelching warehouse grabbed Shae's belly. What was this, middle school? "As fleet admiral of the Space Templar fleet, the fleet you'll be flying and fighting our oppressors alongside, I can't have you second-guessing me." He looked at each officer and gentleman. "I come from a system that has technology you couldn't fathom, and wars that would tear your heart out. I'm a reasonable man, but don't cross me, don't speak behind my back, and don't say my name in vain. You won't like what I'll do to you."

A few men shifted, including the perfectly manicured politician, undoubtedly not used to being spoken to in this manner. Shae meant business, and if these people wanted to stay alive, they ought not to inflame their egos during training and combat.

He paced in front of them, his hands behind his back. "Address me as 'Fleet Admiral' or 'Admiral.'" He thumbed over his shoulder at the door had Truman exited. "I have a family to get back to after this shit is over, and I mean to get back to them. I assume you are all in similar situations. If you want to hug and do whatever you do with your family again, you pay attention to every damn word I say. Every. Damn. Word." He halted and stood straight. He wanted to wipe the sweat that was cascading down his face. But any action at this moment, other than those strong and confident, may lose one or two of them. He eyed the politician that had whispered in his colleague's ear. "Do you understand?"

All the men nodded, including the politician. A few voiced, "Yes, Fleet Admiral."

"Good. If you don't understand, you'll find yourself locked up. I have full authority to put all of you behind bars if I see fit. Again, do you understand?"

"Yes, Fleet Admiral." More voices picked up.

"Excellent. Now man the transports. We leave for the moon." The men turned and walked up a ship's ramp, Shae following them. Before entering the cabin, a wide warehouse wall slid upward like a garage door. The sun beamed in, and in the background stood a red mountain range, hiding what Shae figured was a blue, cloudless sky beyond.

He walked in the cabin and sat in a transport seat, the chair automatically adjusting to his size and weight, matching the curvature of his spine for a comfortable fit. Armrests extended, and a restraining belt wrapped itself around Shae and clicked in place.

He wanted to crack a smile at the surrounding men, all startled by the chair's movements and automatic seat belts buckling them in. The cabin door closed, and the hum of the engines purred. The craft lifted off the ground and blasted through the warehouse opening, heading for the moon.

1 4

EDEN

Starship Swift

A flash of light and movement carried across the sleeping quarters. Eden opened her eyes, sleep weighing her eyelids down. She lay comfortably tucked under her covers. What the Guild flashed?

She looked around in the darkness. She shook her head, figuring she'd imagined the flash. Perhaps it occurred in her dreams. She closed her eyes, taking in calming breaths, slow and deep. A soft rustling echoed in the room. Then silence. Eden opened her eyes again, then examined with the Sight outward. Her mind's eye detected a presence, someone who sat frozen and waiting.

Swift, who's in my room?

Sleuth, replied Swift.

Yes, I know. But why hiding and waiting for something?

Before she fell asleep, Skye had swapped out her bed with a bunk bed. Sleuth arrived shortly after under a guard's escort. Eden and Sleuth didn't say a word before going to bed. To say the entire situation was odd was an understatement. What did the Bali Masters want her to learn?

Eden sat up. "Sleeping quarters, illuminate." The lights turned on, though dimly, allowing her eyes to adjust without squinting. She glared at Sleuth, who sat at a dining table that extended from the crystalline wall. In front of him rested a black box, no bigger than a shoebox.

Sleuth put his hands up. "Sorry, just working on something." He walked across the room to the bottom bunk and sat on his bed.

"What are you working on?" How did he get that box inside her quarters without her knowing?

"Just tinkering."

Eden threw the covers off and flung her legs over the edge of the bed. She hopped off the bed to the floor. The walls brightened a tad more, giving off a more substantial glow. "Since you're being vague, I'll check your tinkering myself." She could trust this guy as far as she could throw him. She sat at the table and eyed Sleuth, her brow wrinkled. "What exactly is this?"

"Don't worry about it. I'm sorry I woke you. Just go back to bed."

She went to get up, then sat back down. This was Sleuth. Sinister might as well be his middle name. The guy did nothing to help the galaxy unless it somehow helped himself.

Her hand touched her holster, something she wore before going to sleep, her gun attached. She flicked off the weapon's safety as she studied the box. Two rods jutted out from the top, one on the far left of the box, the other on the far right. She lifted her finger to run between the rods, just in case the rods detected movement, acting as an on-switch. She'd seen simple on and off switches like this before in Tech Lab when she practically lived on Starship *Brigantia* during her Star Guild military days.

Sleuth stood in a lurch. "Don't do that. You'll electrocute yourself."

She paused, her finger hovering just in front of the invisible connection line between the rods. She lifted an eyebrow, focused on Sleuth. She couldn't see auras yet, something many Space Templars had trained in and learned. The little auric teachings the Masters had given her allowed her to see auras momentarily, usually when a person experienced a sudden fright or an unexpected joy. Or a concentrated long and hard lie. Each had its own color.

Sleuth had lied. The color she called puke green dazzled above his shoulders and head. She pushed her finger between the rods, and a spark danced off her fingertip. She pulled back, wiggling her hand in the air. "That smarts."

"I told you."

"You—" She cut herself off as a holoscreen beamed and extended upward in a square the width of the box.

Sleuth stood, taking a step toward the box. "That has my private diary on there. Do not—"

He lied again. She pulled her plasma blaster out of the holster and aimed at Sleuth's chest. "Sit back down."

He did.

Eden's chest tightened when she saw paragraphs and paragraphs of text on the holoscreen and a blinking dash after Enlil's name. She stood, the chair tipping over. "You piece of ebb. I knew it."

He sat expressionlessly. "Guess you pegged me right."

"You're telling him we're on our way."

"I did."

"Did you send it?" She searched the text, trying to figure out if he'd pressed send or not, and if so, how would she possibly know?

"Guess you'll never know. Plus, I was experimenting. You know, having a bit of fun."

Eden spoke under clenched teeth. "What was the experiment?"

Sleuth looked off, his eyes darting everywhere but to her. "I'm trying to patch into the Anunnaki holonet system. There I can hack and get whatever I need off their servers."

"Bull crap." She didn't believe him, but his aura didn't flash a disgusting green. She might have missed it. This aura Sight had been hit-or-miss, mostly showing itself as it pleased.

"Okay, then take me to the brig. I don't care. I was more comfortable there, anyhow." He started patting his head, though harder than needed. "I was starting to feel a little better, to think more clearly. Now I can't." He flapped his hands in jerky movements, hitting his thighs.

"Stop, Sleuth."

He calmed, a sheen of sweat on his cheeks and chin.

For a moment, she felt sorry for the guy. "Are you okay?"

He nodded, his eyes cast to the floor. "Yeah. Just leave me alone."

"All right." She studied the screen, her eyes widening. At the bottom and in small italics was a word she hadn't seen at first glance. **DELIVERED**.

"You sent it." If it wasn't clear before, it was crystal-ebb'n-clear now. He wanted to work for the other team, for Enlil, the new ruler of Nibiru. She swallowed hard. Adrenaline hit her body and saturated her hands and feet at the implication staring back at her. No doubt, Enlil would send a mass of ships in their direction soon. "How long ago did you send this?" Sleuth walked toward her, and Eden stood, the gun pointed at him. He didn't stop. "Back away, Sleuth."

He shook his head, his gaze bouncing from rounded wall to rounded wall, his bottom lip trembling. "No."

"I'll pull this trigger."

He didn't halt, moving slow and calculated as if each step carried a single question. Will she shoot me at this step, or this step, or…

Eden backed away from the table, moving toward the compact kitchen inside the dome. "One shot and you're dead."

"Good." He glared into her eyes, his thoughts practically penetrating her mind.

She paused as a sense of clarity came to her. "You sent Enlil to kill you and, in so doing, killing all of us, didn't you?"

He shook his head, lips shaking as if he were shivering from cold. "No matter what I write, he won't help me, he won't save me, he won't give me the reward I deserve."

"He takes you out, he takes us all down with you. That's what you want."

"To blow this ship into a million blasted chunks, scattering mine and your crew's bloody corpses across the stars? Yes." He took a wobbly step forward.

"What do you want, Sleuth?" Eden backed against the rounded wall, not able to move any further. She concentrated on the Sight, her hands shaking. She sucked in a deep breath. Her mind was spinning too fast, too wild for her to concentrate. She dug deep into her emotions, doing her best to focus on the energy around Sleuth, and breathed her emotions outward. Nothing happened. The Sight didn't throw him back as she'd wanted.

"I don't want to live." He took another step, now a meter from Eden.

She cringed, doing her best to push the surrounding energy, to throw him on his butt. It wasn't working, and her nerves were getting the better of her. She held on to her gun. If she needed to use it, she would. "The Masters want me to help you for some reason."

He walked closer. She wanted to shoot and end this guy's miserable life. Oddly, the Sight showed her something deep in his soul, a piece of him that matched something in her. They both had horrible childhoods. How could she know this?

A scene came to her. Sleuth was on the floor, maybe six years old, and his father was beating him with a belt. He screamed in pain, not knowing what he'd done wrong. The smell of alcohol wafted from his father's breath and seeped from his sweaty pores. Eden jerked back and came to. She calmed, and her heart went out to him.

"Masters," he said. "You said Masters. Who are they?" He paused, looking as if a tinge of hope coursed through his mind. It lasted a second if that. He lurched forward, and Eden let her guard down, lowering her weapon. She pulled in the Sight, partnering with the energy around Sleuth. She tugged as if tugging the rug out from under him. He fell and landed on his back, grunting and wincing.

Her gun hand felt lighter, and she glanced down. Her weapon was MIA, missing in action. She swept her eyes to his hand. She couldn't fathom how, but his fingers were wrapped around her gun.

He flattened his lips, his eyes bulging as if gathering steam and willpower. He held in his breath, and his face reddened. He thrust the gun to his forehead. "Maybe I'll see you on the other side." He squeezed his eyes closed.

She dove for the gun. The blaster went off, and blood splattered. She screamed.

ALI

<u>Lowell, Michigan</u>

Ali stepped inside the building, and the lights flickered overhead. A musky smell drifted to her nose. Furniture covered in dust filled the complex. Couches, chairs, lamps tall and short, dressers, tables, and everything an abandoned furniture warehouse could want.

Picking out furniture wasn't why they asked her here. In front of her stood several men in sport coats and trousers, fedoras atop their heads like CJ. They were in conversation when Ali entered and quickly hushed. A few looked her up and down, then their eyes fell on Daf—the beauty queen.

One man, small with a white mustache, hair on end as if he'd been electrocuted two minutes ago, wearing a dark suit and tie, stared at her. He brightened in a smile, his happiness flowing outward. He extended his hand, bowing as he shook Ali's grip. "My name is Albert Einstein. I'm here to meet you and observe for posterity's sake."

Another man stepped forward. He had deep brown eyes, and slick, brown hair. "Dexter Huntley, ma'am." He swung his arm at four others. "My archeology team under the Blueline Project. We're glad you're here to help. I look forward to learning much from you. We'll sort out names later as we're in a bit of a hurry." He took his hat off, dipping his head toward CJ and Daf. "I see you brought friends with you."

She cocked her head to the side. The man was the spitting image of Gary Cooper.

"I'm fascinated by your story, miss," said Einstein. His voice was soft, with compassion that rivaled Skye's, though his eyes were more serious. "Where did you go for all those years?"

Ali gave him a curious look. "What do you mean?"

Einstein looked at CJ, then Daf, and finally rested on Ali as if he searched their souls for an answer to another question only he knew. "We've read your file, miss, so understand we know more about you than most people you've met. We know the United States government sent you on an expedition by the Joint Chiefs of Staff before the war in conjunction with the University of Michigan. What baffles us, is you contacted the United States legation out of Iraq in 1939 and disappeared shortly after. No trace. No word. I've met one of your colleagues, Skye Vortek, and he's as much a mystery to me as your vanishing. My question to you is, where did you go?"

Ali glanced at Daf, who shrugged, silently telling her it was up to Ali to let the frazzled-haired man know where she'd been.

Ali grinned. "Mr. Einstein, that's classified."

He shrank back and shuffled away from her. He dipped his head a few times. "My apologies, miss."

Dexter rubbed his hands together. "Ali, our tools and supplies are on the plane. We're ready when you are."

She stared at him a moment too long, taking in his features. Then she breathed in deeply, blinking rapidly to get her thoughts on the plan, and off the man who appealed to her a lot more than she'd ever hoped a man would. Dumb crushes were just that, dumb sprinkled with silly and garnished with childish. She'd add a little waste of time ingredient to the recipe as well.

"Right, I take that as you're ready." Dexter gave a nod to her silent reply, a side grin capturing her heart as he walked by, his team in tow.

"Yes, right," she said, rolling her eyes at her stammering heart.

He stopped at the door. "Are you coming?"

She nodded. "Yes, yes." She motioned to Daf as she tipped her head toward Dexter. "Get my stuff out of the car?"

"Am I your servant?" asked Daf under her breath.

"Do I know where it is?" She wanted her sword, and Daf knew its whereabouts in the car, as did CJ. Her sword kept her safe, more confident.

"I got it." CJ walked to the door, facing Dexter. "You okay if I load a few things on the aeroplane?"

Dexter furrowed his brow.

"Airplane," said Ali. "He has a speech impediment." He didn't, but her heart raced at the Gary Cooper doppelganger. Her mouth was now spouting things out of her control.

CJ stood tall. "No, I don't have a speech impediment." He gave Ali an odd look, then looked at Dexter as if suddenly seeing her attraction to the guy. His eyes hardened for a moment. Thumbing over his shoulder toward his car, he said, "I'll load up."

Dexter sighed impatiently. "Do your best." He eyed Ali, his eyebrows raised. "We can talk more on the plane." He motioned to the door.

Einstein lifted his hand in the air. "I would like to talk alone with Alison for a minute."

Dexter folded his arms. "I'm sorry, Albert, but we have to get that plane rolling. You insisted on meeting her for reasons you won't explain, and here she is. If it hadn't come from the top, I'd rather you stayed home. So, here you are. You met, and now we have to get to business. What's coming to Earth waits for no one."

"Understood. If you load up and get the engines a'roarin'," Einstein made a fist and jabbed it toward the ceiling as if he were a sports coach giving an inspirational speech, "by the time I'm done chatting with the lovely lady, you'll be ready to go."

Dexter continued to stare at Einstein while tapping his finger on his elbow.

Einstein held up five fingers. "Give me five minutes."

Dexter dropped his arms by his side with a distaste that told Ali that Einstein had been an irritating pill Dexter had been forced to swallow. "Five minutes. No more, Albert." He flicked a look at Ali, the side of his mouth rising in a half-smile. "I'll see you soon." He exited, his men trailing him.

Daf stayed by Ali's side, leaning slightly in Einstein's direction, obviously waiting for the conversation to start. Einstein clapped his hands together several times and gave a jovial laugh. "I would like this to be a one-on-one conversation, dear."

Daf looked the man over from his shoes to his face and back down. "You're harmless." She gave Ali a soft punch to her shoulder. "You heard the man, five minutes, and no more."

"I heard." Ali watched Daf exit, the door's slam reverberating off the building's walls. She gave Einstein a long hard look, waiting.

He grabbed her arm, his face changing from jovial to serious. He pulled her away from the door and toward the middle of the facility and behind an armoire.

"I've been with these men for almost a week, and I've taken mental notes." He pulled out a folded piece of paper and placed it in her hands. "I've written something on here for you. Hide it."

Ali straightened her lips. "Why?"

He leaned into her ear, whispering. "We're being listened to at all times in this place, okay?" He continued to talk in a low hush. "As you know, Skye sent me to observe these men."

"What did you observe?" Ali whispered.

"It's all in the letter. Just know I pay attention, miss. It's what I do best. Understand that these men and the agency they work for have top-secret clearance even above the President. They know things and do things the President will never be privy to."

That didn't surprise her in the least. She was used to secret people in the background running a government, using political types as puppets. It happened on Starbase Matrona, and most likely occurred on Earth. "Understood."

"Skye let me know you'd understand. You, oddly, have first-hand experience."

"You've spoken with Skye, so you know what's coming?"

"Yes. Skye informed me of everything. I know where you disappeared to and when you came back to Earth. I know about the Anunnaki. I know you've held back an invasion once, and you mean to do it again." He pulled out a pocket watch, a chain attached from it to his belt. He huffed. "Two minutes." He held up his index finger. "Be careful. Watch everything. And good luck with the glyphs."

"Cuneiforms," she corrected.

He bobbed his head up and down. "Yes, those. Tell your friends, Daf and CJ, to watch your back, too. That black-haired woman seems like she can hurt someone if need be, and that need might be."

"CJ can hold his own too."

"Good. I notice CJ's a good man." He looked at his watch again, then shoved it in his pocket. "Now, go."

"Are you staying here?"

He gave a hearty grin. "My car is out front and I don't like planes."

"So, you're not getting on the plane?"

"The noise. I'd rather stay inside when it shoves off the ground and into the air."

"Got it." Ali turned to leave.

"Oh, one more thing," he said. "I saw how your eyes glittered when you looked at Dexter. Don't fall in love. That's the worst trap in a situation like this."

Ali crinkled her nose. "I'll be fine."

"One last thing."

"Yes?"

"Don't show anyone my letter, not even your friends."

She held the paper up and pushed it into her pocket. "Done."

"Good luck, Ali." It sounded almost as though he cut himself off at the end of his sentence, as if he were about to say, you're going to need it. He held up his hand. "Go, Ali. Make Earth proud."

1 6

SHAE

Earth's Moon, Solar System

The ship shuddered when it connected to the docking bay. A drill-like sound vibrated across the ship's inner walls. Shae glanced past Sabra to the cabin door. The door and the surrounding area sucked in, and then slightly pushed out. A bang carried across the cabin. The airlock attached, and in a few moments, they'd all walk across the pressure vessel to a lunar base.

Sabra sat next to him and patted his leg. "I bet you never thought you'd be on the moon." She winked. "Or, should I say, the other side of the moon."

"Not in a million years."

From Shae's previous views from Earth, the moon had always been bright from the reflection from the sun. He was able to see pock-marks from his front yard when he stared at it, figuring like most did that those craters were likely formed from meteor impacts. He never imagined the dark side could also light up from the sun, or that it carried more impact wounds.

But why was this side of the lunar surface lit up? He shrugged, guessing "dark" meant "unseen from Earth" rather than lacking sunlight.

When they had hovered for landing, he eyed the base. Tucked into a gigantic crater, it was comprised of three equally sized domes that rivaled Detroit, Michigan skyscrapers in height. The domes were kilometers wider. In true Space Templar form, the domes glowed from gold to silver, back to gold, then silver again. A sizeable Space Templar fleet orbited the moon. As they landed, he noticed hundreds more ships, big and small, on landing pads around the crater.

Sabra unstrapped and stood. "Everyone, time to exit." She made her way to the door and pressed her hand on the control panel. The door hissed and opened to reveal a short, translucent joining vessel leading to a dome.

They made their way through and past another doorway. Shae's footsteps clanked on the dome's floor.

Sabra motioned down a long, cobblestone walkway. "This way, Admiral."

Shae eyed the area. "What the hell is this place?"

Shops and markets, along with other buildings, lined the walkways as if he'd stepped inside a massive city metropolis. High skyscrapers reached toward the top of the dome's tinted ceiling, and hovercars zoomed overhead.

"We're inside a Space Templars' base. Keep in mind we're all Beings with needs here. We shop, gather in groups for enjoyment, watch holomovies, play games, listen to live concerts and live life as normally as possible. Space Templar family members need places to work, too, hence the office buildings."

"How many people are here?"

"I haven't counted, but a lot. The Space Templars' network is vast, and because of the size of the galaxy, we have millions upon millions of people working, fighting, and training in the Space Templars' ranks."

They walked down the stone path, bright street lamps lighting the way. The Earth politicians and military men walked behind them, led by another Templar who gave instructions and spoke about the buildings and views, much like a tour guide.

Shae dug into his pocket, feeling the vidcom President Truman gave him. His heart went to Helen. He wanted to call her more than anything and to let her know he was safe, ask if she's safe, how she felt, and how her day went. He paused as Ali came to mind. "Where's my daughter? Is she here?"

"She's on Earth with Dexter Huntley."

"You've got to give me more than just a name."

"An archaeologist from the Blueline Project, a highly classified agency out of your government."

"Why?"

"We have to keep walking. They're waiting."

"Who's waiting?"

"For time's sake, you'll be training right away. We need to get your people up to speed." Sabra led him toward a medium-sized dome, its glow and pulse like everything Templar.

"And about my daughter? Why is she with the Blueline Project?"

"Yes, about that. There are locations all over the Earth with portals that lead right to Enlil's feet, his armies, to his most elite soldiers, you name it. This we know, but even with our technology, we can't find the portals. They're well-hidden or not activated. We're not picking up anything other than from the one at the Ruins of Madkhal, which we've since deactivated. But there may be hundreds or thousands of potential hotspots the Anunnaki can use to teleport their troops if Enlil so wishes. And he will. He's not dumb. Your government, however, believes they've found Peruvian tablets that might help the cause. They suspect these tablets share maps to portal locations scattered around the world."

"Why would they suspect that?"

"Ali can translate better than most, but Dexter can translate too, though not at Ali's caliber. He's uncovered a few locations. One at Machu Picchu, one at a place called the Grand Canyon and another at Mount Shasta. Two more in Africa, one at the Great Sphinx. But they want to find more. They want to find them all, and much of what Dexter can't decode, Ali will do for them."

A massive ship flying overhead shook the ground. It towed metal beams that extended past the sides of a hovertrailer. It was headed toward a building under construction. Shae dropped his eyes from the craft to Sabra. "Top secret organizations give me a little pause, Sabra. Are we sure we can trust this Dexter guy and the project he works for?"

Sabra stopped in front of the dome she'd been leading him to. "It's what we have thrown at us. We'll go with it until they show us otherwise. Right now, there's nothing to fear."

A tingling went through his stomach, nerves wanting to jump out and tackle him. "My daughter is with this Dexter guy, a man I've never met, so I have plenty to fear."

"She's with two Space Templar-trained assets. She'll be fine. If anything goes awry, I'd fear more for Dexter and his crew than for Ali."

"Good." He crossed his arms. "So, they find these portals, and then what?"

"It's the Blueline Project's conjecture that destroying them will prevent further kidnappings and potential Anunnaki ground troops from jumping through these portals for surprise ground attacks. We agree."

"Perfect." Shae looked down at the round rocks making up the walkway, noticing some red, gray, and blue. He pinched the bridge of his nose. "Does the President know about the Blueline Project?"

Sabra nodded. "He's aware of it, but he mentioned it was above his pay grade."

"Do you need Ali to find these portals for the Space Templars? We could use her for something else, something more important, like captaining Starship *Tranquil* when Enlil's fleet arrives." He looked down. What was he saying? That'd put her in more danger than the potential with Dexter. Around his daughter, he needed to stop thinking like a father, and more like an admiral.

"If they deactivate these portals, that's one less stressor off our shoulders, and less potential issues we need to deal with regarding the protection of your citizens on Earth."

Shae shook his head. "You realize Ali won't be happy about the destruction of ancient sites."

"We gave them the technology to destroy the portal connection, not the site. What they'll destroy is the link from one location to another. Nothing more."

Shae let out a sigh, his thoughts on Ali. Something didn't feel right about her situation. Perhaps he wanted her near him, a father wanting to protect his daughter. Better yet, she'd be at home protecting Helen. They'd support each other during the coming times.

He touched his vidcom again, wanting to take it out and see his wife's beautiful face, to chat, to laugh, and share their love. He wished he had a vidcom for his daughter.

"Your aura keeps changing, Shae. You're bleeding fearful colors."

Aura? Colors? He didn't know what she was talking about. He put his hands out. "I'm sorry?"

"What do you fear?"

"I have a bad feeling about the Blueline Project. I don't know why."

"Well, good. Because you'll get to know some of them soon enough. A few are here for training." Sabra opened the door. "Welcome, Shae. These are the top military leaders from Earth."

Shae frowned and stepped inside. He hesitated, wanting to take a second look at the structure. The dome didn't look the size of the grand assembly hall he'd stepped into. In fact, it looked like a basic house-sized dome, but inside the dome, the sizeable room expanded wide and deep.

He surveyed the room, observing the military leaders of all nations sitting in auditorium style chairs that cascaded down in rows, stopping in front of a stage and podium. He figured that's where he'd stand and teach.

"Teach them. Train them." Sabra exited the dome and walked away. "I'll be right back."

"Teach what, exactly?" he said under his breath, shaking his head. He relaxed. He'd improvise like he did when leading a fleet during battle.

Everyone stared at him, the room quiet as he made his way down the steps, passing military minds from all over the world. The men were sitting comfortably on their chairs and he saw some had basic translators.

Good.

He stepped to the stage. His eyes found a person he met several times during his service as an admiral in the United States Navy before the Anunnaki had stolen him to Starbase Matrona. He gave a nod to Admiral Richard Byrd. The man was wearing a decorated Navy uniform. Richard smiled and gently lay his hand on his heart, then moved it outward toward Shae.

Another man sat next to him, dressed in blue, with a gray fedora and tie, and black suit pants. He abruptly stood, took off his hat, and set it on the chair. "Fleet Admiral Shae Lutz. My name is—"

The entrance door shut. In walked Sabra, the politicians and military men who had accompanied Shae to the moon behind her. She showed them to their seats and took one herself.

Shae gestured to the man standing. "Proceed with your question."

"It's not a question, sir."

Shae stood tall, hands behind his back. He extended upward on his toes for a moment and pressed back down, his feet level on the stage. "Proceed anyway."

"I'm Lloyd Winters of the Blueline Project. We aren't here for you to train us. We're here to assure Earth's survival, which we believe should be led only by Earth's leaders." His face reddened. "You are the most experienced person on Earth who has dealt with the creatures about to attack us, so they say." He shot a look at Sabra, who shifted in her seat, her brow crinkling. "If this invasion is real at all, and not some ploy by these Space Templars."

Shae frowned. "What are you getting at, Lloyd?"

"Trust me, Admiral. I do not wish to do this, but I do so for Earth's sake. Until we can get a definite on the potential targets, and a definite on Space Templars' well-wishes for us and all of Earth, we can only trust Earth's leaders." He turned, eyeing the crowd. "It's time."

Several military leaders, including some soldiers who followed Sabra inside the building, raised their guns and pointed them at Shae.

Sabra stood. "What's the meaning of this?"

Admiral Byrd slowly stood and put his hands on his hips. "Put your guns down." A few military leaders not in on the gun-pointing-plan similarly pushed to their feet.

Lloyd backed away from Richard. "Sit down, all of you." He eyed Sabra. "Or we'll kill Admiral Lutz on the very stage where he stands." He shifted his aim at Shae.

"After you kill me, what will you do?" asked Shae, his lips pursed. He moved his hand slowly and cautiously to his holstered gun, only to find neither holster or gun, something that'd been happening all too frequently lately.

Lloyd's face hardened. "We're taking over this operation until further notice." He motioned toward Sabra. "This is for the safety and security of our own kind." He brought his glare upon Shae again. "And we'll kill you or as many Templar leaders as necessary to prove our point."

ENLIL

Nibiru

Enlil stared at his brother from inside the jail cell. This time he sat across from Enki on the bench, his head in his hands. "Tell me if you did it, brother."

Enki leaned against the wall, a calm expression on his face, one that Enlil wanted to smack upside down and every which way. "Why do you keep going over this?"

Enlil eyed the holopad in his hand. The holographic vid extended outward and displayed Enki stepping a few paces closer to his father and raising the gun, his finger pushing through the trigger guard. The vid paused, the techs not able to unveil any more. "You didn't love him?"

Enki's lips downturned. "I loved him very much."

Rage filled Enlil, and he did everything in his power not to throw the holopad across the jail cell. "Then why did you kill him?"

Enki cupped his hands. "I heard you pushed my execution up a few hours."

"Why won't you answer my question? You'll answer every other question I ask, but you skip the most important."

"You know why."

Enlil leaned back, wiping his face. "I haven't been this stressed since we nuked a portion of Earth thousands and thousands of years ago."

Enki laughed, then slowly shifted his expression. "Many humans and Anunnaki died. That's when I learned about life and how the smallest part affects the whole. I've done my best to keep people safe across the galaxy. That's why I aligned with the Space Templars. They're the only ones protecting the weak, protecting others from people like you."

"From slavers. But Father didn't enslave anyone." He eyed the holopad. "I see your finger on the trigger. You shot him, and he had nothing to do with slaves."

Enki shook his head. "He was, and so was I. But we stopped when we saw the error of our ways. You can't control the souls of others for your own benefit. It not only disrupts life and goes against Universal Law, but it also affects karma. Like all things, what you do to others will return to you threefold."

Enlil pushed off the bench and paced the floor. "I need to know if you killed father. Just speak the truth. Answer my question." Spit came from his mouth as he clenched his teeth, huffing.

"Again, why? It won't make a difference."

He halted and took several long strides toward Enki. He reached forward and grabbed his brother's shirt by the collar to lean in, face to face. "I don't want to kill you. It's destroying me. Every time I think about it, a piece of me feels like it's burning away. I don't like that feeling. I don't like that my brother, Enki, the son of Anu, will die by my orders." Maybe that's why his brother wouldn't answer. Perhaps to do what Enki always insisted on doing, teaching him a valuable lesson. Enlil hadn't expected these feelings to surface. That was probably his brother's intention, a plan to change Enlil's stance on Earth. Enlil wanted to laugh. Nothing would change the fact they needed Earth and her gold resources.

Enki looked into his brother's eyes. "I love you. Whatever happens to me, that love won't change. Although I don't see eye to eye with you, it doesn't change my heart." He wrapped his hands around

Enlil's. "I won't confess to murdering father, and I won't deny it either."

Enlil let go and pushed Enki into the wall. "You frustrate me to no end. No, you make me irate. You killed father to pull me away from my slave operations, didn't you?"

"I'll confess that I killed him or didn't kill him under one condition."

Enlil raised an eyebrow. "Go on."

"Call off your invasion."

Enlil stiffened. "I won't."

"Why?"

"I'm not diverting from my plan, which is to keep Nibiru and the Anunnaki alive and well."

"And here we go in circles again. Enslaving other races to do the gold mining for us." He paused, rubbing the back of his neck. "So, when do you invade?"

"Shortly after I…" Enlil swallowed, his voice cracking. Was that a tear falling from his eye? He wiped it away.

"Shortly after I'm executed."

"Yes."

"Why not sooner?"

"You know why."

Enki bobbed his head up and down. "Because if I'm alive, I have some say. And if I have a say, not all the military will go along with your invasion."

"Sad, but true. That's why I don't understand. If you killed father, then why? It takes away your weight with the council and your weight with our people."

"You'll understand in time why I do what I do. When you understand ruling by your gun, by fear, will be counterintuitive to your wishes for our people, perhaps my sacrifice won't be for naught." He looked down, then shot his brother a look. "You wanting to instill fear into the public will send you down a winding road, brother. That only lasts for so long. They'll follow you wherever you want to go until they've had enough."

"Trust me. They have no other option. It's that, or we die here on Nibiru from lack of an adequate atmosphere. I'm attacking Earth after the execution. It's more than written in stone."

Enki grinned. "So, if I yell from the rooftops that I'm innocent, and you drop all charges, who will you kill in my place? Because if you want the people to fear you, me going free won't do it. You'll need to kill someone almost as high up as me."

"Senator Gronis." Killing him wouldn't be as effective as ending Enki, but it'd do, and he wouldn't have his brother's death on his hands. Or the pain that consumed him even with the thought.

Enki slightly jerked back. "He was our father's right-hand man. Of all people, he's not one who should be executed, especially not in public. He's done nothing but to show love to our entire family. He watched us when we were kids after mother died."

"I'm not stepping back from my plan."

"If I plead my innocence, then where will I be when you execute Gronis? Because you know I'll fight you tooth and nail to keep him alive."

"You're here until the invasion ends."

"Then, I'm guilty."

Enlil pursed his lips and crossed his arms. "You're not guilty, are you?" He could see it in his brother's eyes. If Enlil couldn't pull the trigger on his own father, then Enki sure as hell couldn't.

"I'm guilty as charged."

"Damn you, Enki." Enlil spun on his heels and exited the room, telling the guard to shut and lock the cell. He hurried up the steps to the upper floor, a knot filling his throat. He hadn't felt that sensation since he was a child when their mother died from a rare sickness. The staircase spiraled, and he stopped and sat on a step. He put his hands over his eyes. "Father, I can't do it. I can't kill him."

Anu didn't answer.

He stood, shaking off the odd sadness that surrounded him. He walked up the steps and entered the lobby. He eyed Kamina standing behind a counter, her long, red flowing hair touching her shoulders. Her blue eyes beamed back at him.

"Kamina," he said. "The execution doesn't change. Let the council know and make sure they invite all the military leaders as witnesses. I need them to see my power and how we rule the Anunnaki people. Do you understand?"

She nodded. "Understood."

"Good." He turned, heading for the elevator. Something came to mind, and he stopped and eyed Kamina. "Let Senator Gronis know I need to have a chat with him. I need him to execute my brother. It'll be a king's order, something he can't refuse."

He walked to the elevator and pressed the button. He was losing the council day by day. The head of the council pulling the trigger would force them fully on his side.

1 8

EDEN

Starship Swift

Eden wiped the blood off her face and blinked several times. Her heart pumping fast, she grabbed the blaster that lay next to Sleuth's arm.

What had he done? Did he kill himself? She pushed to a standing position, Sleuth's eyes staring into hers, blood dripping from his shoulder. She lifted her hand to her mouth. *"Swift, get medical here immediately."*

Already notified and on their way, Eden.

She didn't know how, but Sleuth had shot his arm clean off at the shoulder. He breathed shallowly, stunned. Blood oozed, and she rushed to press on his chest, hoping to slow the bleeding.

"Let me bleed out." His eyes vacant, Sleuth looked at the ceiling. "I want to die."

"No." She gave him a few gentle slaps across his cheek. "Stay with me."

"Why?"

She didn't know. It would probably be best if he just went and died. It'd take the stress off her life, and off the Space Templars. But

115

the Master's orders were orders, and she needed to teach him some-thing, though she couldn't figure out what. "You're staying with me."

He winced in pain. "I don't like you."

"Feeling's mutual." The blood continued to ooze. She pressed her knee on his lateral pec, wondering if she was doing more harm than good.

"We have a similar past." He gave her a wink, then his eyelids fluttered.

She slapped at his cheek. "Stay with me." She lifted her pressure for a moment as his comment took her off guard, then pushed down harder.

His eyes opened wide, and his voice slurred. "Eden, you were… abused. I was…too."

How would he know she had been abused? She'd never opened up to anyone about her past other than the Masters. They had somehow known her past rather than her spitting it out to them.

She looked up to see men and women rushing into her dome. A stretcher followed, hovering in the air. A woman dashed to Sleuth's side and pushed Eden away. She pulled a gun from a belt saddled with medical equipment and shoved the gun against Sleuth's open wound.

Sleuth screamed, cringing in pain. "I…want to…die. Just kill…me." Tears dripped down his upper cheek to his ear.

The medic pulled the gun's trigger, and a web of electricity spun around his wound, then faded, cauterizing the shoulder and stopping the bleed.

The stretcher lowered, and the medical staff hoisted Sleuth on to it. They left, one person carrying his severed arm out with them.

Eden splayed her fingers across her heart and sat on a chair at her dining table. She breathed heavily, replaying the event in her mind. She wiped the blood off her face with her forearm, shaking. Swal-lowing and taking deep breaths, she walked to the bathroom and shut the door. The walls glowed, lighting the small room, and she stared at the mirror. There was a streak of blood on her forehead and drops across her cheek.

She turned on the faucet, continuing to look into her tired eyes, as her mom's voice echoed in her head. "You'll screw this up. Give up. Go home."

"No," she said as she cleaned the blood off. She grabbed a towel. "Leave me alone, mom."

She leaned forward, her palms on the counter as the tears came, her heart bleeding.

"Eden," said Nyx's voice over her dome's intercom.

Eden looked at the ceiling and wiped her eyes. "Y-yes." She cleared her throat. "I'm here. What is it?" She stood alert, her captain hat back on.

"We've arrived at Pluto."

"We jumped already?" Eden instructed *Swift* to take hyper-hops, a Space Templar term for short jumps from one sector to another until they jumped to a final destination. It allowed for quicker NMJ charges after each hop and a more cautious approach. In one more jump, they'd enter planet Nibiru's system.

"We jumped while you slept. We need you on the bridge as soon as possible."

"Can you give me a minute?" She opened the bathroom door and glanced at the blood splattered across her crystalline floor. She blew spent air, shaking her head at what had just occurred. She was slow and careless, and several times her nerves had gotten the better of her because she couldn't conjure up the Sight to stop Sleuth. Had she lost her touch?

"I'm afraid we can't wait. Enlil is on the screen. We've been compromised."

"Dammit." Enlil had received Sleuth's messages sooner than she expected. She ran out of her dome. "I'm on my way."

Up the elevator, through several corridors, she made it to the bridge. The door whooshed closed behind her. She passed Skye and Jantu, who both sat at their stations. She picked up Nyx's gift, a Templar weapon—a bow, no arrows—from her seat and set it on her lap when she sat at the captain's chair. Nyx was at the helm to her left. Eden eyed the vidscreen.

Enlil stood with his full red beard, blue eyes, and long, curly locks flowing over his muscular shoulders. He held out his hand to Eden. "So, my friendly Space Templar chaps, do we need to wait for anyone else before commencing our talk?"

"No," said Eden, her lips frowning.

"You didn't notify Anunnaki or Nibiru authority that you were entering our system." He crossed his arms, his bulky biceps flexing.

She straightened. "Who said we're flying to your planet?"

"Minutes ago, I received a message from my old friend, Sleuth. I know you're traveling to Nibiru, and I know why. Thankfully, he gave me a way to your ship's commlink. Isn't it nice we can chat?"

Eden's chest tightened. "Release Enki, and you'll have no quarrel with us."

Enlil laughed, his shoulders bouncing up and down. "Anything you want to exchange for Enki? How about your special Grand Master, Skye Vortek?"

Skye stood and walked toward the screen. He bowed. "Nice to see you again, Enlil. I'll offer an exchange."

Enlil lifted a brow. "Yes?"

"We don't negotiate for prisoners, so we'll do one better. You stay your armada from Earth's system, and I stay Ali's sword from your neck."

Eden's eyes widened in surprise. Skye went from bowing to the new Nibiru king to threatening him. Of all people, Ali ruffled Enlil's feathers more than anyone.

So much for diplomacy.

Enlil's nostrils flared. "Stay my fleet from taking Earth?" Enlil shook his head, his eyes practically beaming laser beams at Skye. "Sorry, you can't have her. That planet is mine. Anything else you want to propose?"

Skye smiled. "We're coming for your brother, Enki."

"If you want to live, I'd suggest you don't come near my planet and that you leave Earth's system altogether."

Skye tilted his head back. "Understood." He turned and swiped his hand in front of his throat in a slit-like gesture. "*Swift*, vidscreen off."

The vidscreen blipped off, and Enlil disappeared, leaving the expanse of space in front of them. Pluto's icy sphere hovered in the distance.

Skye strode past Eden. "Enlil will hurry the public execution now."

Eden nodded, her chin high, chest out. She gave Nyx a side glance. "Are the crew on board ready for a jump?"

Nyx nodded, a wry grin on her face. "I've notified them and set our coordinates. They won't know where we jump in, or when. Let's rock and roll."

Eden took a breath, then exhaled, calming her nerves. "*Swift*, prepare to jump."

19

ALI

En route to Peru

The airplane jostled. It lifted upward as if a gust of wind raised the plane and then dropped it with a jerk to its original position in the sky.

Ali rubbed her face. Her hands were clammy, and her stomach was swirling in knots. She swallowed nausea down and leaned her head back against the headrest. "If I'd known airplanes were hell, I'd have hitched a car ride all the way to Peru. It's like we're in a constant stream of anti-air fire."

Daf nodded, her eyes wide. "How do these people travel like this? We'd be there by now had we taken a Starjumper or another one of the Star Guild's transports, and without all this silly turbulence."

Daf sat next to Ali, the cabin lights low. They both held on to the armrests, their fingers squeezing a little too hard. Ali glanced out at the dark night sky through the window. She saw a light blinking at the edge of the wing, and rain flying through the light's intermittent glow. She let out a sigh, nerves picking up more. They couldn't get to Peru soon enough. She wanted to translate those cuneiform tablets to see what she could find to stave off the coming war, if possible. She couldn't help but think she'd be more suited shooting down

Anunnaki ships in Starship *Tranquil*, than decoding information for Dexter and his team. They, along with the President, thought it could curtail the Anunnaki armada and their infantry. From what little Dexter told her, she better get to these tablets sooner rather than later.

The plane bounced again. Ali gripped the armrest tighter, wondering when the plane would either land or break apart.

She eyed Dexter, who sat a row diagonally in front of her, his eyes closed. An hour after liftoff, Dexter briefed Ali on what he believed were Anunnaki portal entrances all over the world. He just didn't know how to translate their exact locations, or what he figured was a map on two of the tablets. Dexter had been given Space Templar technology to unlink the portals. Apparently, thousands of these devices lay in the Blueline Project's headquarters, and thousands of people were on standby to fly all over the world to these portal locations to turn them off.

CJ's snores brought her back to the present. He sat in front of her, conked out, his head leaning to the side. She took her eyes off of him and scanned the cabin. She'd done this too many times during the flight.

The seats were spaced out nicely, two per row, and the cabin was bare, the walls silver. Two pilots sat in the cockpit about twenty rows in front of her. The four other men on the archaeology team sat in random seats, spread out. They slept.

Ali had been in the air for nearly twelve hours by her count. She understood the basics of fuel in cars, but not planes. Two hours ago, when she asked Dexter how long they could stay in the air before they ran out of fuel, Dexter leaned against his chair, his pearly whites sparkling. "We have three-hundred-gallon drop tanks on each wing, in addition to the 'Tokyo Tanks' mounted in the outer wings, holding 3,400 gallons of fuel."

"What does that mean?"

"If you're worried that we'll run out of fuel before we get to Peru, don't. It means we have almost twenty-five hours before we run out, and it only takes fourteen hours to get there."

She moved in her seat, doing her best to get comfortable. CJ woke and turned. "You all right?"

Ali gave him a thumbs up. "Yes, thank you."

"Way to be Johnny-on-the-job, CJ," said Daf, sarcastically.

"If anything goes wrong, regardless if I'm asleep or not, I'll be on the job to protect you two."

Daf snorted. "Really? My hero." She touched her heart, fluttering her eyes jokingly. "Listen, if anything goes wrong, I got mine and Ali's back just like I did at the bakery."

CJ flashed a smile, twisting back around. "You're still sore over that?"

"Not sore," retorted Daf. "Just don't be late next time."

CJ dipped his head. "Gotcha, but I've been at this a lot longer than you. There's a time for training, and a time for action. You trained, and I didn't need to act."

Daf leaned forward, her mouth opening into an 'o'. "You were testing me?"

"More or less. You passed. Time to move on."

Daf leaned back and crossed her arms. "We almost died."

"I can't hold your hand every minute of the day. I need you to understand you're a fully capable Templar," said CJ.

Daf looked off. "I kinda kicked ass, didn't I?"

"Surprised the tarnation out of me." Ali rested her elbow on the armrest and looked Daf up and down. "More than capable is an understatement." The note in her pant pocket crinkled. She rose. "I'll be right back."

"Where are you going?" asked Daf, looking to the front of the plane and the back.

She thumbed over her shoulder. "Another seat, two rows back. I need to think." She shimmied by Daf, eyeing a row of seats lit well by a cabin light. She made her way there and sat. She pulled out Einstein's note and unfolded it.

Ali, for the last few weeks, I've been a thorn in Dexter's side at a newly constructed building labeled the Pentagon. Under the orders of the heads of the Pentagon, Dexter was ordered to show me around, to answer questions if they weren't over my security clearance and allow me to eventually meet you. All in exchange for solving mathematical theorems they couldn't figure out. I was like a puppy dog at Dexter's feet. Where he went, I went. Yet, he's good at what he does. He doesn't let much slip, but I see everything. Where he hid the key to his briefcase, for example, under his office mat. On day twelve, during lunch, I went into his office undetected, grabbed the key, and opened the briefcase that—

The plane lurched, and lightning flashed, brightening the sky. A hand came down on the seat in front of her. Ali looked up with a start. Dexter stared at her, his eyes falling to her note. "What do you have there?" His chest was against the backrest of the seat in front of her.

Ali folded the note and tucked it into her pocket. "My mom wrote me something."

"She misses you, I bet." He smiled a Hollywood smile.

"As moms do."

"We descend for landing in thirty minutes. We'll reach Limatambo International Airport soon. We arrive around zero-two-hundred hours. We'll be chauffeured in two cars to someone's home as guests."

Ali tilted her head, scrunching up her brow. "Why not a hotel?"

"My agency makes sure we get the best of the best."

"In a house? Won't that be cramped?"

"It's a mansion. So, I need you to be on your best behavior." He looked over his shoulder at CJ and Daf. "I know you'll be fine, but please mention appropriate behavior to those two."

"Sure."

"Can you tell me anything about your friends there?"

"No." Ali wanted him to buzz off so she could finish the note. His handsome face only took him so far, and perhaps short answers would give him a hint she didn't want to talk.

"I'm serious. I didn't expect them to come with you. I thought when they drove you to the warehouse, the woman was your friend, and the guy a driver. But they're on my plane. I didn't ask questions because you're here to help us, but a little clue to who they are will lower my hesitations about them."

"Daf is a colleague of mine. She helps me document my findings. I think fast, and she writes faster. She'll be with me when I translate the cuneiforms. And CJ, he's my bodyguard."

Dexter's eyebrows drew upward. "Since when do archaeologists need bodyguards?"

"Since my run-in with the Nazis on my last expedition." Ali couldn't believe how easily she lied to the man. It burned her soul but giving important information to a guy she just met wouldn't be a smart move.

"About that expedition. You disappeared off the face of the Earth. Where did you go?" He gave her a curious look, almost as if he knew more than he should.

"What do you know?"

He put his hands up as if in surrender. "That's it. Did you go back home to your parents and call it quits?"

"More or less. Took on another job."

"What did you do?"

"I mined."

He paused, cocking his head sharply. That took him off guard. Good, thought Ali. Maybe he'll leave now. She hoped he'd think she was a dirty, coal mining woman.

"You mined?" He hesitated as if abruptly realizing something. "You're not telling me the truth, are you?"

Ali didn't respond.

He let out a giggle. "You were throwing me off." He nodded. "Understood." He tapped the headrest with his hand and shoved off. "I'll see you when we touch down." He turned and walked to his seat.

Ali watched him sit down and dug into her pocket. She pulled out the note and read quickly, skimming through what she already learned.

...day twelve, during lunch, I went into his office undetected, grabbed the key, and opened the briefcase that always sat by his chair. I found a document labeled Blueline Project, Confidential. I read it. He's not what he seems. In that document, the agency—

A hand reached forward and snagged the note from her. Ali gasped and went to grab it, but a hand blocked hers. A man with a black hat, gray striped shirt, and beard glared back at her. He crumbled the note and held it behind his back.

Ali stood and grabbed his shirt by the collar. "Give me that back."

"Boris," yelled Dexter. "What are you doing?"

"Zis voman hide somezing. I sniff it."

Ali stiffened. A Russian? What the hell was a Russian doing inside an American agency? She bared her teeth. "Dexter, tell him to give me my note back, or I'll do something he doesn't like."

The Russian grunted and fell back, slamming against the seat behind him. CJ stood over him, the crumpled note in his hand, and the Russian's arm bent oddly in CJ's other. "You take something from the lady again, and I break your arm." CJ winked. "All right?" He let go of the man's arm and let him waddle down the aisle to Dexter.

"Here you go." CJ handed Ali the note.

She opened it and gasped. The note was torn. She held the upper portion, and the lower portion which she hadn't yet read was missing. She looked up in time to see the Russian hand Dexter the bottom half of the note.

"CJ," said Ali. "Get the rest of the note. It's in Dexter's hand."

CJ twisted around and dashed toward Dexter, who had his head down reading the piece of paper. He finished before CJ made it to him and dropped the letter on the ground at CJ's feet.

Dexter glared at Ali. "I knew I couldn't trust Albert. Boris, Sam, Phillip, Carl…get up and find whatever else she has on her, including her bags."

"I don't think so." Daf stood and stepped in front of the men. "Take another step and lights out."

20

EDEN

Starship Swift

Swift shot into the Nibiru System, smooth and easy. The colors filling the vidscreen from the jump dissipated, and Eden stood. "What am I looking at?" A brown object hovered in front of *Swift*, its axis tilted toward the starship. Ice covered the majority of the planet's northern hemisphere.

Nyx cupped her hands. "That's a Nibiru moon, a dwarf planet. They call the moon Yomogi. Behind the moon sits Nibiru, so we're using Yomogi as cover."

She could see Nibiru's golden glow highlighting space from around the moon's uppermost edge. A glowing sun, a quarter of the size of Earth's bright star, blazed in the distance. It looked like Nibiru had its own system, though it was small.

Eden stood. "Skye, you ready?" Skye nodded. Eden faced Nyx. "You have the bridge until I'm back." She pulled off her crystal pendant and handed it to Nyx. Intermixed with the bloodline, the crystal would allow Nyx to pilot and command *Swift* without Eden.

Nyx dipped her head. "Don't forget your bow. I left you some ammo in the Starjumper, along with a utility belt."

"Thank you." She grabbed the bow from the captain's chair and headed to the door, Skye close behind her.

Skye had given her the plan a few days ago. Several Enki and Space Templar sympathizers worked in Nibiru's Ranging Control Towers. Once notified by *Swift*, the sympathizers would mask Eden's and Skye's Starjumper from Nibiru radar, giving them safe passage. They would touch down in a forest near the capital city, Anka.

Eden and Skye would meet up with more Enki sympathizers, and head to Anka to save Enki. They hoped Enlil would be surprised and hence, react slowly, but that idea faded shortly after Sleuth contacted Enlil. One question Eden had was, why the heck were she and Skye going instead of someone else? A Grand Master and an up-and-coming Grand Master? It didn't make sense.

Eden and Skye exited the bridge. "Remind me why you and I are going again?"

"The Space Templars lead by example. Like George Washington or Alexander the Great, we—"

"Who?"

He nodded. "That's right. You're not an Earthling. They were important leaders trained by Space Templars disguised as officers or mentors. There's a reason why good George and Alexander lived so long in conflicts, their actions speedier than their troops, their strategies cleverer than the enemy. That's why you and I go. Training never stops, and we evolve during each battle, bettering ourselves, becoming more lethal, more experienced. It's the way of the Templars."

They turned down another corridor. "And if we die?"

"A monk steps in."

"And if that monk dies?"

"Another monk steps in."

"How many Space Templar monks do you have?"

They rounded a corner. "We span thousands over the galaxy."

She almost stopped in stride. "And they were at one time Grand Masters?"

"Yes. Some lasting a year before moving on, some lasting twenty, and a few over fifty years."

Eden shook her head. She couldn't believe her ears, but Skye didn't lie. "How old are they? How old are you?"

They approached the entrance to the launch bay. "We have anti-aging technology, and we've discovered ingredients in nature all over the galaxy that extends our lifespans significantly. You need not worry about that. You'll be given such things when needed. Right now, focus. You train under me during this mission. But to calm your nerves, if we die—which we won't—a monk steps in and leads just as well, if not better, than me."

The door whooshed open, and they stepped inside the bay to the sounds of mechanic hover vehicles and artificer bots . Space Templar engineers busy on ships slowed in their work and watched Eden and Skye make their way to their Starjumper. A few bowed when they strolled by. Reaching the Starjumper, its almond-like body thrust out a ramp from its already open starboard door.

Skye marched up the ramp, Eden stepping in stride. She came to an abrupt halt when she entered the cabin. "How?"

There, in the cabin, sat a dozen Space Templar Marines, their Templar armor camouflage fatigues melding into the seat's colors. Rifles, blasters, and stun grenades magnetized to a rack near the cabin's stern.

But that's not what gave Eden pause. In a seat in the cabin's front row sat Sleuth, one gleaming arm silver, the other normal. He looked his arm over. Other than the metallic finish, the artificial limb looked as human as his other. "I've got a cybernetic arm now, Eden." He had a wide grin on his face.

Skye stopped just before entering the cockpit. "Monk's orders."

"What?" Eden just about jumped out of her skin. "Sleuth's coming along?"

Skye sat in this pilot's seat. "Not much time to argue, here, Eden. It's zero-six-hundred hours right now. We have until eight-hundred hours when Enki's public execution takes place." He flicked a few switches on the ceiling and said, "Close."

The Starjumper vibrated as the door shut, and the ramp sucked in. Eden didn't budge after the door clicked shut a few inches behind her.

"He shot off his arm a few hours ago, and now he's coming with us to save Enki? I don't think so." She put her hands on her hips. "He'll jeopardize the entire mission."

"The Masters are throwing everything they can at you to make you the best Grand Master you can be, Eden." He motioned to the co-pilot seat in the cabin. "Nothing's a walk in the park, but no matter what occurs in the outside world, you can remain at peace in your inner world." He tapped his head. "Now, please take a seat."

"He'll compromise the mission. He can't shoot. He can't run. He can't do anything a Space Templar is trained to do. He'll be dead weight. We'll carry him the entire mission."

Sleuth shook his head. "I'm so glad I'm wanted." He eyed his arm again. "This thing is powerful. I mean, look at this?" He squeezed his armrest, and the end broke off as if made of dried clay.

Eden bit her cheek, her face reddening. Regardless of whether the monks wanted Sleuth with her, she wouldn't let him off the Starjumper when they landed. Enki's life was at stake, and she wouldn't let Sleuth be the deciding factor between Enki's living or dying.

She rounded the co-pilot's seat and halted. A couple dozen rounded tipped detonation arrows, a few stunner arrows, and a utility belt sat on her chair. Her lips flattened at the idea of Sleuth coming along, but her inner smile shone when she eyed the beauties before her. "Thank you, Nyx."

She snagged the belt and tightened it around her waist. She grabbed one of two blasters attached to the middle flight console and holstered it to her side. She touched the arrows, and they shrunk from tip to tip, now measuring about a quarter of a meter. Bundling them up, she placed them onto her belt, each one magnetizing in place.

Skye leaned into the commlink. "Clear main deck. Potential zero gravity in thirty-seconds. Bots and equipment, fully magnetize now."

Fully magnetized, said *Swift. All Space Templars off the deck. I'm opening the launch bay door now. But zero gravity won't happen on my watch.*

"You never know," said Skye.

The door opened, and the dwarf planet cast a shadow inside the bay, the ship's amber lights illuminating to offset the change.

Skye pushed the throttle forward, and Eden sunk into her seat as the ship gained speed. It shot through the gravity field and burst into the black expanse beyond. He pulled back and accelerated, pumping more energy into the boosters to counter the dwarf planet's gravity well.

They crested Yomogi, and a dazzling planet the size of Aurora, the Space Templars' stronghold, extended a golden aura outward, inviting them for a visit. One Enlil wouldn't enjoy.

Eden turned in her seat. "How can Sleuth function? He just blew his damn arm off." She couldn't make sense of him joining the troop.

"Space Templar technology," said Skye, steering the ship toward Nibiru. "We put him inside the infinity coupler. We—"

"The what?"

"When we attached his new arm in surgery, our team of doctors also placed him in a tube apparatus, we call it the infinity coupler. We attach anodes to his skull. It not only calms him, but it also eases stress levels induced by such an incident and alleviates any potential mental trauma as well. He'll be fine."

"He's Sleuth. He won't be fine."

"Granted, he's Sleuth, I give you that. But he's well-rested, as if years have gone by after the trauma, and as if during those years, he went to weekly counseling sessions to work on any post-traumatic stress he suffered."

Eden's heart abruptly grew a size bigger for the worm behind her. Maybe he'd changed, evolved, and grown more compassionate. "So, he's a different, better person then?"

"No. The personality doesn't change, just the emotional stress. You'll need to help him with his personality and get him in line to help us, not hinder us."

"Yeah, I thought it was too good to be true." She sat back, watching the planet grow closer. Satellites roamed in orbit, and a few outpost stations hovered at the edge of Nibiru. She dug her heels into the floor. "We're masked, right?"

"Yes. The sympathizers did well. Nibiru sensors aren't tracking us." He pressed forward on the control stick, angling them at forty-five degrees. "We hit the upper atmosphere in five minutes." He reached down, unattached a holopad from the side of his seat, and tossed it on her lap. "Study the map. We join the rebels when we land. They'll lead us to a tunnel system under the city that leads to the execution point. Once there, we'll overwhelm the stage and extract Enki, then back into the tunnels."

Eden held the holopad and eyed the image displayed before her. A map of Nibiru zoomed in on the landing site, and a line cut through the forest. Several lines split off to what appeared to be about a dozen tunnels under the city. The lines weaved in and out, sometimes connecting and breaking off, and all clearly underground. They intersected at one point, which Eden assumed was beneath the execution stage. "Does Enlil know these tunnels exist?"

"Yes, it's right under his nose. We think it'll be the last place he'd expect us." He thumbed over his shoulder. "We're leading a group of elite soldiers, so if things go wrong, we'll pack a mighty punch."

Eden looked over her shoulder. The Templars sat ready, their expressions neutral. Then there sat Sleuth, enamored by his new arm.

"We better not give Sleuth a gun," she said.

"That's a certainty," replied Skye. He leaned toward his comm. "Ranging Control Tower, this is Skye Vortek. S-A-F-E, I repeat S-A-F-E."

"Skye Vortek," came a voice over the comm, "this is Halm from Ranging Control. We confirm your password, you have safe passage. Land at the specified coordinates. We have you masked. Safe travels, and good luck. Free Enki."

"Affirmative. Free Enki." Skye dipped the ship a few degrees, and it vibrated as fire lapped at the craft's nose, highlighting his face in oranges and yellows.

The fire died down, and Skye leveled the ship, gliding it through a mess of clouds. A moment later, under cloud cover, a black forest came into view. It went on for kilometers, looking as if it had recently burned to a crisp. It edged up to a metropolis, no doubt Anka City.

The horizon was filled with gold colors, sparkling as if gold particles filled the atmosphere. A volcanic mountain range covered the city's backdrop, smoke coming out of several of the open mountain peaks. With little galactic travel and experience under Eden's belt, she imagined Anka must be one of the largest, most spectacular cities she'd ever eyeball.

"Coordinates point there." Skye threw an index finger at a clearing in the forest below. They approached fast and slowed to hover at the leafless, charred canopy tops.

They lowered into a landing, touching down with a jostle. Quiet filled the cabin as Skye brought up a scan of the area. He leaned back, letting out a gush of air. "The sympathizers either haven't arrived, or they've been found. I don't detect Anunnaki or sympathizer soldiers anywhere in the vicinity." He closed his eyes, concentrating. He opened them with a jolt. "Everyone, strap back in, we find another place to land." He flicked levers, and the ship lifted into the air.

"What's going on?" asked Eden.

"I used the Sight. The Starjumper doesn't detect Enlil's men, and for a good reason."

Bots, small and quick, rolled into the opening. Painted black, they resembled large, round balls. Their apexes opened, and cannon barrels lifted and began turning as if on a turret.

Skye yanked on the control stick. The ship shook and whined, then bounced up and down as cannon slugs raked off the underbelly.

"Hold on," yelled Skye. "When we land, everyone get your weapons. We head into a fight."

Smoke drifted from the ship's belly, and the flight console blinked off. The ship plummeted toward the ground, heading for a patch of trees close to their specified landing coordinates.

Eden braced for impact, her eyes wide, the canopy coming in fast.

21

ALI

En route to Lima, Peru

The plane descended, and Ali grasped the chair in front of her to keep her balance. It seemed everyone else did the same.

Dexter looked out a window. "We're coming in for the final approach." He gazed around the plane, and so did Ali. Everyone stood and eyed one another as if waiting for the first move. Then all hell would break loose.

"I don't know what's on the rest of the note, Dexter." Ali moved around her seat and stood in the aisle. "I couldn't read the rest because your Russian stole it from me. All I know is that Albert had his suspicions about you. If you want my help, you better let me see the rest of Albert's note."

Dexter relaxed and dipped his head at his people. They eased back and took their seats. Daf and CJ remained standing.

The plane bounced, and Ali gripped a seat harder. "Care to explain what's going on?"

Dexter stepped around his chair and walked forward. Daf stood in his way. He looked around Daf and at Ali. "Can I get some help here?"

"Daf and CJ come back here. Sit with me while Dexter and I have a chat."

"I prefer to do this alone," said Dexter.

"It's nice to prefer things, but again, you need me to decipher some cuneiforms, am I right?"

Dexter bit his tongue, and Daf moved out of the way, letting him go by. CJ swiped the ripped portion of the note off the ground and slid it into his pocket. Ali noticed Dexter didn't see CJ's little stunt, or if he did, he didn't make any gesture that it mattered. Daf and CJ followed the man down the aisle, and Ali took a seat, Dexter sitting next to her.

"Explain yourself," said Ali. "Why would Albert write me a note telling me not to trust you?"

"I thought you didn't finish the note?"

"I didn't finish, but I got that far."

Dexter leaned to the side and away from Ali, looking up at CJ, who stood a row in front of them. CJ kept his eyes on Dexter's men. Daf sat in the row next to them, listening intently as the plane jostled back and forth, the rain coming down faster as the plane descended.

"Look," said Dexter, moving closer to Ali, his voice in a hush. "Albert didn't trust me for several reasons. I have nothing to hide other than what I hide from the Blueline Project. I had to keep him away from the confidential materials associated with this project, not only for his safety but for mine."

"What do you mean?"

He looked around and keeping his voice low, continued. "The project wants whatever technology they find for themselves. That's fine and dandy. They want to stop the portals from allowing the bad guys on our planet, but after this is all over, they'll want to use it for their own gain." He patted his heart. "I can't in good conscience do that, so I'll do my best to keep the hounds at bay."

"Who are the hounds?"

"The project's leaders."

"And what's so bad that you don't want them to have this technology, or whatever creates these portals?"

"Mind you, there are some good people in the Blueline Project, but none of them head the project. What if the Space Templars' devices they gave us permanently disabled the portals? The Blueline Project wouldn't like that, so the call would go out to stop disabling the portals."

"What? Then the Anunnaki could easily send their armies through."

"They have protocols in place. They'd leave a few portals open and kill the rest. At the portals they'd allow to remain open, they'd send troops, tanks, you name it. Anything that pops through, they wouldn't let get far before they took them out."

"That's insane on so many accounts."

He wrinkled his nose, a surprised glint in his eyes. "Really? Why?"

"The Anunnaki are at least a thousand years ahead of you in technology. They'd flick your armies away like ants."

Dexter looked away. "They're that much farther ahead of us in technology?"

Ali nodded. "Don't think for a moment that we have a chance against these people without Space Templar help."

"Then why didn't these Anunnaki people eliminate us before now? Why did they wait so long?"

"There used to be a galactic treaty to leave Earth alone. If they violated that treaty, which they're about to do, the Space Templars come down on them hard. But we're talking Enlil here, the new Anunnaki leader. He's batshit-crazy and probably finds it amusing to start an intergalactic war, and I'm confident he thinks he'll win. If we don't stop him, billions of our species die." She flicked her index finger at him, pointing. "Tell that to your Blueline Project."

He let out a gush of air. "I don't think it will matter. The heads of the project want the portal technology, and we all know what happens when a group of greedy people takes something as their own. They use it to their own advantage and to the disadvantage of the many." He put up his hands. "That's all I know, so that's all I can say."

Ali shook her head. "You know more than that."

He looked Ali deep in her eyes, his gorgeously chiseled face practically sending her off into dreamland. "Ali, I know how this sounds, but I'm just an archaeologist, and so are the people on my team. They want to do good and stop the coming invasion heading our way. Some of those very people you almost had a tussle with may be the reason we live through this or stop what's coming. So I need them in one piece, all right?" He shot a look at CJ and then Daf.

Ali grabbed his forearm. "Then why do you have a damn Russian on your team?"

"Because this isn't just a United States issue, this is a world issue. We need all the top scientists we can get. And he's a damn brilliant one."

She patted his thigh, more so to touch the handsome guy than to let him know everything was fine on her end. "Okay. I believe you." She tipped her head to the side. "You can go to your seat now."

He rose. "We land in a few minutes. I'll see you on the tarmac. I'll have umbrellas ready."

"Thank you."

He walked off, and Daf took the now empty seat. "Do you believe him?"

Ali stared at Dexter, walking down the aisle. "Yeah."

Daf snapped her fingers in front of Ali's eyes. "Get your head out of the clouds. Close your eyes and feel your heart, and let me know if you feel truth from him or not."

Ali shot Daf a look. "I can tell he's not lying."

Daf sighed and scrunched her nose, crossing her arms tightly. "You like that guy a little too much, and it's blurring your judgment."

"No, it's not."

"You missed every tell he had."

"What tells?"

"One, I can feel he wasn't entirely truthful with you. But two, how many times did he look off when he spoke with you? Did you see him rub his nose two or three times when answering your questions?"

Ali shook her head. "No, because he didn't."

"He did."

"Miss," said CJ, handing Ali the rest of Albert's note. "I think you should read this."

Ali opened it.

He's not what he seems. In that document, the agency known as the Blue-line Project wants this technology as their own. In the confidential letter, it stated that Dexter was to use you to decipher, and once they didn't need you anymore, to get rid of you by any means necessary. I didn't know why they'd think of doing something like that until I read further. They don't want to destroy the portals. They made some kind of deal with the Anunnaki. What deal, you may ask? The Sumerian tablets speak of the past, and that the Anunnaki used humans as slaves. The Blueline Project would like to run the slave race in exchange for money and privileges. But beforehand, they want to understand the portals so well that they can turn them on and off as they please, also using that as leverage to keep the Anunnaki honest with them and on their side. This isn't a sprint to permanently turn off these portals before the Anunnaki arrive, it's a sprint to understand these portals before the Anunnaki arrive. So be careful. Dexter is a scoundrel, and as head of the Blueline Project agency, he'll do anything to follow this through.

She closed the letter, glaring at the back of Dexter's skull. "Shit." She'd been talking to the one in charge the entire time. Not once did he mention that, always acting as if he was in the lower echelons of the agency. She looked at her friends. "Daf, CJ? When we land, get my sword."

2 2

SHAE

Earth's Moon

Shae stood on the stage, his hands up. Lloyd Winters of the Blueline Project had a weapon aimed at him. Admiral Richard Byrd lunged for Lloyd, grasping for the gun.

Shae jumped off the stage just as a Blueline soldier side tackled Richard, and laid him out on the floor, a rifle in the good admiral's face. Shae backed up, not wanting to be the cause of a bullet to Richard's forehead.

"Get everyone lined up, including Sabra." Lloyd pointed to the stage, and one by one, men from high offices, top military backgrounds, and political leaders from all over the world were shoved against the stage at gunpoint.

They raised their hands, confusion and fear in their eyes. Sabra stood next to Shae, her height almost twice his. She beamed him a smile without a tinge of fear. "Your race has some pep." She leaned down and whispered, "Should I tell him this isn't such a good idea, especially in a Space Templars' base?"

Shae winked. "Let them learn the hard way."

"Don't talk, Fleet Admiral," said Lloyd. "We're running the show

141

from now on, and if we need to keep you here under guard the entire time, I'm fine with that."

Dozens of troops and several political types held weapons, surrounding the men and women butted up against the stage.

"You'll take on the Anunnaki Armada? If so, please enlighten me how?" asked Shae.

"She's an Anunnaki, Shae." Lloyd jabbed his gun toward Sabra. "She claims to be a leader of the Space Templars, and here she is, sister of the very king who wishes to kill us all." He squinted his eyes at Sabra. "If she's telling the truth about that, too."

Shae sighed. "Listen, we held off the coming armada before, and we'll do it again. However, we can't with you holding us up like this." He raised his voice. "We don't have time for this, Mr. Winters."

"My guess is that you have all the time in the world. If I were a betting man," he jutted out his bottom lip, "which sometimes I am, then frankly, I think you're the ones who'll invade us. You're the problem. Or you're the sideshow, a distraction to the coming invasion. You're here to throw us off."

Shae shook his head. "You think I'll lead an invasion on Earth?"

"Anything is possible."

"So, we'll play the what-if game?" Shae glanced at Sabra. He didn't understand fully how the Space Templars intuitively spoke to each other, but he knew they did. "Are the Templars coming to the building?"

Sabra nodded. "Indeed, Admiral. They're surrounding the dome as we speak."

Lloyd stepped back. "Don't do anything stupid."

Shae stood still. "Trust me, we're far from stupid."

Lloyd put one hand in the air to shut Shae up. He looked around, backing up. "If you want us to trust you, then make us the lead in this operation. We watch everything. We make the decisions, we direct the troops, and no one, I repeat, no one but those in the Blue-line Project will be given access to the operation rooms on this base."

"We don't hold anyone back from watching everything," said

Sabra. "But we stop there. You won't be the lead. We want to win this war, Mr. Winters, not watch Earth go up in flames."

"Tell your Templars outside to back down, or one of you dies right now."

Sabra dipped her head. "We don't negotiate, Lloyd. We don't fear death either."

Shae could tell the people up against the stage didn't feel the same as Sabra.

"But," continued Sabra. "If you take your fingers off the triggers, we can find some agreement."

Lloyd shook his head. "No. My way or the highway, miss."

Sabra's lips twitched. "So be it." She thrust her arm outward, and a translucent shield materialized from her wrist band, whirring loudly. The lights in the structure turned off. A zipping sound slashed and echoed in the room, and footsteps pounded on the floor as gunfire went off.

Shae twisted and jumped to his side, tackling the person next to him to the ground. He covered him, keeping the man low, hoping bullets didn't meet his back or the person he attempted to keep safe.

He turned to see bullets flash from guns. Slugs sank into something in front of him, stopping as if caught in midair. They were absorbed, then turned into ash, one after another.

There were a few screams and yelps. A pound and a clank. Gunfire. Shae kept low, crawling in the darkness and pulling someone along he couldn't see. More gun shots. He stumbled against someone in front of him. He pushed the person forward. "Get out of the line of fire." He didn't know if anyone could hear him over the chaos. He heard more yelps and hurried faster. He slipped and face planted in the ground.

The lights turned on, and black ropes hung from the ceiling. Shae glanced around, his mouth dropping open. Space Templar Sirians and humans stood over Lloyd and his companions, rifles pointed at their chests. At the stage, the prisoners were on the floor, either crouching or lying face down. In front of them stood Sabra and a dozen Templars, their shields extended.

Sabra walked over to Lloyd, who lay face up on the ground, his gun in another Space Templar's hand. She bent down. "We're here to help, Mr. Winters, and if you can't handle that, if you can't relent your egotistical control, then you're the problem." She shoved a thumb over her shoulder. "Get them out of here."

The Templars cuffed dozens of Blueline soldiers and agency members and lifted them off the ground. Lloyd flattened his lips as a Templar gripped the back of his shirt. "I see through you."

Shae pushed up on one knee. "You'll see through me from behind bars." He tipped his head toward the exit. "Now get him out of here like Sabra said."

The Templar nudged Lloyd forward and followed the other Templar Marines out of the dome. The door shut with the last of Lloyd's men out of the auditorium.

Shae stood and wiped himself off. "Is anyone injured?" He glanced around, noting the shocked faces as foreign leaders pushed themselves to their feet. He helped Admiral Richard Byrd up, realizing he was the man he tackled. "You all right, Richard?" asked Shae.

He nodded. "I've been in combat. I'll shake it off."

Shae lifted his hands to get everyone's attention. "My apologies. This is a bump in the road. Today I was supposed to speak and then train you, but you received a training unlike I imagined. You now see the strength and quickness of these Space Templars. We couldn't have asked for better equipped, more experienced soldiers. We'll give Enlil and his fleet another terrible memory when they arrive. But today, I'm calling everything off until tomorrow. I assume you have rooms. I'll have a Templar personally escort you to your dome."

Richard raised his hand. "Sir, this isn't a frequent occurrence within the Space Templars' ranks, is it?"

"I assure you it's not."

Sabra chimed in, "We took the Blueline Project Agency in on good faith. Little did we know they had something up their sleeves. Let this be a lesson. We react fast and get the job done. We'll train you in this way too, but we have limited time. Tomorrow, you enter the simulators."

A young Asian woman leaning against the stage, her face slack from the recent turmoil, raised her hand. "We weren't told about simulators." Her moving lips didn't match what came from the translator attached to her chest. Shae hadn't been told about the simulators either.

"They'll enhance your training," said Sabra. "It's a new technology. With the simulators, what we learn in a month in Space Templar training, whether it be piloting, weapon use, hand-to-hand combat, etcetera, you'll learn in a day. It's harmless, but you'll advance faster than anything else we can do for you." Sabra looked around. "Any other questions?"

Everyone raised their hands. Shae went to call on someone and fell to his knee. His vision spun. He looked up and was surprised he now stood inside Starship *Brigantia*, watching Thunderbird starfighters dash in and out of combat, many blowing up on the vidscreen in front of him.

His heart sank at each explosion, and he squeezed his pant leg. The vidscreen zoomed in on a Star Guild cruiser, taking Anunnaki blasts. Its hull was breaking, and internal explosions shot outward.

He gasped and came to, his eyes wide, and sweat dripping down his temples. Sabra crouched at his side, her hand on his back. "Are you with us, Admiral?"

Shae nodded, using her shoulder to help himself up. "Flashbacks. Or I don't know what they are, but they haunt me when I least expect it."

"We can help you with that."

"I need to talk with Helen."

"Understood. But get back to me soon. We need to work on you."

A Templar helped Shae up the steps and out the door. He stood amid the skyscrapers and buzzing city, as hover vehicles zipped overhead. He thanked the soldier and walked around the dome, his boots clicking on the cobblestone street.

He grabbed at his heart as pain ripped through his chest and down his arm. The side of his face went numb, and he stumbled, falling to the ground. He reached for his pocket, pulling out his vidcom.

He weakly pressed a few buttons, his breaths coming harder at each inhale. Helen's beautiful face came on the screen, and he smiled. He closed his eyes as she called out his name.

"I love you, Helen," he said, his words coming out like a drunken sailor. Then everything went black as his heart stopped.

23

ENLIL

Nibiru

Enlil sat on a couch in his father's home, staring at a raging fire in the fireplace. He counted the time before his brother met his end, a blaster slug to the back of his head. He held a glass of mead and swirled the liquid. Taking a drink, he savored it in his mouth before swallowing.

His holopad beeped. He searched the couch as it beeped again. He glanced up to see it sitting on his father's favorite chair. He walked over and snagged it. Turning it on, the holographic display pixilated and rounded upward. "What is it?"

"Hello, King Enlil."

Enlil snorted. "So, you show yourself. What do you have to say for yourself? You run when I order you to kill my brother? It was a king's order, Gronis. You don't turn a king's order down without your head on the chopping block."

Gronis' wrinkled face glared back at him. "I know you don't understand mine and the rest of the council's position. I can't say it enough, we won't support your invasion or your brother's execution."

"Where are you?"

"I can't say."

"Because you know I'll kill you."

"Precisely."

"How long do you think you can run?"

"I'm still around you, watching everything you do. I'll be there when you fail."

"And you'll take my place as king."

"Yes, and run the government properly. Or sweep your sister in your place. A lot is going on underneath your nose that you can't sniff."

Enlil tapped his shoulder comband twice, a signal he set up with tech. The techs would receive the two taps, then track the caller on his holopad. In confirmation, his shoulder band would buzz. "My sister is a female. That wouldn't sit kindly with the populace."

"The populace is changing. They'd accept her."

Enlil's band didn't buzz. He tapped it again.

"I know your trick, Enlil. You won't be able to track me. I have many eyes and ears in tech, and they told me of your little tracking idea in case I called."

"You took a few of my captains. That doesn't sit well with me."

"You should be happy. We tried to take more."

Enlil stood and paced, his face reddening. He had at least two hundred intelligence officers searching for Gronis. The senator had left in the dead of night with all council members, who were now hiding like cowards. Several military leaders went with him and dozens of soldiers, maybe more. The world was vast. It could take weeks, if not months, to find them all.

Then there were Enki's sympathizers, an underground network of people from all walks of life. They annoyed him more than Gronis and the council. The sympathizers busied the streets, infiltrating the business sectors, and had started to make a name for themselves. They left propaganda wherever they dwelled and whispered lies to anyone who'd listen. They'd soon die—all of them. But dammit, more people on his plate to murder took up valuable time in his already loaded days. And he thought running slave worlds was stressful.

"None of my fleet has left to join you," said Enlil, walking to the bar. "I heard you tried to take as many of my ships as you could." He set his glass on the counter and pulled a bottle of mead from a cupboard.

"Your fleet remains intact, yes, but many won't be following you when you invade."

Enlil poured mead into his glass. "You lie."

"You'll see."

He snorted, seeing through Gronis' bluff. "Why are you calling?" He took a swig.

"To give you a chance to see the error of your ways. It's your last chance. We can help you lead your people, or we can help the sympathizers fight you."

"I'll weed out those sympathizers, and when I do, I have a feeling I'll find you."

Gronis sighed. "You had your chance. Your father's rolling in his grave right now, I promise you that. You're a disgrace to his family and his lineage. Enki deserves the throne, not you. Take care, Enlil."

"I'm king, so call me by my title."

"You won't be king for long." Gronis ended the call, and black filled the screen.

Enlil sat on a stool at his father's bar. He'd have to monitor his fleet when they attacked Earth to see who cooperated and who didn't. If he had to blow holes in some of his own ships, so be it. Somehow, he'd have to keep an eye on his soldiers when they went through the portals. Who followed orders and who purposely disobeyed would be the difference between two slugs in the chest or none.

"Running a kingship is proving impossible." He flexed his fingers and made a fist. He groaned his eyes on his whitening knuckles. He couldn't be in two places at once. Gronis had taken the two best fleet group captains he had, the ones he trusted to run the armada's attack. He'd have to place his trust in another.

He nodded to himself. A man came to mind, one he barely knew, but the guy showed class and loyalty. "Captain Fin will be my eyes above." Enlil would head to Earth with the ground units, popping through one of the portals, and making life miserable for Earthlings so Nibiru could stay alive for her people.

He stared at the walls, feeling like they were closing in on him. "I don't like this, Father."

"Get used to it."

Enlil looked up to see Anu sitting in the seat he was murdered in.

"Why can't they just follow my lead?"

"There are two ways to lead, my son. With love or fear."

"I love my people." Enki stood his hands out. "My past actions more than show that love."

Anu leaned forward. "If you love them, you listen to them and the council. You weigh their needs and desires above your own. That's how I led."

"You led with an iron fist."

Anu laughed. "When your mother was alive, she led me with an iron fist. If I treated my people through fear, your mom would have given me a lashing. After she died, I remembered her wishes, and I remained in love with my people, treating them with respect and honor. That's a true king."

Enlil looked down. "It's me against my entire family." He shook his head. "You can go now, Father." He looked up to see his father gone. He tapped on his skull, wondering why he hallucinated Anu. He'd been stressed before, and it never conjured up spirits of dead relatives.

He made his way back to the couch and sat. Bringing up his holopad, he typed and an agent came on the screen. "Yes, my king."

"Any luck finding the sympathizers or the council?"

"No luck with the council. But the sympathizers won't like what's about to hit them."

"Excellent." He tapped the screen off, and stroked his beard. "Father, the difference between you and me? I'd never let mom stand in my way."

24

EDEN

Planet Nibiru

Eden lurched forward, her seat's restraining belts pulling her into her backrest. The ship's bow crumpled like paper as it crashed into a boulder. The cockpit window shattered as a portion of the stone found itself inside the cockpit, inches from Eden's face.

The ship's jostling eased, and Eden heard Templars gearing up, grabbing weapons, and magnetizing them to their utility belts. She swiped the shards of glass off her. The smell of boiling tar rose to her nose and perhaps the forest's scent.

She unbuckled her restraining belt and slid under a portion of the boulder. Her bow lay on the floor, and she shouldered the bowstring, the bow now hanging by her side. She crawled to the middle of the cockpit, meeting Skye. He gestured with a tilt of his head toward the cabin.

Clear of the boulder, she stood and took the bow into her hand. She pulled a detonation tipped arrow from her belt. It elongated to full size, and she notched it. She lowered it toward the ground.

Sleuth sat in his seat, frozen and unable to move.

Yeah, so glad you came along, thought Eden.

"All ready?" asked Skye. The Templars dipped their heads, rifles raised. Outside, a slug cracked across the air, and a bang sent the ship rocking back and forth, signaling that the bots had arrived at the crash site.

Skye cleared his throat. "Shielders, ready us for exit."

Three soldiers went to a knee at the closed door and thrust their fists outward, their gold bands flashing. There was a whirring sound and a translucent shield materialized from each band.

"Open," ordered Skye.

The Starjumper door opened, and a few Templars that stood behind the Shielders sent plasma bolts down on an arriving bot. The bot extended its cannon, but the bolts met the cannon's muzzle before it could get a shot off. More bolts hammered the bot. Sparks blew out at its seams, and it cracked apart, blasting shrapnel and debris and turning into a metallic mess on the scorched ground.

The Shielders jumped out of the craft, their shields absorbing cannon slugs, disintegrating them in a spiral of energy. Three more troops jumped out of the ship, exchanging weapon fire with the bots, each using a Templar Shielder as cover. The Templars' fatigues changed in color, matching the terrain they walked upon, their once-white boots now black as the burnt ground.

Three more Templars exited the ship, materializing shields, and three more followed, raining fire down on the bots. One by one, bots flared into a fiery mess. More came through the forest, colored the same black that made up most of the trees and plants.

Skye jumped down from the craft, Eden in tow. She raised her bow and targeted a lone bot making its way into the fray. She let loose, and a scream erupted from her belly and passed her lips, sending the arrow faster and farther.

The bot's apex opened and freed its cannon. It let out a shot that singed a tree near a Templar. Eden's detonation arrow met the bot's exterior, and it erupted in a ball of flames.

A hum filled the sky, and Eden looked up, nocking another arrow. Anunnaki starfighters raced toward them, and Eden pulled back on her bow and released. The arrow soared faster than the last, hitting the lead fighter in the nose. A loud bang and fire overtook the craft. It went into a downward spiral and crashed nearby, a fire cloud forming.

"So much for the Enki sympathizers. They either ratted out our location or Enlil planted a person in their ranks." Skye waved his arm. "Let's go."

Eden looked around. Where had Sleuth gone? Did he run off to Enlil, crying for help? She turned toward the Starjumper. Its body was worse than she realized. The front sizzled, cracked in half, split around a boulder. The bow was pushed in a heaping mess into the cockpit, and the small wings had been completely ripped off. They'd need a ride back to *Swift* after this was all over. This Starjumper was more or less out of commission.

She saw movement inside the cabin and paused. "Skye, I think Sleuth is still in there."

"Get him."

She wanted to scream, "I told you so," to Skye. She knew they'd have to carry Sleuth on their backs, but she didn't think in the literal sense.

She hopped into the cabin, and there stood Sleuth, his mouth open. "You're all idiots. You thought Enlil wouldn't be on the alert after he heard you were coming?"

"Idiots?" She grabbed his arm, pulling. "You're the one standing in the line of fire."

He jerked back, his face going pale. He took a step forward and slipped, falling flat on his chest. His artificial arm came down as he fell and slammed through the seat next to him. He stood, eyeing his arm. "Holy crap, did you see that?" He pulverized the chair into a gnarled mess.

Eden kept her expression as neutral as possible, wanting to get him out of the craft quickly. "Let's go."

She twisted on her heels, not caring if he followed or not, wondering why she'd attempted to retrieve him. She nodded to herself, thinking the Masters wanted him around, so she should probably feel the same. She looked over her shoulder to see him following her, and jumped out of the craft, her mind spinning over Sleuth's new weapon, his arm.

A purple raindrop-shaped energy projectile rocketed against the ground. A loud bang and dirt and roots flew in the air, throwing Eden, Sleuth, and a few Templar Shielders against the ship she'd just exited. She pushed up quickly, her ears ringing. Helping her fellow Templars to their feet, she tugged them away from the growing fire in front of them.

The bots volleyed pulse weapons into the Shielders, the pulse fire sucking into their shields, fading away a moment later. A few shots flew past Eden, singeing boulders. The starfighter's hum grew louder as they reared around, heading for another pass.

"We move now." Skye rushed forward, and the Shielders took up the rear, extending their shields behind them. Skye led them down a make-shift path between crooked trees, large spiral hanging vines, and giant plants all the same blackened color.

Eden ran behind him, Sleuth behind her, already heaving in and out as if he just finished a marathon. Skye dashed to the right to follow another trail between enormous boulders, and then down a rocky incline, pebbles jostling loose and cascading.

Starfighters buzzed overhead, and zap sounds of pulse weapons blasted from their cannons. All the Space Templars activated shields, including Eden. She twisted and pulled Sleuth into her and tumbled backward, sliding on her back down the hill. Extending her shield, she covered her and Sleuth's bodies. The cannon blasts from the starfighters littered the surrounding ground, throwing eruptions of rock into the air.

She came to a stop, and Skye grabbed Eden's shirt and pulled her to a standing position. "We keep moving," he said, pulling her along. "I've been in this area before, and the cave is to the east. We can defend ourselves there, but the Sight is also telling me there's something else that can help us in that direction as well."

Eden glanced behind her as she hurried behind Skye. Sleuth raced after her, but a few Space Templars found death's doorstep from direct hits by the starfighters.

A bot's beeps, along with crunching sounds as they rolled over dried branches and twigs, came to Eden's ears. The bastards were in pursuit, and the whir of Templars' rifle fire flew. The Templars were crack shots, stopping several bots dead in their tracks.

"It doesn't look like we'll get to Enki in time," shouted Eden, pumping her arms, jumping over a root sticking up from the path.

Skye dug his foot in the ground and dashed to the right. "We'll get there, trust me." He came to a grueling stop, his hands up and legs bent, about to use the Sight to his advantage.

Eden halted by his side, bow and arrow at the ready, conjuring up the Sight. In front of them stood dozens of Anunnaki giants with scarfs around their heads. They wore raggedy clothes, all in different colors, and none matching the terrain. They leveled spears with glowing ends, the Anunnaki rifle of choice, and aimed.

"Get ready, Eden," ordered Skye, about to send as many people off their feet as he could with the Sight.

"Ready." Eden narrowed her eyes, ready to end the lead man with one shot.

25

ALI

<u>Lima, Peru</u>

Ali woke and glared at the clock on the bedside table. She blinked several times. The night before seemed a distant memory.

"It's evening already," she said to herself.

They had exited the plane at Limatambo International Airport around three in the morning. They arrived at the Atemporal Mansion an hour later with CJ, Daf, and with Dexter and his crew. She carried the long suitcase housing Sol up the stairs, and the owner's hired staff carried her other bag.

"What's in the long bag?" Dexter had asked.

She batted her tired eyes. "Woman things."

Dexter bid her and her friends a good night. CJ and Daf took separate rooms. Ali couldn't fall asleep until around ten in the morning, Albert's note, Dexter's dishonesty, and Enlil's insanity swirling in her mind.

She brought herself back to the present and eyed the falling sun through the window. The rays beamed past soft pink curtains with pelmets. A floral upholstered chair and a small, white loveseat faced the window. A bookshelf butted up against a wall, and a dozen books were spread out on the shelves.

Ali stretched and yawned. She sat up and stared at the sword against the wall next to her. She had placed it there for a just-in-case situation. Trust in Dexter had fallen sharply after reading the rest of Albert's letter, but there was something trustworthy about him she couldn't shake. She'd do a little more digging to find out if her gut spoke the truth, or if her fluttering, dumb crush masked it.

A knock on the door. "Ali, are you up and ready?" Dexter stood on the other side.

Ali's eyes widened. She reached for the sword and wrapped her fingers around the hilt. She stood and hid it under the bed, the bed's wooden frame only a quarter of a meter above the floor. "I'm getting ready."

"We're going to dinner soon. I've talked with CJ and Daf, and they're famished. My men are just as hungry."

"Yeah." She looked around for her bag of clothes, something she'd neither searched through nor packed herself. CJ and Daf took that responsibility before they snatched her from the bakery. They better have grabbed the right outfits, including her field garb.

"Are you hungry?" he asked. "I bet you're just as raring to eat as your friends."

Ali shook her head. "I'm not." Her stomach growled.

A pause. "Are you sure? From my calculations, you missed yesterday's lunch and dinner. And today's breakfast and lunch. I'm sure you need some food in you."

She found her bag against the dresser. A mirror reflected her disheveled red hair, and a line from her pillow ran across her cheek. She'd slept in yesterday's clothes and looked a mess. She rummaged through her bag, picking out a blue-striped t-shirt and beige high waisted, wide-leg pants.

"Ali?"

"Still getting my things in order." She stripped her clothes off and threw her shirt and pants on.

"Can I come in?"

She turned and fussed with her hair. "Just a minute." She shoved her dirty clothes under her bed with her foot and twisted to face the door, nearly out of breath. "Come in."

The door swung open. He smiled at her, and her heart just about flew out of her chest. He held his hat in his hand. "I apologize for last night. If that's what's keeping you from coming with us, then know it's all a misunderstanding on my part, on Albert's part, and well, all of our parts." He wore a three-button notch lapel sport coat, chevron checkered, and dark pants, all fashion, handsome, and ready to go. He motioned toward the door. "We have a few cars waiting."

"Where are Daf and CJ?"

"In the cars."

Daf and CJ thought Dexter was a liar. They wouldn't leave her alone with Dexter and his crew inside the mansion. "And your men?"

"In the other car. Look for yourself." He pointed toward the window.

Ali stepped around the chair and pushed the curtain aside. Outside, on wet pavement, steam drifting upward from the now warming asphalt, idled two Packard Clippers, one car painted black, the other painted blue. The driveway was circular and had a statue with green plants stuck in the middle. A well-manicured, green lawn bordered the drive, and a few Peruvian men in white sweaters and white pants stood on the grass pruning red-flowered oleander shrubs.

All she could see from the second-floor window was Daf sitting in the backseat of the blue Packard Clipper. The Russian was leaning against the nearest passenger side door of the other car, his face and shoulder in view. Apparently, Daf's and CJ's hunger trumped their lack of trust in Dexter and his team.

Ali sighed, rubbing her stomach. "I'll stay back and rest. My stomach's queasy from the plane ride."

He raised his brows. "Are you sure?"

"I'm sure." Ali could do with two plates of food, but she could do more with finding out how much this guy had lied. Being an archaeologist and scraping up the truth didn't stop at ancient artifacts.

He gave a crooked smile. "It would be nice getting to know you a little better, even if you don't eat."

She frowned, holding her stomach longer. "I may run back and forth to the toilet if you know what I mean."

He dipped his head. "Understood. Have a good night, Ali." He turned and left, gently shutting the door behind him.

She leaned against the window, playing with the curtain. She imagined Dexter being an honest man, touching her, holding her, kissing her neck. She stepped back and let out a sharp breath. "Dammit, Ali. Grow up," she told herself.

She watched Dexter walk to the black car. He gave Ali a look and waved. Opening the passenger side door, he sat, and the cars drove off down a drive bordered by cedars.

She turned and walked out the door, halting in front of a smiling, short man. He wore a black suit, bow tie, and black pants as if about to go to a play with his wife. He held out his hand, his accent thick, though his English fluent. "Welcome, miss. My name is Alejandro Garcia. This is my home."

She grabbed his hand and shook it. "Thank you for having us." They stood in a hallway, with stairs leading down to her left, and more rooms splitting off into another hall to her right. Black and white pictures lined the walls, and red carpet with thick gold patterns covered the floor.

"If there's anything you need, just ask my staff."

She held up her index finger. "I need to know where Dexter's room is. We're both archaeologists on a dig, and I need some notes he left for me."

He nodded. "I know who you are and why you're here. It's of utmost importance, I'm sure." He pointed to a room at the end of the hall. "Dexter's room."

She nodded and proceeded forward, thanking him. Reaching the door, she turned the knob. A stream of light lining the wood floor greeted her. She gave Alejandro a nod and stepped inside, closing the door behind her.

She turned the light switch on, the metal switch plate cold against her hands. A small table near the window held a vase of roses, the bed made next to it. Other than the table, the room matched hers. She took quiet, steady steps, searching for anything that might hold secrets.

A pen and book with a green leather cover sat on top of the bedside table. "A diary," she muttered, picking it up. She let out a sigh as she set it down. She looked around, not liking that she'd almost snuck into someone's deepest thoughts uninvited. She surveyed the floor.

A briefcase, perhaps the one Albert mentioned in the letter, sat next to the dresser. It looked more like a leather Swiss Army tool bag than anything else. She hurried to it and crouched, pulling the leather strap from the metal buckle.

She opened it. Inside, documents and papers were divided into several sections between thick, beige sheets. She rifled through them, reading the page titles: Blueline Project Objective, Blueline Project Mission Statement, Blueline Project Notes, and so on.

She read through the objective's first page, not gaining much other than the Blueline Project pursued a method to locate all portal entries, which they called the blueline. She set the Blueline Objective on the floor and pulled out a paper-clipped stack titled Lima's National Museum. She took the paperclip off and spread out the pages, all containing pictures of ancient cuneiforms inscribed with symbols.

She was about to translate one when a letter with her name caught her attention. She furrowed her brow and picked it up. She leaned against the bed's footboard.

Alison Johnson, Chief Petty Officer, Anunnaki blood intermixed with Homo Sapiens. A member of the bloodline.

She lurched back. "How the hell would they know I'm of the bloodline?" She wrinkled her nose. And how did they know the last name given to her when she lived on Starbase Matrona? Her real last name was Lutz, not Johnson. Shae, her dad, had been paired with people matching his last name after the Anunnaki kidnapped him and brought him to Matrona. Instead of doing the same for Ali, Enlil paired her with Captain Diana Johnson.

She read more.

We must eliminate Ali immediately after her translations for each portal location are complete, per the Monarch's orders.

Her mouth gaped open. "What?" Her gut twisted, but she couldn't take her eyes off the letter.

Once portals open, Anunnaki military will advance on Earth, efficiently eliminating specified cities and military sites listed on the Blueline Project Objective pages four through fourteen. As of this writing, the Monarch knows of one portal location, but suspects there are thousands across the world. Ali can translate and locate, and once we get a map of all locations from her, we eliminate her. Be careful. She wields a Space Templar Sword known as Sol. She is dangerous and considered a threat. Caution is advised. Read Blueline Project 'Ali Johnson' pages twelve through eighteen for specific strategies to gain her trust. Her psychological—

She dropped the letter. She stood her hand over her mouth. They're attempting to open the portals and not attempting to unlink or disable them. They had her personality profile. What had she stepped into? What had the Space Templars thrust upon her?

The door to Dexter's room opened. Ali crouched in a start, her fingers curled in a fist, ready to throw down.

"Yeah, Alejandro, I forgot my—" Dexter's smile turned down. He looked at the papers spread out on his floor, and then at the culprit. "Ali?"

26

ENLIL

Nibiru

Perspiration dotted Enlil's forearms and hands. He watched the beads of sweat slowly roll to the underside of his arms, imagining one bead was him hiding, running from the responsibility he had for his people, to kill his brother.

Today was execution day.

He sat atop his father's home, a skyscraper that nearly reached the mountain tops. He stood and walked to the building's edge, placing his hands on the top of the barrier railings. He looked past his father's statue that took up most of the city's center and peered a scant distance away at Ovaro's Peaks, a mountain range that loomed in a semi-circle around much of the city.

Lava bubbled down one side of a peak, disappearing off the back of the volcano. Like most of his race, he enjoyed lava. Anunnaki thrived in the heat, and this planet gave plenty with its constant mini volcanic eruptions. The volcanic frequency gave three thing to Nibiru and her people: a release valve; the release valve easing volcanic intensity; and steady lava streams slithering toward each city, giving off an abundance of heat.

His race built cities at the base of volcanoes. At each mountain range, the Anunnaki created lava funnels that led to deep tunnels veining underneath each great metropolis.

"They're here," came Kamina's voice through Enlil's shoulder band.

He tapped the band. "Tell them to meet me at his cell." He turned and took long, heavy strides toward the elevator. Stepping inside, he voiced, "Level one." The elevator descended, and he put his hand on the wall, leaning against it, his head lowered.

He took a deep breath, his heart racing. He didn't want to look into his brother's eyes for the last time. Enki had confessed to his father's death, but knowing if Enki spoke the truth went beyond Enlil. The techs had worked on the holovid that recorded his brother holding a gun in his father's presence. No matter what they did, the vid came to a standstill with Enki's gun raised just above his hip.

It proved nothing, other than the possibility that Enki pulled the trigger on their father. Knowing Enki, he'd probably come to their father's rescue. Maybe he arrived too early, on a tip to stop their father's assassination. Perhaps Enki left before the assassin entered the building, and then his father's murder took place.

The elevator stopped and dinged open. The usual frantic lobby was empty. The busy workers and businessmen and women were in the stadium at the town square, awaiting the public execution.

He strolled across the lobby, his boots clicking on the floor. Kamina stood behind a counter, and like always, held a smile and a pleasing look. But Enlil wasn't pleased. You could pull a fast one on him for so long. He unholstered his blaster, flicked the safety off, and aimed. He pulled the trigger, and the plasma bolt exited the muzzle. Her expression changed to horror.

The bolt struck her forehead, and she jerked back, her eyes rolling. She dropped behind the counter. He spun on his heels and headed toward the stairs near the entrance. This morning, Nibiru Secret Intelligence had come to him with urgent information regarding the woman he just killed. She'd had several discussions with Enki's sympathizers, giving them execution date and time intel. Each exchange had gone from Enlil's mouth, out of hers, and into a sympathizer's ears.

He bit down a yell, wanting to punch someone. He couldn't trust a damn soul nowadays. He pressed his hand against a door panel, and the door slid open, revealing the spiral staircase that led to Enki's prison cell. He hurried down, glaring at several guards with long rifle spears at the bottom of the steps. "Get Enki."

All four nodded. They marched to the cell, opened it, and pulled out his brother. Chains bound his wrists to a metallic ring around his waist and clanged at each step. His brother's eyes penetrated Enlil's.

"Hi, brother," said Enki, his long greasy hair twisting down his face, partially covering his eyes and cheeks. He didn't smile and only gave his brother a nod.

Enlil dipped his head, his heart dropping. The guards marched Enki past him and through a doorway behind the stairs. Enlil extended his hand to the lone guard sitting behind a desk. "Give me your holopad."

The guard stood and hurried to Enlil, holopad in hand. "Here, my king." He bowed as he handed Enlil the item.

"I like your haste."

"Thank you, my king."

Enlil faced the stairs and hurried behind the others, entering a dark tunnel. Reaching the guards, he slowed to walk with them. The guards stopped at a platform, and Enlil stepped onto it. He eyed the guards, the dim tunnel's light showing nothing more than black outlines.

"You can all go now," said Enlil.

"Sir?" said a guard.

"Leave," Enlil barked.

The guards stepped away from the platform.

"Hover," ordered Enlil. The platform lifted into the air. "Forward." The platform flew down the black tunnel, carrying Enlil and Enki.

Enlil brought the holopad to his face, and tapped in several commands, bringing up the recording of Enki and his father. He sighed. No progress. Enki held the gun at his hip, his father's arms out wide, excited to see his boy.

"Why did you lift the gun?"

"To kill Father."

Enlil grabbed Enki and pulled him close, nose to nose. "You're covering for Senator Gronis because you hold something dear in your heart for that cowardly man. Keep in mind, you hold more weight in the council than Gronis."

"If you don't kill me, will you still kill Gronis?"

Enlil looked away. "No."

"You lie."

Enlil didn't argue and tightened his lips. A hum echoed, and their boots magnetized to the platform. The platform sped up, the wind whipping Enlil's hair across his face.

Enki straightened in his posture. "I love you, brother. I loved Father and Mother, and I love our sister. No matter what happens, it won't change that."

"I know." In a strange, screwed up way, he loved Enki. He didn't know how much until he wanted to kill him. But want carried a strong tone. There wasn't a want, there was a must, and that must traversed across a hundred reasons. Power. Strength. To harm the Templars. To gain his people's trust and fear. For his people to do his bidding. To show leadership. The list went on and on. But the desire to prove his strength and leadership to his people waned at every passing moment that marched him closer to his brother's death. "I know that Skye and Space Templar Marines are on Nibiru, heading our way."

"They're good people."

"I'm slowly killing them. They won't make it to your execution. Skye will die if he's not dead already."

"When you don't fear death, death doesn't exist."

"It exists."

"Not if you surrender to the mind. Our souls carry on after our body's breath ceases. Energy doesn't vanish. It transforms."

"I've heard your philosophies before. Rubbish." He swiped the holopad to check the vid. Again, stalemate. No movement, no progression. "Was anyone else in the room beside you and Father?"

"Yes."

"Who?"

Enki didn't respond.

"Did you kill that other person?"

"No."

"But you killed Father." It became a statement now, not a question.

"Yes."

"Was the other person there to kill Father?"

"He was."

Enlil stretched his neck, the stress getting to him. "You didn't kill Father, then. You killed the murderer after he killed Father."

Again, Enki didn't speak.

Enlil's eyebrows drew together. "I don't understand."

His brother blinked a few times and smiled. "You will. In time."

The platform slowed. "We're almost here."

"Let the fun begin." Enki winked.

Enlil tilted his head at Enki's comment. The platform stopped, and in the darkness, he looked up. "Are the Templars up there?"

"Perhaps."

Enlil swallowed hard and pulled out his blaster. "If some of them got past our combat units, I have something in store for them in the form of explosives right here in the public square. You know, just in case. It'll be a spectacle no one will forget." He winked and tapped his chin on the shoulder comm. "Do we have eyes on the building tops? Any strange activity?"

"Building tops empty except for our snipers. The perimeter is clear," came a voice. "The only Templar activity we see is our current military engagement in Ebol Forest."

"Good." Enlil eyeball his brother, his lips close to the comm. "We're ready. Lift us."

The ceiling opened, and sunlight poured in, highlighting his brother's serene face. The platform raised and clicked into place in the middle of the city square. Black spindly trees surrounded a large fountain with a statue of their dead mother, water pouring from a bowl she held into a pool. A crowd sitting in stadium seats circled them. The people stood and erupted into a cheer when they saw their king and his brother.

He shot his blaster into the air as his voice boomed through the speakers. He swept his eyes around the two hundred thousand spectators. "Keep your damn mouths shut." Spittle flew from his lips. "Today isn't a day to celebrate. Today is my brother's death. If I hear a peep of excitement from any of you, I'll hunt every one of you down like dogs."

The crowd fell silent. He eyed them, doing his best to pinpoint Skye or anyone else on the Templars team. Perhaps they had taken a seat. He shook his head. There were too many people.

"And to all of you," he shouted. "Do not cross me. Do not disobey. Do not go against my well-wishes for Nibiru and her people, my people. If you do, my brother will be an example of what I'll do to you." He eyed his brother, his tone flat and soft. "Get on your knees."

"This quickly, huh? No more words of wisdom for our people?" He grinned, his sarcasm more than apparent.

"I want to get this over with and move on with my life."

"You won't move on. Not after this."

"I will."

Enki went to his knees and bowed his head. "I'll miss you, brother. I'll miss our people. Tell Sabra I love her."

"I'll miss you too." Strangely, he meant it.

He rounded Enki and held the gun against the back of Enki's head, his finger on the trigger. He squeezed his eyes shut, his lower jaw quivering. He let out a heavy gush of air and pushed the muzzle harder into Enki's skull. "Goodbye, brother."

2 7

EDEN

Nibiru

"Hold on," yelled Skye, his hand up, halting Eden and the remaining Templars from ending the giant men and women standing before them.

The giants lifted their spear-like weapons, aiming at the starfighters. The spear muzzles flashed, and the enemy craft veered away. Several direct hits sparked off the ships' exteriors, but the starfighters continued onward, flying overhead, shaking the ground.

A handful of giants jumped down from a boulder and rushed past Eden. They went to their knees and blasted several bots coming down the path, cracking them open and sending black smoke into the air.

"Let's go," said a gruff voice. Eden turned and watched the Anunnaki run in the opposite direction of the bots. One was clearly the leader and waved her onward. "We need to save Enki. We have very little time."

Skye nudged her as he ran after them. "These are the sympathizers."

Eden grasped Sleuth, who was bent over, his hands on his knees. "If you don't come with us, you die right here." A Templar ran by. "Get your ass moving."

Sleuth nodded, drops of sweat dripping off his nose. "Okay."

They moved swiftly down a hill, while starfighters screamed overhead, dropping more tear-drop energy weapons.

"Shields up," yelled Eden. She activated her shield and slowed her run to allow Sleuth to catch up to her. She aimed her shield toward the sky, covering them both. The energy weapons dropped behind them, and explosions riddled the ground. Her stomach fell. "Oh, no."

Three Templars met their end, their shields doing nothing against the big weapons that pulverized them into the ground.

"Go, Eden. Go." A Templar hurried by her.

She rushed ahead and looked over her shoulder to see if Sleuth ran at her pace. Her eyes popped wide, and she skidded to a halt. "What the hell?"

Sleuth ran in the opposite direction, his metallic arm reared back in a punch. A bot came around the path, and he swung at the machine, his fist slicing through it. The bot spurted sparks and rolled down the side of the hill like a perfectly round tumbling rock. Sleuth's mouth hung open as he studied his silver fingers.

Eden reached him. "What are you doing?"

Sleuth rushed forward, in the direction the rest of the Templars and sympathizers had gone. "I don't know. I couldn't control myself. It's as if my arm dragged me there."

She ran to his side, keeping pace with him. "You have legs, so use them and don't split off from the rest of the group."

"It's stronger than my legs. It pulled me, and I didn't have the strength to pull back."

She shook her head, not believing a word Sleuth spoke. The guy probably wanted to test out his new toy. "Can you keep up?"

"I think so."

"If you don't, you'll die."

Eden moved farther through the forest, dashing by boulders, jumping over roots and through the brush. They made it to the edge of the city, where a group of Templars and sympathizers waited. A throng of black, twisted trees, thick and wide stood between them and the metropolis.

Skye looked around the group as if counting. He eyed Eden. "Any more of us coming?"

Eden put her hands on her knees, her bow over her shoulder. "We lost three Templar Marines back there, and two near the crash site." They lost five elite soldiers in a short time. Not good. She looked up. "Where are the starfighters?"

"They won't drop their bombs this close to the city," said the sympathizer leader, a scarf over his head and face, only his sharp, blue eyes exposed. All the sympathizers wore similar scarfs in different colors.

"And the bots?" Eden looked behind her.

"We have something special for them." As if on cue, a line of fire lifted from the ground in the distance. Trees, shrubs, and smoke were thrown toward the heavens.

Skye grinned. "Good man. What's your name?"

"No Name."

Skye tilted his head. "No Name?"

"Yes. Ain't no one going to know who we are, no matter what."

Skye dipped his head. "Understood."

A large black hovervan came from down the street, a man sitting in a large turret on top, his hands gripping a hefty double-barreled pulse weapon. It was headed their way.

Eden crouched and whispered, "A friendly?"

The leader nodded, his hand up, waiting to give the order to proceed.

Skye glared at him. "We weren't told about this. We're supposed to navigate the lower tunnels with a band of your soldiers."

"Things changed, and those bands of soldiers are dead. Enlil infiltrated our ranks and overran us down below. He moved up the execution time. It goes down in ten minutes."

Skye stiffened. "We won't get there in time."

"We'll try." The leader dropped his arms. "Let's go." Everyone dashed forward as the van descended. It landed on the edge of the road. Several sympathizer soldiers fanned out on all sides, their weapons extended.

The door opened, and No Name threw his hand across the opening. "Not all of us can fit. Pick two of your best, and I'll pick two of mine." He pointed at two large men near the hood of the vehicle. They rounded the van and jumped inside.

Skye flicked his thumb at Eden and Sleuth. "Get in. The rest of you get to the rendezvous point and wait. Stay safe. That's an order."

Eden shook her head furiously. "You can't take Sleuth."

"We don't have time to argue." He grabbed Sleuth, picked him up, and threw him in. He stepped inside next and eyed Eden, daring her to say another word.

"The damn monks." She hopped inside, and the door shut. The van hovered in the air, then flew forward at a quick speed.

Inside, the van was empty of seats, yet still crowded with the gigantic Anunnaki men on their butts, weapons cradled in their arms. More weapons were magnetized along the walls. Silence filled the van, except for Sleuth's heavy breathing. He glared down at his metal hand. His other hand was shaking and picking at the silver.

"What's our plan now?" asked Eden.

No Name, sitting behind her, shifted his position. "Enlil's soldiers overran our men down in the tunnels, so we're dead in the water if we go with Plan A. Kamina, Enlil's assistant and second-hand-woman was Plan B. She was to follow him to the execution and put a slug in his head. She's dead. We're on our last plan, which isn't a plan in the slightest. We head blind into the execution stadium."

"How high can this thing fly?" asked Skye.

"Over the stadium. We'll use the element of surprise if we can get there fast enough. I have a gunner atop the van right now, and he'll zero in on Enlil once we have him in sight. He'll put a slug in Enlil's head for Kamina."

"And if he doesn't?" asked Eden.

"We land and grab our target, and get out," said No Name.

Skye giggled as if this were an everyday thing. "That's not much of a strategy." He shook his head. "But miracles happen."

"It's not a plan, but that's all we have in such a short time. I'll gladly sacrifice myself for Enki. He's the only hope we have, and the only one with enough political power to stand up against our new tyrant king."

"We're coming up on the stadium," said the driver.

Eden's muscles tightened, and she checked her sidearm. She pulled off her bow and notched an arrow. "Sleuth, if you can use that arm, do it."

"I don't think it gives me much of a choice."

"Good," she replied. Because if Sleuth had a choice in the matter, he'd hide behind Enlil.

The van rose higher, and out the front window, Eden saw the stadium. It's large cement-like walls rose high into the air, and windows lined the structure up and down. She could see Anunnaki sitting, their backs to her, and some standing and cheering. She swallowed hard. "Did the execution already happen?"

"I don't think so," said No Name.

They lifted above and over the stadium walls, and the van dropped, descending. She eyed a stage in the middle of a public square. Enlil was holding a gun to the back of Enki's head.

Enlil shifted and pointed at the van. The gunner on top of the vehicle fired at Enlil, tracers sparking off the stage. Enlil jumped out of the way.

"Dammit, Halm," yelled No Name, eyeing the van's ceiling. "The objective was not to miss."

"Get ready," said Skye.

Tracers hammered the van from Enlil's troops. Halm flipped over the front of the van and rested dead on the windshield, his eyes open and lifeless. Blood drooled out of his mouth, and bloody marks pocked his body. He slid off the side of the van, disappearing from view.

More tracer fire hit the hover vehicle, ripping through the walls, and zipping out the other side. A slug hit Sleuth's arm and sparked. He twirled away, fumbling backward, and tumbling toward the rear of the van.

"Shields," ordered Skye, activating his. Eden did the same. The shields didn't extend far, exposing the driver and the men behind her.

Dozens of slugs ripped through again, cracking against No Name, several puncturing his side and skull. He leaned over, dead. More slugs poked holes through the walls, disintegrating into the shields, one slamming into the driver's neck. He grabbed his wound, then slumped over onto the passenger seat.

"This was a shitty plan," yelled Eden, getting up, shield still activated. She moved toward the driver's seat, shouldering her bow and holstering her arrow. Her mouth gaped open as the public square's asphalt rushed toward her. She lunged for the control stick and pulled back.

Skye stood. "No time, no plan. Sometimes that's the demons of the game." He rushed forward and dove shield first into the windscreen. It shattered, sending shards of glass outward. Some sucked back toward Eden from the van's speed. Eden thrust her shield in front of her to block the glass, simultaneously pulling the control stick toward her.

Skye twisted in the air, landing on the asphalt and rolling, the shield to his side, blocking more shots. The van's front end buckled as it slammed into the ground, and Eden flew through the vehicle's front window frame, her hands extended, her shield blinking off.

ALI

Lima, Peru

Dexter lifted his coat and reached around to his back. He pulled out a gun and pointed it at Ali. "What are you doing?"

Ali raised her hands, taking a step forward. She was only a meter or two from him. "You're—" She lunged at the gun, and grabbed his wrist, knocking him back into the wall.

She brought a knee to his groin, missing and hitting his stomach. He grunted, and a gush of wind exited his mouth. He took in a gulp of air as Ali thrashed his gun hand into the wall. The gun dropped, and Ali dove for it, her arm sliding across the wood floor, scuffing her skin.

Wincing in pain, she grabbed the gun and rolled to her back, aiming it at him. Already in midair, he landed on top of her, slapping at the gun. It went flying across the room. A thud and the weapon dented the fine wood on the lower dresser drawer.

Dexter leaned into her arms, holding them down. His face reddened, and the veins in his forehead extended outward as if about to burst. Ali tried to move, but her hands were pinned, his strength too much for her. "Get off of me." She strained to twist and turn, to do anything to get up and knee the guy or race out of the room.

She screamed. If Daf and CJ followed him in the mansion, it would give them a heads up that shit just hit the fan. His hand came down on her lips, pushing hard on her nose, and stifling her voice. She kicked her legs, and he shifted, landing his knees on her arms. Now both of his hands covered her mouth.

She tried to bite his finger. She couldn't get the angle and he didn't sink his finger or palm too far into her mouth. He shushed her several times. She wiggled her head, her strength draining, and her energy fading.

She went to take a breath, but he had her mouth and nose covered. She flailed, and moved her head back and forth, gasping for air, unable to grab much-needed oxygen before he covered her nose and mouth again.

He shushed her more. "Ali, be quiet." He looked behind him as if making sure no one was coming down the hall. "Just shut up and listen."

She shook her head, frantically wanting to break loose of his powerful grip and heavy weight. She screamed again, but her voice hit his palm and fell back into her throat.

She couldn't breathe, and her vision faded. Her body went limp. He jumped off of her in fright. She took in a deep breath, wheezing in and out as her energy came back. He bent down, tapping her cheeks, his eyebrows drawn. "I'm so sorry." He rubbed her forehead. "Keep breathing. There you go. In and out."

Her life slowly came back, her vision clearing and her wheezing less.

"Are you okay?" he asked.

Ali nodded and swallowed, her throat sore. She turned her head, her eyes catching the glint from the gun. She twisted and crawled toward it. A knee came down on her back, and she screamed. He reached around and covered her mouth again, muffling her voice.

"Dammit, Ali."

She reached for the weapon, and he swiped at her forearm, grasping it and pulling it behind her. He lifted her arm high behind her back, and pain rushed up her arm to her shoulder.

"I don't want to dislocate your shoulder, so don't move." He grabbed her by the back of the shirt and tossed her on the bed.

Ali bounced and moved backward, butting up against the headboard. Her heart beat quickly, her adrenaline soaring. She breathed in and out, gripping the bedspread into her fists. "Leave…me…alone."

He held the gun in her direction, though not pointing it directly at her. It didn't matter. He had the gun and the leverage. "I don't want to hurt you." He stepped on some papers and looked down. He took several looks at what she read, moving his eyes back and forth between her and the pages. "This isn't what you think."

Ali breathed heavily, unable to catch her breath. "It's…exactly what…I think."

"Yes, and no." His shirt was untucked, and his hair stuck out every which way. His face lost its redness, and his breathing slowed. "Listen carefully. I know what you read, and it doesn't look good. There's a reason I insisted on this job. Unbeknownst to the heads of the Blueline Project, I plan on keeping you alive and using the Space Templar device to turn off as many portals as I can. I won't give them a map to any of the locations you find."

She shook her head and narrowed her eyes. "What do you mean, heads of the Blueline Project? You are the head."

He scrunched up his brow, his lips drooping into a frown. "What do you mean I'm the head?"

"I read the rest of Albert's note."

"You said you didn't."

"CJ picked it up after you dropped it."

"That's why you didn't want to go to dinner. You wanted to spy on me and get as much information as you could." He paused for a moment, continuing to point the gun near her. "I would've done the same. But to make something clear, I don't know where Albert got the idea that I was the head of anything. I volunteered for this project. I'm not even getting paid. I'm an archaeologist like you, and so are the rest of my team members. Not one of them will harm you. They just don't want any hiccups."

"Why would Albert say you're the head then?"

"I don't know." He let out a sharp breath, looking down for a moment. "I had my suspicions about him. I think he may work for Lloyd Winters and be acting as a double agent."

"A double what?"

He put his hand up. "Did you see my name as head of anything on those documents you read?"

She looked away. "No."

"Did you see my name anywhere on those pages?"

She shook her head.

"Because I'm not the head of anything, except for this team."

"But Albert—"

"Don't trust that guy. He's a snoop for the wrong team." He put his gun behind his back and tucked it into his pants. "I won't kill you, and I never planned to. I've never even killed a fly."

Ali pointed to the papers on the ground. "But, your Blueline Project aligned with Enlil." Even if this guy didn't have evil intentions, he knowingly or unknowingly worked for the very team that took orders from the Anunnaki king.

He crinkled his brow. "Who?"

"The Anunnaki leader." She crossed her arms at her stomach, her lips and nose aching from when he had covered her mouth.

"Is that who they call the Monarch?" He scratched his temple. "I wondered who or what that was. But no, I'm not aligned with whoever that is. Lloyd Winters and the other leaders of the agency have a deal with that Monarch guy. I don't know who contacted who first, and I don't care. We'll use the Templar devices to shut down these portals when you find each location. That's my mission. Don't tell a damn soul, not even your friends. Word gets out and we're all dead men." He flicked a hard look at Ali. "And women."

Ali tightened her arms around her waist. "Let me see the device."

He cocked his head to the side. "What?"

"The device the Space Templars gave to your agency to kill a portal link."

He flattened his lips, now crossing his own arms. "No."

"I'll call for CJ."

He went rigid for a moment. Good, it meant CJ was nearby. "Ali, I don't know you from Adam."

She looked at the door, ready to yell CJ's name.

He backed up. "All right, just relax." He went to his hands and knees and pulled out a wooden box from under the bed. He lifted it and set it next to Ali. Running his hand over it, the cherry-stained lid opened on its own. He grabbed a round orb about the size of a bowling ball. It glowed and pulsed, like everything Space Templar.

Ali went to touch it. He pulled back. "Again, I don't know you from Adam."

"Understood." She eyed the orb and saw Space Templar sacred geometric designs etched on the surface. She gave a satisfied nod. "How does this work?"

"By commands. A man named Skye gave the Blueline Project thousands of these to use all over the planet. He said he was a Space Templar. He gave me this one and said if I voice the words—" He cut himself off. "I'm probably not supposed to voice the words, just in case it does something we won't like."

"Did Skye voice the words to you?"

"No, he spelled them out."

"Then do that."

"A-U-R-O-R-A."

"Their home planet."

He shrugged. "Sure? I don't know. When I say those words out loud while in the portal's vicinity, it shuts down the portal for good."

"Are you sure?"

"No way to know. It's what he said, and I can only go on blind faith." He put the orb back in the box, and the lid closed. He picked it up and shoved it under his bed.

Ali let her arms drop to her side. The only reason she was giving an ounce of trust to this guy was because of Skye. For reasons she didn't know, Skye had trusted him enough to give him an orb. She gave a curt, "Sorry." She didn't mean it.

He sat next to her. "You had no way of knowing."

She leaned away from him. "When do we go to the excavation

site?" She'd rather knock him out with the rest of his team and take Daf and CJ herself. But she didn't know its specific location. She needed them like they needed her. Skye gifting the orb to them caused her to pause at her total lack of trust in the guy.

"Tomorrow we head to the site. We have tablets to translate. Our military is there, more or less guarding it against local authorities who either want to steal it to sell to the highest bidder or place the tablets inside a museum. It's a quick ride to the site from here, and you'll—" he stopped talking, his eyes coming to her lips. "Your bottom lip is swollen." He gently touched her cheek, his finger slowly moving toward her lip. "I didn't mean to. I just didn't know what to do. I didn't know if they sent you to kill me."

Ali touched his finger and pushed it away. "I'll live."

Dexter looked deeply into her eyes, his voice low and sweet. "It pains me that I hurt you." He leaned closer for an obvious kiss. She leaned away, her eyes widening. "What are you doing?

The door opened. CJ stood there, his hands cupped in front of him. "I'm sorry to interrupt you two. We wanted to know what took you so long. I came up here to see if everything was okay?" His eyes drifted to Ali.

Dexter stood immediately. "My apologies, sir." He gave Ali a dip of his head. "We're late for dinner. Would you like to join us?"

Ali pushed off the bed. "I can do that." She could watch him and see what Skye saw in him or didn't see.

CJ stood aside, his eyes set on Dexter, who avoided eye contact and marched out of the room. Ali went to follow, but CJ blocked her. "Don't fall in love." He looked away. "Not with him."

"I'm not. The piece of shit just tried to kiss me."

"What happened to your lip?" He looked around the room. "And what happened to this room?"

Ali eyed the floor. Crumpled papers were everywhere, no doubt from her and Dexter's tussle. "Tomorrow we have a long day. Let's get some food. I need to translate those cuneiforms as soon as humanly possible."

CJ nodded and Ali went to walk past him. He gently touched her elbow. "Ma'am, don't trust him. I have your back. We get this done and then leave his presence immediately."

Ali let out an exasperated breath. "Do you think he's as bad as you think? I mean, Skye—"

"He is."

"How do you know?"

"I've been trained with the Sight. I can see through him. He must have guarded himself well with Skye because, for the life of me, I don't know why Skye didn't see through him like I do. Or perhaps he did. Skye has his ways. But I'm here to protect you and keep you safe, and I'll do that with every ounce of my being. Yes, the man is as charming as he's handsome. All the things a woman crushes over. But Daf and I see he's not telling you the truth."

"I see it now." She nudged CJ out of the way. "Let's go. Tomorrow we find some portals, which gives us one more way to defeat Enlil. Because we don't have much time, and I may be clumsy, watch my back even more so."

Ali walked out of the room and toward the stairs, her stomach growling. Instead of two meals, she may go for three keeping one eye on her food, and one eye on Dexter.

EDEN

Nibiru

Eden hit the pavement. Pain went into her wrists and up her arms as she attempted to cushion the blow with outstretched hands. She rolled out of the way, the scream of the van's metal crunching behind her. She activated her shield with a twist of her hand.

Skye raced toward Enki, his arm positioned behind him, shield extended. Tracer fire and pulse weapons sizzled off the shield.

Eden ran backward, her shield outward, doing her best to block the incoming fire from snipers positioned on building tops surrounding the stadium. The beams and tracers sank into her shield, and her arm vibrated at each impact. With her shoulder feeling a tinge lighter, she took a quick glance for her missing bow. She looked at where she'd rolled on the ground. Her bow was lying there, but too far away for her to safely retrieve it.

She glimpsed several spectators, their jaws open, looking confused as if they didn't know if this was planned entertainment or a rescue attempt.

Enki stood and spun, sending a roundhouse kick to the side of his brother's head. Connecting hard, the chains around Enki's wrists jangled, and Enlil dropped to the stage floor. Skye ran and jumped on the stage, grasping Enki and pushing him out of the way of fire.

Eden rushed the stage, not knowing where they'd go next. Their escape vehicle was out for the count. If she aimed a weapon at Enlil's skull, she assumed it would stop the incoming fire. She couldn't get too close as he was twice her size and five times her strength. She couldn't wrap an arm around his neck and pull him along with a weapon to his head, hostage style. He'd just throw her off. Plus, she couldn't reach his neck even if she tried. She eyed Enki. His arms were strapped to the metal band around his waist, essentially useless.

Eden jumped on the stage, blocking several more blasts with her shield. She unholstered her sidearm and went to a knee, the shield activated in one hand, her gun pointed at Enlil with the other.

He pushed to a standing position, and Eden closed her eyes. A soft wind swirled around her, and she partnered with the energy around Enlil and pulled it back. He slipped off his feet, cracking his head on the asphalt.

Dazed, he attempted to stand again. Eden shot above his head, singeing the cement wall behind him. He ducked down, then looked at her. He narrowed his eyes, rage practically growling from his pupils. Eden took another shot, and he flinched. "Don't move or you're dead."

Enlil put his hands up. "All right." He lifted his chin, his voice barking through his mic and booming over the stadium speakers. "Stand down."

The weapon's fire died, and Eden chanced a glance at the hover-van. It was a mess, smoldering and smashed against a black tree just off the stage. No way anyone survived that crash, including Sleuth.

Enlil stayed put. "What are you going to do with me?"

Eden stood, walking closer to him. "Turn off your mic and toss me the keys to free Enki."

"No." His voice blared over the speakers. "I'm not giving you a damn thing."

She shot his leg and the plasma bolt cut into his thigh like acid. He screamed, grasping at his wound.

"Change your mind yet, Enlil?" She glanced over her shoulder.

Enki had his hands out and away. Skye was pressing his gun's muzzle against the chains and pulling the trigger. The chain broke, and Enki's hands were free.

Skye gave her a nod. "No need for a key." He looked around, as if figuring out how they'd escape the hell they'd plopped into.

A pounding sound reverberated off the stadium walls, and the van shook. Another pound and the back of the van broke open. Out stepped a beaten and battered Sleuth. He stared at his metallic arm and walked as if drunk, blood dripping from several cuts on his face, legs, and human arm.

Eden jumped off the stage, her eyes on Enlil. She moved toward Sleuth. She'd need to carry the skinny bastard through this mission if the monks wanted him alive and well.

Enki stood in the middle of the stage, Skye crouched with his activated shield in front of them both. "Stay your trigger finger, Eden. Don't shoot...yet."

Eden dipped her head, her eyes trained on Enlil. The Monarch stood, pain riddling his face and his mouth downturned. He limped off the stage away from Enki, blood dripping down his leg.

"Don't move," Eden yelled. Enlil ignored her and hobbled away. She shot a look at Enki. "Let me shoot him."

Skye pointed his free hand at Enlil, and Enlil lifted off his feet. He slammed hard against a cement wall no more than five meters behind him. He slid down the wall onto his rear. He groaned, his hand went to the back of his head. He grunted and pushed back up, trying to gimp away.

"Shoot his other leg," said Enki. "But if you kill him, we all die."

It was true. He was the only leverage they had, and if they wanted to keep it that way, Enlil needed to survive. She zeroed in on his good leg and pulled the trigger. The gun whirred, and a plasma bolt exited. Enlil fell, grabbing his leg, grimacing in pain and falling again to the ground.

Sleuth made it to her, his breathing fast and hard. "What do we do now?"

"Aim your weapon at Enlil. But don't shoot to kill. We need as many guns on him as possible while we find a way out of this."

"I don't have one."

"You don't have what?"

"A gun."

She looked at him. A van full of weapons and he left the most important item he would need in a situation like this. She spit at his feet. "You're worthless."

"Stay calm, brother," yelled Enki. "Keep your hounds at bay. If you don't, my friends will fill you full of holes."

Enlil raised a hand, his face twisted in pain. "Where are you going to go from here, Enki? Where the hell can you escape to?"

"It wouldn't be wise to tell you."

"You killed Father." He shook a fist. "And I have you on record confessing more than once."

Enki shook his head. "Nothing is as it seems, brother."

Enlil's face hardened, his eyes narrowing. "I'm sorry, but it's time." He glared at a building top in the distance. "Detonate the explosives."

Enki opened his mouth as if about to speak. The middle of the stage lifted upward, Skye and Enki going with it. Skye's eyes widened in a start, and Enki grabbed his friend's shoulders, pushing him forward to throw him off the stage.

Red fire engulfed them as the stage continued to blast up and outward. In seconds, flames were everywhere in a dazzling display, hiding Enki and Skye from Eden's view. The concussion pushed her against Sleuth, and they fell to the ground. She covered her eyes from the bright flash with her forearm, gasping.

The blaze grew and Skye, covered in fire, stepped off the stage and fell to his knees, his arm reaching for the heavens. Tracers from the rooftops riddled his body. He jerked from the impacts, then dropped forward. Enki fell off the stage a moment later, his body limp and charred. He hit the concrete face first and didn't move.

Eden screamed in horror, and gunshots rained down on her. She lay on her back, positioning the shield over her and Sleuth, the impacts shaking her violently.

A slug cut through her exposed arm, and then her leg. The bullets and pulse weapons were like a storm of fury. She blinked her eyes shut, knowing she'd never open them again.

ALI

Pachacamac, Peru

Ali sat in a small bus, staring out the window. It was early morning, and they'd been bouncing up and down in the old shanty vehicle for half an hour, maybe longer. Outside, brown, sandy hills covered the landscape. They'd gone from Lima's green beauty to a coastal area Dexter called Pachacamac.

The bus jostled as it grumbled over the dusty road, which also served as a donkey trail. Small indentations and hills made up a majority of it. Dexter drove, slow and methodical in some areas, and fast and straight in the smoother stretches.

Earlier that morning, he asked the mansion's owner Alejandro for a bus to take them to an excavation site. Alejandro came back with a rusty, beat down bus that CJ and Daf scoffed at. It didn't look stable, and as Ali rode to the site, it didn't feel it either. The constant squeaking sounds and clatter of empty loose bench seats nearly drowning out any other sounds that could present themselves.

She eyed Dexter, who gripped the wheel, his eyes set on the winding road. He bobbed up and down along with her and the rest of Ali's team and his crew. Her lips wanted to curl downward. Dexter almost kissed her last night. For a moment, she thought he wanted to kill her. The jury was still out. Last night they also went to dinner, and he acted like nothing happened. She sighed. Good guy on a bad team or bad guy on a bad team? She'd do her job, watch him and his team like a hawk, and find the portal locations to dismantle their links. CJ and Daf better watch her back.

Dexter's four colleagues took up two seats in the front, while CJ and Daf shared a seat across the aisle from her. The Russian turned and gave Ali a quick look, one eye squinted as if studying her. He turned, running his hand through his hair. Ali glimpsed the guy's palm. A portion of it was burned as if he placed his hand on a perfectly straight, scalding level surface.

A sensation of someone staring overwhelmed her. Ali shifted in her seat. "What is it, Daf?"

Daf pursed her lips. "You know what it is." Her voice was muffled over the bus' creaks and whines, but Ali read her lips.

"I don't fancy the guy."

Daf flicked a look at Dexter, then back at Ali. "Good. I have my eyes on him."

The Russian turned again, his eyes burning a hole in Daf as if over-hearing their conversation, which Ali thought impossible. But who knew? Daf tilted her head and gave the guy an unblinking stare in return. The Russian shook his head and faced the front.

"Ali," said Daf. "Make sure your sword is with you at all times."

Ali pointed underneath her seat. "It's not my first rodeo." She'd brought it on the bus with her, case and all.

Daf gave her an odd look, not knowing the term. Ali threw a dismissive hand, telling her to forget about it. When she hopped on the bus holding the case, Dexter eyed her strangely, but she ignored him, not wanting to explain why she brought her things with her.

The bus slowed, and Ali glanced out the front window. A dozen tents lined the base of a deserted, lifeless hill. Jeeps were parked around in a chaotic cluster, and United States Army soldiers walked around, helmets on, and rifles in their hands.

Dexter rolled down his side window and came to a halt as a man walked up. They spoke words Ali couldn't hear. She could only see the top of the man's helmet. Dexter nodded, rolled up his window, and the soldier windmilled his arm, telling Dexter to proceed. The bus lurched and whipped Ali slightly forward.

Dexter raised his hand, driving the bus slowly. "Sorry." He turned the wheel, parking away from the jeeps, by a green tent that billowed in a soft breeze. "We're here." He stood and opened the door with a pull of a lever, giving Ali a quick look before walking down the steps.

Ali withdrew the long, rectangular suitcase housing Sol. She wanted to open it, pull out the scabbard and wrap it around her waist, then sheath her sword. She didn't want to carry around the box wherever she went. But precautions were precautions.

Dexter's men walked off of the bus, and Ali followed CJ and Daf. She went down the stairs and hopped onto the dusty, dirt-covered ground. She surveyed the area, barely seeing anything resembling a plant in sight. Had this area been salted long ago? During ancient times in the eastern Mediterranean, sprinkling salt over cities after an invading army sacked them had been standard procedure for centuries. It was a symbolic way of completing the destruction of a culture and rendering the site barren. Glancing around, she thought another culture may have used the same approach here.

She turned, glancing up a hill, hearing the nearby ocean. Her eyes came down on Dexter, who approached a tent.

"Ali." He raised his hand, motioning for her to accompany him inside. "I have some cuneiform tablets I'd like to show you."

Ali gripped her sword case's handle more tightly and marched toward Dexter. She walked by CJ and Daf, her eyes set on the beautiful man opening the tent's entrance.

"We'll make sure you're safe." Daf glared at Dexter's men, who stood around watching CJ and Daf.

Ali nodded. Passing a soldier, he looked her up and down, giving her a smile. "Welcome, ma'am."

Ali dipped her head and went inside. A gas lamp lit up the darkened tent. There was a table with two large tablets set on top. Ali's heart melted, her eyes about to burst. Two perfectly held together tablets with etchings on top in a long line, and more symbols spread throughout, grabbed her soul, and danced.

She gathered herself, and set the suitcase by the table, eyeing the practically sparkling specimens. Whoever had cleaned these up did a job better than she'd ever seen.

"Why did you bring the suitcase?"

"Good luck, I guess. I don't leave home without it," she lied.

He grinned. "You're attached to your things."

"At the moment, yes." She peered over the tablets.

Years ago, she studied select Sumerian tablets different from the rest, and they gave her what she believed were secrets of the universe. In them, they spoke of a divine source who sent dignitaries from across the Universe to the Milky Way. There they inspired several extraterrestrial races to create an experiment on a school-like planet known as Earth.

Past translations pegged the Anunnaki as human creators, but she didn't find that to be entirely true. A few tablets suggested the opposite, as if some Sumer scribes disagreed with other Sumer scribes. She found the Anunnaki had only dabbled in the human makeup, and that other, unnamed ET's created the human genome.

They had created more than one species on Earth, finally coming upon one that could survive the harshness of this planet, Homo Sapiens. She wrote about her findings, only to walk into closed and locked doors from her peers. What she found went against all theology, mainstream archaeology, and accepted history books.

If the coming alien invasion had any good at all, it would be to teach humanity that other technologies, other Beings, and other truths existed outside cultural bubbles. Or not, because she wanted to stop the attack before it began and save countless lives.

She ran her hand over a tablet, the bumps and indentations of ancient art, words, sentences, and history telling her that people long ago had a story to share. As she looked closer, she realized she wouldn't be reading stories. She'd translate two large maps made of stone. Past the myriad symbols, Earth's continents were outlined underneath, not identical, but similar in shape to current maps.

She looked at Dexter. "I thought you said your team would go out on their own?"

Dexter nodded. "Not today. They're excited about the maps here, and the portal locations you'll be able to find." He scratched the back of his neck. "I can translate most of what I find, but not all. I've not studied these particular symbols before, or it's laid out in a way I can't decipher."

Ali touched an owl carved into the first line of the stone, her fingers gentle and delicate. To Ali, a cuneiform tablet was worth more than the world's most expensive paintings. "The owl tells us to be careful. There's good and bad magic here."

"Here?" Dexter pointed to the ground.

Ali puffed out her lower lip, crinkling her brow. "No, not here, but here." She circled her hands in the air above both stones. "Surely, as an archaeologist, you'd realize that."

He looked away. "Yeah, but I didn't get that inference with your tone."

Ali eyed the next symbol, that of a raven. She tilted her head. This symbol alone probably told Dexter these were portal maps. "You recognize this one?"

Dexter nodded. "The Raven."

"And?"

"You're the expert."

Ali placed her hands on her hips. If anything, Dexter was a shitty expert in his own right. "Raven can mean several things, and since these are the only two birds or animals that I see on these tablets, they're important. The Raven is the link between two worlds. Magic holds the links together. But magic didn't mean 'magic' back then. I think it meant a very sensitive, incredible technology."

She eyed more etches in the stone, seeing symbols that spanned across all cultures. There were three swirls touching, meaning Earth, a circle with a dot in the center and arrows pointing off, signifying Nibiru, and several more symbols to other planets she knew nothing about. One with two wings represented planet Eos, and day, night, air, fire, wind, portal links, arrows, and more symbols smiled at her.

She traced her hand over one location and stepped back. "The hill."

"What was that?"

"We see a location, a line with a ball on top. That means here, you know, the here you thought I inferred before." She stepped back farther, taking a longer look at the two tablets and the maps they exposed. "From the hill representation, I believe the hill we're standing next to is a portal, especially because it has this symbol etched onto it." She pointed at a half owl, half raven. "You found these tablets in this location, correct?"

"We did." He pointed easterly. "Buried at the base of the hill over there. But I don't see a raven next to the hill on that tablet, and that doesn't even look like a hill."

The guy had never seen Anunnaki maps before. That didn't matter entirely, because the way these symbols worked were unlike the symbols she'd seen in hieroglyphs or other cuneiform tablets. These symbols mixed almost all worldly symbols, as if a culture traveled the globe and stole written languages from one society to the next. "We see half an owl and half a raven, pieced together to form one bird. Now, do you see those all over the map?"

Dexter rubbed his chin. "I do."

"Those are portals, and they're all over the world."

She eyed several more portal placements. They'd take some time to translate, but eyeballing the map, she could see hundreds of portals throughout North, Central, and South America. She hadn't taken more than a glance at the other continents, but that would come later. They'd need to hurry to close all the portals before Enlil stepped through. "You mentioned we have thousands of volunteers waiting to close these portals?"

"Yes. I tell the sergeant out there and he lets the agency know, and they let the volunteers know the locations. We're then on a race to close each one."

"The Blueline Project doesn't want these portals closed. Why would you tell the sergeant?"

"I want these portals closed. That sergeant knows the situation and of all people, doesn't want the portals left open for a mass invasion."

"Because he and the majority of humanity wouldn't survive an invasion." She fixed Dexter with a stare, making sure he understood the severity.

"Yes, no games. I'm being honest here."

"Okay, so now that you see the portal locations, I need you to translate the other map. It'll speed things up."

Dexter shook his head. "Like I said, I can't figure out what they're telling me."

"What?" These were basic symbols, easily translatable. Yes, some were rare, and ones he'd probably never seen, but he could get past that and make good guestimations, slowly coming to more accurate conclusions the more he translated. That's how translating worked.

She gave him a cute half-smile, wanting to kiss his lips. "You're pulling my leg, aren't you?"

"No, Ali. I really can't figure these out."

She frowned. "You don't know any of these? Including tablets that I assume are in the other tents?" Something didn't seem right. The guy either didn't work as an archaeologist or played around the lower echelons of the profession, unable to figure out his left foot from his right. He figured out this was a map of some sort, but after about a minute of study, she figured most people could point that out. It brought up a valuable question. "Who figured out this was a portal map and not just a map?"

"I did."

"How?"

Dexter bit down on his lips, taking his eyes off Ali and to the map. His neck pulsed, moving his skin rapidly. He continued to stare at the map.

"Who translated this map?" If it was buried for thousands of years, how was it in such pristine shape as if stored in an icebox?

He walked toward the exit, pushing aside the tent canvas. "Boris, get the coupler."

Ali cocked her head to the side. "Coupler?"

Dexter faced her and gently squeezed her arms, looking down at her. "Listen, I'm trying to help you, not harm you. Can you please trust me?"

Ali pushed his hands away. She backpedaled toward the suitcase that stored her sword. "You're not an archaeologist, are you?"

He sighed and looked around the tent. He rubbed his face, finally taking his eyes off everything else to look at her. "No." He gave her an innocent look, like a puppy wanting attention. "My team doesn't know a single thing about tablets, archaeology, or geology, for that matter. We're part of a special ops team to help you. We've infiltrated the Blueline Project. You find us these portals, we close them. That's what we're here to do, ma'am. So, please, I keep asking, will you trust me?"

"You lied to me." She scooted closer to her suitcase.

"Not because I wanted to. I had to. I needed to get you here. I lied to the Blueline Project. They think I'm a famous archaeologist, but Truman set that up. President Truman and his team put together my resume and handed it to the Blueline Project team leader, Lloyd Winters. Ali, you and I are on the same team. The Blueline Project isn't." He touched his heart. "We need to hurry, too. Please, I implore you, trust me."

There was that trust word again, yet his heart went out to hers, and she could feel him in a way she couldn't understand, in a way she'd never felt anyone before. "Okay, but after this is over, we need to work on your lying. You're too good at it."

"Look, I have this strange feeling about you."

"What do you mean?" asked Ali.

"I've just met you, but I can't help this sensation growing in my heart. I'm trying to ignore it—"

"...but you can't." Ali knew the sensation all too well because it stuck to her like glue around this guy.

Dexter dropped the canvas drape and let the flap close. He took a step forward, grabbed her, and brought his lips to hers. Ali's heart rang a thousand songs. His lips were soft and perfect. He pulled back, eyeing her, and kissed her again, long and deep.

He relaxed his hold, and she opened her eyes, wanting to carry off like a bird into the sunset with her fingers intertwined around his. "I trust you," she said.

He smiled. "I can feel it. You can keep translating. I'll be back." He stepped outside.

Before the flap closed, Ali saw Boris walking toward Dexter with a black, crystal-like orb in hand. "The coupler," she said to herself. Dexter had shown her that orb last night, something Skye Vortek gave to him.

She went back to translating, tracing her hand over a path of symbols that explained the next portal. She mouthed coupler again, thinking what an odd name for something that's supposed to break a portal link. "Shouldn't it be de-coupler?"

She paused, remembering the orb Dexter showed her last night. The crystal orb Skye gave him was white and mostly clear, translucent. The one in Boris' hands was black. "Wait." She bent down and opened her suitcase. She sucked in a sharp breath of air. "That bastard."

Boris' injured hand flashed to her mind. Sol caused it. He most likely grabbed the sword, and since he wasn't of the bloodline, Sol burned the crap out of him. She palmed her forehead. "This can't be happening."

In Sol's place was a long, skinny rock acting as a weight. The sword was missing.

31

EDEN

Eden screamed in pain, her arm and leg burning from direct hits. She opened her eyes, determined to survive. She held the shield over her and Sleuth, as the weapon's fire slammed into the shield, sinking heavier and heavier every impact.

Sleuth grasped at the ground behind him with his metallic arm. The asphalt crunched and cracked, and black pebbles jutted upward as his fingers tore through the concrete. He wrapped his other arm around Eden. "I think my arm has a plan. It's controlling itself." His silver arm pulled, dragging Eden along as the gunfire rained down.

Eden winced in pain, though her wounds numbed. "Where is it taking us?"

Sleuth craned his head, looking behind them. "We're heading for the stage."

It was the last place Eden wanted to go, but perhaps burning up by the stage's fire would be a better death than any other. She glanced at Enlil across the way. He sat on his butt, pointing at Eden, screaming something she couldn't hear over the crowd's uproar.

Good. It meant that his soldiers might not hear him through the speakers. She frowned a moment later, seeing a commband near his chest. He could talk to his men and probably give them orders at this moment.

"The fire is dying down," said Sleuth, continually thrusting his arm out, crushing the blacktop under his fingers and pulling them closer.

"No, it's not. More soldiers are engaging." The tracer and pulse weapons poured on her in a steady stream, attempting to break her shield. To Eden's knowledge, they'd need heavier weaponry to bust through. She hoped No Name spoke the truth when he mentioned starfighters wouldn't fire in the city due to civilian safety. Not that all these shots coming down on her screamed safe to the audience surrounding her.

"I'm talking about the stage fire, not them shooting." Sleuth slid her along the ground at a faster pace. "I see an opening near the middle of the stage." They passed a sizzling Skye, his body dead on the ground, the smell of rotting flesh wafting to her nose.

Eden's heart pushed to her throat, and she swallowed tears. Her mentor, the Grand Master, lay dead beside her. Enki, too. The tall, wide man lay on his back—the very man who had the political power to stop Enlil and prevent the Anunnaki invasion—burnt to death. She weakened at the sight, but Sleuth's arm carried on, moving her closer to the smoking, damaged stage. The heat engulfed her.

"We have to stand," he yelled.

Eden nodded, keeping her shield in front of them as the slug and pulse weapons sent blows like punches at her. She limped to her feet, her adrenaline dulling the pain, her injured arm hanging limply by her side.

They stepped over splintered wood. Sleuth swung at large plank boards, crushing them under his fist and making a path for them to snake through. Out of the corner of Eden's eye, a horde of troops raced through a doorway, their spear-like weapons aimed at her.

She hopped over a busted wooden beam. "At our eleven o'clock."

"What?" Sleuth's arm pulverized a chunk of wood, and he tossed it to the side, glaring at his arm as if it did the work on its own accord.

"Oncoming troops, eleven o'clock."

Sleuth didn't look but stopped in stride as if seeing something peculiar. "Holy Guild. It's not a hole. It's a sunken metal platform." Sleuth pulled her up and over a lip, and they fell back on to something that bobbed up and down as if in a hover.

"A platform?" She eyed what she sat on. She holstered her weapon and stretched out her shaking, pained arm, pressing a control panel on the platform. "Down."

The platform lowered slowly. The sun's light blinked out as the hole above closed like an elevator door. Other than Eden's glowing shield, blackness surrounded them.

They hovered to a stop, the platform clanking when it hit the floor. Sleuth jumped off the platform, his face pained as if he'd suffered a terrible loss. "Enlil wanted to kill me."

"Get in line." She went to move, to hurry around him, and search for a way out of this underground area.

Sleuth held his arm out, stopping her and shaking his head. "No, he wanted to kill me. I thought we were friends. It makes no sense." His lower lip drooped along with his eyes as if he were a child with hurt feelings.

"You can stay here and sulk all you want, but I have to get out of here before we're overrun." Her heart beat quickly, and she looked around, using her shield as a light. She held in a breath as the thrust of Skye and Enki's death hit her like a kick to the side. She wanted to curse Skye's name, wanted to grab the monks, and shake them back and forth for adhering to an insane policy. Grand Masters and Grand Masters in training shouldn't go headlong in a battle.

She dropped her head, her anger growing into rage. She tightened her lips, biting her tongue so as not to scream. She pushed Sleuth aside and marched down a narrow passage that led to Guild knows where. She turned down a corner, Sleuth's boot steps pounding behind her. "Keep it down. Enlil's men are probably on their way down here to look for us." She didn't know how she'd get out of this debacle. Her leg didn't ache, but her arm hung in a heap of pain by her side.

Sleuth's boot steps softened. "Maybe he didn't see that it was me?"

"Do you think he's blind?"

"Of course not."

"Then he saw it was you."

"But he had his men shoot at me."

She held her shield out farther to see a little more ahead. The tunnel descended at a slight grade and went in a straight line with no end in sight. Enlil's troops would no doubt be onto their position soon. With Enki out of the picture and the Anunnaki's screwed up patriarchal belief structure, Enlil now had full power. She wouldn't be surprised if he ordered the armada's invasion this instant.

"Did you hear me?" Sleuth whispered loudly. "He shot at me even though he knew it was me."

"I heard you. And I don't care."

He grabbed her and shoved her against the wall, lifting her high with his metallic arm, his cold, smooth fingers around her neck. He pushed higher, sinking his strength deeper into her neck. Wasn't this arm supposed to be on her side? She couldn't breathe.

As if hearing her thought, the silver hand let go. She dropped to the ground, and a sharp stab grabbed her leg where she'd been shot. She yelped, her wound burning. "You piece of—"

Sleuth leaned against the wall, his forehead in his hand. "I got nobody. No one."

Eden just lost two friends dear to her heart, and she didn't shed a tear because that could come later. In a time like this, immediate action was necessary. Sleuth was here, after saving her like a badass, crying like a selfish prick, his feelings more important than imminent oncoming death in the form of Enlil's troops.

She breathed out sharply. She lifted her arm, bringing her armband close to her lips, the shield bright in front of her face. She tapped the band with her nose, turning on the comm. "Nyx, do you read?"

A whiny sound whistled through the band. She touched it with her nose again. "Nyx, it's Eden. We need your help."

Nothing.

She sighed. "Enlil blocked communications." Her heart just about dropped out of her chest. Her mom was right. Eden wasn't cut out to be a Grand Master and had probably somehow caused the old Grand Master's death to boot. Skye was dead, and everything felt hopeless. Her mom's prophecy of Eden ruining the Templars' order turned out to be true. If she survived this, she'd leave her position and give it to a monk or someone who deserved it more than her.

Sounds and commotion came from down the tunnel. It seemed to come from behind her and in front. "Sleuth, we have to go."

He lifted his head and looked around. "They're coming."

Boots pounding against the ground came closer, and Eden twisted her wrist, the shield blinking off.

"What are you doing?" whispered Sleuth.

"Maybe they'll run by us." It was the only plan Eden had. With soldiers coming from both ends of the tunnel, she didn't have much choice. The bright light of her shield would give them away. The coming troops probably carried lights, so her strategy would only keep them alive minutes longer.

She hugged the wall, bringing up the Sight. No way it could hold them all back, but perhaps some of them being pushed down by an unknown force would scare them into turning around. She wished Skye and the monks would have taught her more. Maybe there was a kill option? Maybe she could create so much pressure or mix the energy together rapidly, then isolate it in one spot and let it loose? Maybe a small explosion, a tornado?

Sleuth leaned against the wall next to her, his breath shaky. "What do we do now?"

"I'm trying something."

"What?"

Eden ignored him and brought in a hefty inhale, feeling her third eye pulse, and her mind open. She connected to the energy all around, watching electric-purple colors spin in her head like a cyclone.

The troops rounded the corner, and through her mind's eye, she could see them shadowed, coming from both directions. Once they shone a light on her and Sleuth, they'd end their lives as fast as they ended Enki's and Skye's.

The pounding steps echoed across the tunnel, and men's voices reverberated off the concrete. She zeroed in on the closest soldier, about to throw him against another. The wall behind Eden disappeared, and she gasped in surprise. A hand pressed against her mouth and pulled her back.

3 2

S H A E

Earth's Moon

Shae walked to a bench in the middle of a park. A fish rippled the water in a nearby pond, slurping down flakes of food. Two trees shaded the bench in the Templar moon base's biosphere. And there sat his old friend, Captain Stan Jenkyns.

Shae approached from the rear. Stan's back was facing Shae. He stopped a few meters behind his friend, his arms behind his back. "Hi, Stan."

Stan dipped his head. "Come around. I'd like to see you." Dried blood caked his upper back, the exit wound Shae had caused with a slug to his chest.

"No."

"Please, Shae."

"I know what I'll see when I walk around. I don't want to see it anymore."

Stan leaned forward, resting his elbows on his knees. "You caused this."

"I killed you for a good reason. When will get that in your thick skull?"

"I only did what I thought was best."

Shae cleared his throat, stamping the grass with the toe of his boot. "And I did what I thought was best."

"There's a difference, Shae. What you thought was best ended my life. You're a backstabber, a no-good piece of ebb."

"I could say the same about you. I don't take kindly to people who sell out their race to the highest bidder."

Stan stood. His chest was slightly caved in, his shoulders forward as if unable stand upright. He turned, and there was a small hole in his chest with dried blood around the wound. His face was peeled, flesh rotting, and his eyes drooped, showing the red under his lower eyelids. The man's bottom lip was missing, his gums worn away. "You did this to me." A gun in his hand shook as he lifted it.

Shae went for his weapon, and a *pftah* whipped the air before he could grab his firearm. He stepped back, the bullet like ice in his chest. He pulled in a sharp breath, and jostled, flailing his arms. Stan laughed and pulled the trigger again and again.

A bright light invaded Shae's vision, and he blinked. Warmth covered him from chest to toes, and he wiggled his hands. He swallowed, his face perspiring. "Why can't you forgive me?"

Sabra rested her hand gently on his arm. "There you are. Welcome to the living. Having an unpleasant dream? You were twitching as if someone attacked you."

He sat up, glancing around. A blanket was draped over him, and holomonitors surrounded the bed, the monitors displaying lines, codes, and things his blurry eyes couldn't yet make out. He rubbed his eyes, yawning. "Where am I?"

"Looks like you had a fall," said a woman running a wand over him. She circled it around his heart, and electric-like impulses zapped him.

Shae stiffened, his muscles contracting. "You can stop that now."

The woman smiled and turned off the wand. "We don't have heart attacks in our society, so this is new to me."

Shae froze. "A what?"

Sabra loomed over him. Behind her glowed a curved crystalline wall. He was in a dome. "You had a heart attack. We found high troponin levels. I mean, Shae, you really ought to eat better. Your arteries were clogged."

"We freed those arteries for you," said the woman.

His lips drooped. "You're telling me I had a heart attack?"

"Yes, you've been unconscious for a day," said Sabra. "But we need you up and ready. You have training in eight hours, and Enlil won't wait for anyone." She pursed her lips. "In fact, do you mind if I move up the schedule?"

Shae touched his chest. "I just had a heart attack." If so, he felt strangely good. Better than he remembered, in fact. "What did you do to me?"

"Flushed your system," said the woman. She bowed and walked toward the exit. "Fixed your heart. Doused you with nutrients. You're free to leave," she said before she left.

Sabra sat in a chair next to his bed. "Your wife isn't happy with me."

"Helen?" He searched his coat pocket, looking for his vidcom. "I need to talk with her."

"I assured her you would come out of this healthier than before. It's two-thirty in the morning where she's at. She's sleeping." She set the vidcom on his chest.

Shae picked it up and brought it close to his face, about to press several buttons to link to his wife. "Knowing Helen, she's beside herself. Let me talk to her."

"We have agents around her, monitoring her and the activity around your home. We know she's asleep."

Shae lifted his brows. "What?"

"Security reasons. Your daughter's demands." She slapped her thighs and stood. "Get up. Let's go."

"Where are we going?"

"Dome three, by the shipyard."

He scratched under his chin and pocketed the vidcom. "Are you sure I can get up?" He felt fine but having never experienced a heart attack before, he didn't know if he should move or not.

"Doctor's orders." She left the room, saying over her shoulder, "And who won't forgive you?"

Shae pushed the sheets off and hurried after her, his body lighter and his legs somehow stronger. His breathing was easy. "What about forgiving?"

Exiting the medical dome, they headed down the cobblestone street. She lifted her hand as if hailing a taxi. A white almond-shaped hovercar descended. The door opened, and Sabra stepped inside. "After you woke, you asked why someone couldn't forgive you." She patted the seat next to her.

Shae sat, the sleek seat like leather against his palms. The door closed, and the cabin walls lit up in soft white, illuminating the area. A divider between the back and front seat lowered. A bot twisted its head, his photosensor on Shae. "Where to, pops?"

Shae's mouth opened slightly, and Sabra raised her finger. "Dome three, outer wing. Thank you."

The bot twisted his head, facing Sabra. "So, you're the lead in this relationship. I see." His head twirled around to the front, and the car ascended into the air. "Dome three, outer wing. I'll get you there in a jiffy." The divider closed, and the car flew forward.

"Where are we going?" Shae glanced out the window. The car was flying by buildings at a fast pace, each structure's edges brightened in different colored lights.

"Not until you tell me who you want to forgive you. I suspect an inkling of your post-war stress may have helped cause your heart attack. Forgiveness may help alleviate the issue."

"How did you know about my post-war stress?"

"It's evident. I can see it in your eyes." She shrugged. "Plus, the doctor detected it when she scanned your brain."

Shae nodded sighing.

Sabra patted his leg. "So, who do you want to forgive you?"

"Stan, a friend."

"What happened?"

Shae continued to eye the buildings, glancing at people walking below. A hovercar passed them. "I killed him."

"Well, that's some way to treat a friend." She winked.

"He was a traitor, plus he almost killed me. I pulled the trigger before he did."

"Sounds like you need to forgive yourself."

Shae nodded. "There's enough I need to forgive to cover two life-times." He faced Sabra. "Where are we going?"

"We have Lloyd Winters attached to a Crown of Accountability machine."

"That's what you placed on Zim to get him to confess to every-thing over the vid channels."

"Similar, but not the same. This one scans memories and shows them to us like a movie. He has documents tucked away in his mind that we want you to look at. We've looked at a document. Part of it concerns your daughter."

"Shit." Shae slumped. "I knew we should have kept her at home."

"There's no learning or personal growth in hiding."

"Yeah, but there's surviving. Staying-alive-to-live-another-day type of learning and personal growth." He bit his lower lip, holding in a grunt. He wanted to be with his daughter, to help her, and to make sure she remained safe. He sighed loudly. This wasn't good.

They approached a tube that looked like it connected one dome to the next. Flying through, several hovercars zoomed by them. The dome was translucent, long and wide, and he eyed the stars, remem-bering what it was like inside a starship.

His stomach sank. He didn't like that he missed that feeling. He wanted to miss Helen or Ali more, but if he was honest with himself, he measured both the love of navigating through space almost equal to the love of holding, cherishing, and being with his family.

Exiting the tube, they arrived in a different type of dome, this one as large as the last, though filled with military vehicles and structures. There were mechs, bulbous tanks, sleek jeeps with blasters mounted on the hood and roof, and more and more domes. Starfighters, known as Avens, also littered the area.

"Arriving in one minute, eleven seconds," came the bot's voice through a speaker in the back of the hovercar. The vehicle lowered and veered off through another tube. "Heading to the outer wing." Blasting into yet another dome, the car slowed and hovered. It touched down on a pad, and the doors opened. "You may exit the vehicle."

"Thank you." Sabra gestured for Shae to get out. He did, and she followed.

Several installations filled the area. Guards with rifles paced, several at stations attached to the buildings. Sabra waved to a guard, and he motioned for her to proceed.

Shae followed her into a domed building, and the door shut behind him. He walked with her down a hallway, passing door after door. The end of the hallway opened to a massive room, and behind the translucent walls sat Starships *Ascension* and *Tranquil*, along with several gigantic dreadnoughts and battleships in the shipyard. He nodded at the two starships, the closest vessels to the building.

A chair squeaked across the floor. A guard sat at a table. He dipped his head at Shae. Several other guards were sitting and eating. One side of the room held a kitchen with cooks preparing meals.

The guards stood when they saw Sabra and greeted her. She nodded pleasantly and walked to a wall, pressing her hand against it. The wall dissolved as if melting away, and she walked inside where Lloyd lay on his back on a table in the middle of the room, a helmet over his head with wires attached to a holodisplay.

Sabra waved Shae inside. "Come in."

"Is he asleep?" asked Shae, stopping at the foot of the hospital-like bed. Lloyd's toes were twitching.

Sabra swiped her hand over the area they stepped through, and the wall materialized as if out of thin air, closing them off from the dining guards. "He's in an induced hypnotic state. He's at Theta wave levels, and we're extracting much needed information from him. He's a threat, and so is the rest of his team." She gestured toward the holodisplay. "Bring up document two." She leaned against a wall near the head of the bed. "We've gone through the first document, but not this one yet. We'll see what this one says."

The holomonitor displayed a document paper-clipped together. The image on the screen looked as though it came from Lloyd's eyes. The papers sat on a table, Lloyd's hands resting beside it. Lloyd's memory read, as his voice came through the screen. It was all about Ali, and that they needed her specific skill set. "And our officer in charge, Dexter Huntley, will use all means necessary to gain her trust. She's a threat to Enlil, and we'll erase her once she completes her tasks. This will win the Monarch's favor."

Shae stepped back. "A threat to Enlil? They're working with him?"

Sabra's mouth gaped. "My brother." She moaned under her breath. "Shae, this is new to me. Lloyd's working for my brother? When did Enlil contact him?" She walked closer to the monitor. "Your government is compromised." She winced when an alert came through the holodisplay. Sabra's lips parted, her hand going to her heart.

Shae's brows lowered. "We have to notify my daughter and get her away from this Dexter as soon as possible."

Sabra put up her hand. "Hold on." She leaned toward the screen. It streamed chunks of new data. Her eyes almost popped out of her skull. She raced toward the wall they entered through. "We have to get out of here. My brother set up Lloyd to blow if his operation was exposed."

"To blow? You mean a bomb inside of him?"

A beep carried across the room. Lloyd's eyes opened, and he screamed. As if in slow motion, his chest erupted outward, the bed he lay on crumbled, and fire expanded as his limbs tore from his body. The wall near Lloyd's head crumbled and exploded outward.

Cold grabbed Shae, and wind engulfed him, pushing him back. He lifted off the ground, the blast increasing pressure and catapulting him out of the dome like a rocket. Shae slid across the sandy ground, his shoulder slamming against a moon rock. He stood, Sabra next to him, her clothes torn and her flesh burned.

He went to get up, to run, but Sabra grabbed his shirt. He twisted to see Sabra shaking her head. She pointed behind them.

Shaking his own head, he moved toward the complex he'd just exited to see more explosions taking place in the wing.

He had a choice. He could blow apart in the closest structure to him—the wing he'd been thrown from—or in fifteen seconds pass out and die out here.

33

ALI

Pachacamac, Peru

Ali threw the canvas aside and marched out the opening, finger pointed at Boris. "Don't move." She glanced at Daf and CJ. "You two, get that bastard."

CJ and Daf were standing next to the bus, arms crossed in conversation. They abruptly turned and rushed Boris, CJ in the lead.

Boris stopped, his mouth shaped in an 'o'. His shoulders rose, tensing, and his expression hardened. He tilted his head at Dexter, glaring at him as if to say Ali had grown into something more than just a pain in his rear.

Dexter put his hands up. "Ali, we need to find every single portal we can to deactivate them. Time is of the essence."

Ali ignored him, barreling like a bull at the Russian. "Give me that coupler." She eyed the black orb. It shimmered oddly, the metal maintaining its shape but moving like goo.

Dexter stepped in front of her. "Now, Ali. I don't know why, but the orb Skye gave us changes color. This is the same orb I showed you last night."

Daf and CJ arrived, along with Dexter's other men. Daf stood by Ali, with CJ in front of the other guys, daring them to make a move.

"Then why is it called a coupler?" asked Ali.

"Wrong word. It's a deactivator, not a coupler," he stammered. "I'm sorry. It came out incorrectly. But right now, we need to turn this portal off and get you to give us the rest of the locations."

"Where's the item in my suitcase? Why is a rock in its place?"

"What?" said Daf, her eyes widening.

CJ lurched forward, and the men he stood in front flinched, jumping back. He laughed. "Why are you scared, gentlemen? Just me against all of you." He took a step forward, and the men took a step back. "Give us the sword."

Silence.

"Daf," said Ali. "Take them out."

"Now, now," Dexter consoled. "No need for that." He smiled a charming smile. "I don't understand this sudden change. Look, we can settle differences after we close these portals. Until then, I'm sorry, but I have to proceed." He motioned with a dip of his head for Boris to get moving.

Daf rushed toward Boris, and Dexter dove at her, wrapping his hands around her waist. She threw him off like a rag doll and grabbed Boris.

The Russian threw an elbow. Daf ducked, sending a fist to his groin. He dropped the orb and bent over into a fetal position as he fell to the ground.

CJ picked up the orb, and the three other men rushed him. CJ flipped a man over his shoulder, connecting a kick to his back before the man hit the ground. CJ's Templar speed was twice as fast as any normal human as he twisted, slamming a knee into a man's stomach, buckling him over. He landed a punch across the last man standing, connecting with his cheek, and sending him spinning to the ground.

A crack whipped across the wind, and CJ arched his back. Four more bangs riddled the air. CJ jerked back and forth as bullets penetrated him. He fell next to Dexter's men, blood caking his back, his eyes open, breathing hard. The black orb rolled out of his hands.

"No," Ali screamed, shock flashing from her heart and through her body. "CJ." She ran to him. Daf had already jumped in front of him, her wrist band shield activated. Ali skidded to CJ's side, her hand on his back.

"We have guns pointed at Daf in all directions. Ali, you make a wrong move, and Daf is dead." Dexter held a gun in front of Daf, smoke spiraling from its barrel. His other men, including Boris, stood around them, guns pointed at Daf.

"CJ," said Ali. "Stay with us."

He breathed hard, his breaths fast and shallow. "I'm…trying."

She heard footsteps crunching toward her. Her heart skipped a beat when several army soldiers with rifles held their weapons steady on Daf and Ali. One guy spat on the ground, his lips curled in a frown. "Hi, ladies."

"You don't understand what Dexter is doing," said Ali. "He'll open up the portals, not close them."

"I trust Dexter. He's a fine gentleman and has done nothing but good things for us and the government." The soldier stood motionless, gun aimed at her head. "Now, be nice. Let the fine gentlemen do their work."

"They'll let in people you don't want on Earth. Trust me."

He nodded.

Ali's eyes widened, her hand resting on CJ. "You know he's opening them, don't you?"

"Just doing my job, miss."

She shot a stare at Dexter. "These aren't the United States military, are they?"

"They're mercenaries. Paid for hire, and they're making more money today than they'd make in a year in the Army." Dexter sighed. "Now, Ali. You're holding things up." He nodded to Boris. "Do the deed."

"Ali, what do you want me to do?" Daf glanced around, backing up to move closer to Ali.

"Have you seen my sword?"

Daf shook her head.

Dexter eyed Boris walking toward the base of the mountain. "Don't worry. Your sword is in safekeeping."

"Why did you take it?" asked Ali, a fire burning up and down her spine.

"I heard you'd slay us in a matter of seconds if you had it," said Dexter.

"So, you're in contact with Enlil."

"I may have talked to him a time or two."

"Lloyd isn't the head of the Blueline Project. You're the leader, aren't you?"

He didn't answer the question and tipped his gun toward the tent. "We still need your assistance."

"Hell no."

"Then we kill Daf." He walked toward her, straightening his gun arm out further. "Gentlemen. When I give you the word, pull the trigger."

Ali put her hands up, palms out. "Okay." She slowly rose. "You need the locations. But I'm not giving them until you let Daf go."

Daf vehemently shook her head. "Ali, no."

"I'm sorry," said Dexter. "I can't do that. But we'll keep you two alive once you translate all portal locations."

"What about CJ?"

Dexter's expression tightened. "No offense, but I don't like the guy."

"You're going to let him die?" asked Ali.

"Yeah, seems about right."

Ali glanced at Daf. "Call the Templars."

Daf huffed. "Not working."

Dexter thumbed toward the black orb. "You can thank the coupler. It does that to our communication devices as well."

Ali gritted her teeth. "You'll get killed."

Dexter cocked his head to the side. "How so?"

"You're allowing swarms of armies to make their way to Earth and take over. That's how."

"We have an agreement." He threw a hand in the air. "But enough of this. Gentlemen." Dexter's eyes narrowed, anger rising in his voice. "On my orders, kill Daf."

Ali took a step in front of Daf. "All right, I'll go in the tent." She shot Daf a look. Daf shook her head, nothing coming out of her mouth. Ali turned to Dexter. "You harm one hair on Daf, you don't get a single translation from me."

He dipped his head. "Deal."

Daf bent down to comfort CJ, and Ali walked toward the canvas, Dexter in tow, his gun at her back. Out of the corner of her eye, Boris stood at the base of the eastern portion of the hill, saying things Ali couldn't make out. The black orb hovered, bobbing up and down, electricity branching out from it.

A heaviness surrounded her as if a dense gravity well had opened. A moment later, a bright light flashed from the hill. A round, black hole materialized and slowly widened.

Dexter gawked at the spectacle as the wind picked up, knocking Dexter's hat off and whipping Ali's hair. He picked his hat up and whacked it on his leg a few times. "Move."

Ali pushed the canvas aside and entered the tent. Tranquil, *do you hear me?*

No response. She winced, wishing she had the sword with her. Maybe then *Tranquil* could hear her and come down, blast the crap out of the hill and save them all, especially CJ.

Her heart went out to the guy, death no doubt taking him minute by minute. She closed her eyes. *Skye, Dad, any Space Templars out there. If you can hear me, I need your help more than ever.*

Dexter shoved her forward, and she nearly fell onto the table holding the tablets. "Get to translating."

"These tablets didn't come from here, did they? They came from Enlil."

"Yes, now do as I said, decipher these."

"It looks like you found this portal just fine. Why can't you find the rest?"

"We had help from the locals. Apparently, this location has been spoken of in their lore for centuries. It gives off strange black magic. We figured this was a good place…"

"…and you don't have time to ask the locals all around the world.

So you have me." The wind picked up outside, pressing the canvas tent wall inward.

"Give us the location of each portal, or Daf dies. You lie to us, and we find a location isn't where you said it was, we kill Daf. The way I see it, you have your friend's life in your hands."

She leaned forward, her stomach a hard rock. She pointed to a location. "Jaguaruna in the Brazilian state of Santa Catarina." She shot him a pissed off look. "You writing this down?"

He pulled out a round device, definitely Anunnaki technology. A small portion in the middle of the device glowed bright blue. "Keep talking."

If she had a bomb on her, she'd detonate it now, blowing the entire site sky high. But she didn't. She touched another location. "Cahal Pech, Belize." She wiped her face, the sweat beginning to drip from her forehead. Regardless of Daf and CJ's life, she wouldn't give this man the truth. Earth depended on her lies, and she'd continue to point out incorrect places as she went.

ENLIL

Nibiru

Enlil sat in a hover vehicle, emergency medical staff working on his legs. The craft zoomed over the city, heading toward an underground portal gate beneath the Black Gap military installation at the edge of the metropolis.

He cringed as a man in scrubs sealed up the plasma wound, injecting his legs with fast-acting collagen. "Give this a day, my king, and you'll be better."

The vehicle vibrated the faster it flew. Enlil watched the military base grow bigger as they approached. "I don't have a day."

The medical tech straightened, his eyes wide, and his expression worried. "It needs to heal. You'll tear the wound if you're on your legs too much today."

"I can handle a lot more than a tear."

Earlier, when the hover vehicle picked him up at the stadium, his commband vibrated. Through the comm, Nibiru intelligence informed him that an Earth portal had activated and was opening. Immediately, Enlil sent a brigade to Black Gap, along with military hovertanks, hoverjeeps, and striders—small starfighter-like craft.

Killing Enki garnered Enlil more support than he imagined.

Outside of the council, he thought he'd get some kickback after the execution, but that was far from the case. The military seemed to be at his beck and call now, not a dissenting voice around. Enki was wrong. Fear did wonders for leadership.

Plus, with Senator Gronis and the council in hiding and his brother out of the picture, he figured it gave him more freedom to lead his people, more weight to rule his military. But his brother—his poor brother—burned to death.

Enlil's lips curled downward. His heart was heavy. "It didn't have to come to that."

"Excuse me, my king?" said the tech.

"I wasn't talking to you." He scowled, his face relaxing when he saw a holopad attached to the tech's belt. "Give me that."

The tech handed him the pad. Enlil pressed several buttons and pulled up the vid of his brother and his father, the last time Anu was alive. He jerked back when the vid no longer remained on pause and moved forward.

He flinched, his eyes widening as he watched his brother send a piercing shot into his dad's skull. "Why did he do it?" About to throw the holopad out the window, he glimpsed another man on the vid, Senator Gronis.

The senator came from behind Enki, and touched Anu's neck, checking for a pulse. Enlil's chest tightened, and his brows furrowed. He didn't understand. Why would someone kill such a loving man, let alone his brother?

Enki bent down and took his father's hand and pressed it against his forehead, sobbing. Gronis rubbed Enki's back, consoling him. Enki stood slowly, wiping his eyes with his sleeve. He walked closer to the hovercam. "Brother, when you see this, I'll either be dead or rescued by the Space Templars. I'm fine with either. The only way to stop your slavery was to control you with the heavy chains bound by ruling a world and a people you love. Father, and maybe I, have given the greatest gift for the galaxy's cause. Our lives. I'd rather this be you, dead, on father's favorite chair. He didn't deserve this. However, you've proven too difficult to kill, too hard to find in almost every instance but a few. Father kept your slaving ways behind the scenes, veiling it as best he could. He loved you and couldn't tell you no when he knew he should. Without his blessing, your slavery will die with him." Enki bowed, and he and Gronis walked out of the vid.

Enlil dropped the holopad. He drew in a deep breath. He wished Enki was alive so he could wrap his fingers around his brother's neck.

He nodded to himself, knowing he'd done the right thing, burning his brother to a crisp. He handed the holopad back to the tech. He moved his legs and stood, cringing in pain. "It still hurts."

The tech reached into a pouch attached to his belt. He pulled out a wafer. "Eat this."

Enlil plopped it in his mouth and chewed. He paused for a moment, as a sensation swirled through him, easing the ache in his legs and everywhere else in his body. He swallowed. "Much better."

A Black Gap hoverpad came into view, surrounded by military buildings and hangars. A wide entrance led into a tunnel in the middle of a landing strip near the pad. Thousands of troops in military garb stood around, spear-rifles in hand, mingling amongst each other. Black hovertanks, cannon barrels long and wide, and gun turrets on the top were parked in front of the soldiers. Jeeps hovered near the rear of the brigade, missile turrets attached to the roofs, and pulse cannons on the hoods. Further behind the jeeps stood heavy mechs, twice the size of an Anunnaki, looming above the massive army.

Enlil's hovervehicle touched down, slightly bouncing when it landed. He walked to the craft's exit, pulled a rifle from the magnetic strip against the wall, and strapped it around his shoulder. He grabbed two plasma bolt action double barrel blasters and shoved them in his holsters. "Open."

The door opened upward, and he walked out onto the landing pad, eyeing his men like the leader he was, chest out and chin high. The pad lowered and clanked on the cement. He stepped off, walking through the parting soldiers. He made his way past the tanks and into the tunnel.

The tall walls and high ceiling made it easy for ground units to access the portal gate he'd see soon. Exiting the tunnel, he came to a wide room twice the size of a warehouse and stopped in front of scientists monitoring a square metallic device. It reminded him of the galaxy's largest picture frame.

Dozens of scientists stood in gray coats, staring into holopads. They passed the holopads amongst each other, looking up at a growing blackhole-like phenomenon happening inside the portal gate, and then back down at the holopads.

A few scientists walked toward the gate to view monitors that scrolled data positioned on the wall. A scientist walked to Enlil's side. "In thirty minutes, maybe less, we'll send our first troops through."

Enlil kept his eyes on the portal gate. "I'm going with the first wave."

The scientist hesitated, a strange look in his eye before he peered down at his pad again.

Enlil looked him over. "Is there something wrong?"

The man cleared his throat. "No, my king."

He grasped the man by his neck and lifted. "What are you hiding from me? I just killed my brother, so I'm a little edgy."

The man couldn't talk and grabbed at Enlil's arm. He kicked his legs, trying to shake loose. Enlil dropped him, and he hit the ground with a thud. He crawled backward. "I'm sorry, my king. I was worried about you going through the portal with the first wave."

He pointed at the scientist. "Are the rest of you scientists a coward like this man?" No one answered, keeping their eyes away from Enlil, doing their best to avoid eye contact. He twisted around, waving his arms at the waiting army. "Everyone get ready. In thirty minutes, we invade."

He leaned his lips close to his shoulder band. "Captain Fin, do you read?"

"Yes, my king."

"On my command, jump the fleet into Earth's system. We attack soon."

35

EDEN

Niburu

Eden fell back into someone's arms, her mouth covered by a gigantic hand nearly the size of her face. Her nose pressed down by a wide finger, she glimpsed the translucent wall between her and the dark tunnel she'd been in moments ago. The wall then materialized solid.

"Be quiet, you two," came a low voice. "They haven't detected us, and we want to keep it that way. We can talk when the wall seals fully."

The hand slid from her lips. She turned to see a large man in dark robes and several more individuals behind him highlighted by torches attached to the wall. A hiss sounded like a cockpit door closing and sealing. The large man walked by her, pulling a device off the wall and tossing it to a person at the back of the group. The person caught it and shoved it in a backpack.

She gazed at the dozens of men in the damp, sweltering room, her heart beating rapidly. "Who are you?" She eyed Sleuth, who looked wild-eyed at a man who grabbed him. She brought her focus back to the man who spoke to her.

"We're Enki sympathizers." The large man lowered his hood,

showing a wrinkled face with a long, gray beard, and eyes hard and empty. "I'm Senator Gronis."

"You're King Anu's council." Eden looked around, as the rest of the councilmen lowered their hoods.

"And you're Eden," said Gronis. "I've heard you're the Grand Master now. You must be wise and strong, and as a woman, that's quite a feat."

Eden dismissed the odd compliment. "Are we safe in here?"

"For the time being, yes."

"We have to stop Enlil. He's sending his armies to Earth."

"We're on the same page." Gronis motioned for Eden to follow. "We have a plan. It's a long shot, but we've got nothing else."

Eden nodded, taking another glance at Sleuth. "You all right?"

"I heard her."

Eden scrunched her brow. "Heard who?"

"Your mother. Well, not her, but the thoughts in your head. They're similar to mine."

She put her hand up and walked toward Sleuth. "What are you saying?"

He lifted his strong, silver arm, examining it. "This thing, whatever it is, is more than an arm. I can hear things in your mind, sense things around, but only you, Eden. Your thoughts. Your feelings. That you want to give up and forget this Grand Master business. You don't feel worthy." He lowered his arm and moved closer. "Your mom haunts you, doesn't she?" He shook his head like an insane rat. "The same with me. Not your mom. I hear my parents. They torment me every day, screaming in my head, telling me I'm wrong no matter what I do. They're doing it now. Can you hear them?" He leaned toward her.

"You don't want to be Grand Master?" echoed Gronis' voice. "Do your Templar knights know this?"

She shoved a finger at Sleuth. "You shut it. I didn't want you on this mission and—"

"Skye was a good man," roared Gronis. "Did he know that you doubted your role as Grand Master before he gave his life? If so, you're not worthy."

She swallowed the truth of his words. She wasn't worthy.

"Answer me," demanded Gronis, his face reddening.

She'd have to lie to the senator. No telling what these men would do to her if she gave them an inkling of the truth, that she feared leading millions of elite warriors and that her orders determined the fate of a knighthood. "No. I don't doubt. He's been training me for months. I'm fully capable—"

"She's a liar," said Sleuth. "I'm the reason she's alive. I saved her. She'd be dead if it weren't for me."

She narrowed her eyes at Sleuth. The Templars had linked her and Sleuth together via that damn arm. "Whatever the Space Templars put in that new arm of yours is what saved me. It dragged you, practically controlling you to do the right thing."

Gronis stepped around Eden. "What's this about his arm? It looks peculiar." He went to touch it.

Sleuth pulled away. "It can kill you with one punch, big guy. Stand back." Sleuth curled his lips in a snarl, his arm back, ready to throw a fist.

"This guy is a problem." Gronis turned, gesturing to a councilman. "He'll get in our way. We need to end him now."

A larger man than Gronis pushed his robe away, pulling out a blaster. He aimed and walked toward Sleuth.

Eden jumped in front of Sleuth, wincing, the quick movement hurting both her wounded leg and arm. She twisted her wrist, activating her shield. "He's an asset. If he didn't have that arm, I'd agree with you. I'd pull the trigger myself. But that arm controlled him to do things to save my butt that rivaled a Space Templar. It, not him, can help us." She couldn't believe she trusted this arm so much. She bit her lip and held back from cursing Skye's name for putting her in this position, going along with the monks and placing Eden as Sleuth's babysitter. But her wonderful friend was dead, burned to death, Enlil's sharpshooters ending Skye for good.

Gronis put his hand up, halting the councilman. "We'll listen to the Grand Master."

Even though Gronis called her Grand Master once before, the

second time hit her like a blaster slug into her heart. She scratched at her arm, her gut twisting. She wasn't ready. Skye and the monks never had finished training her. She cringed, imagining her mom laughing at her, voicing to Eden an "I told you so."

"See," said Sleuth. "Her mom runs her mind and—"

She slammed her shoulder into Sleuth, pinning him against the wall. "Shut your damn mouth." She glimpsed his metal arm. It could throw her across the room or pulverize her if it wanted. If it were up to Sleuth, it would. But the Space Templars probably installed a fail-safe of some sort. Somehow and in a way she didn't understand, she controlled it too.

Sleuth went to speak. She shoved her hand against his mouth. He mumbled, trying to wiggle out of her hold.

"Keep your mouth shut, or I'll tell them to shoot you like they'd prefer." Eden moved away and spun around, seething. Her eyes rested on Gronis. "You wanted to show me something." She heaved in and out, her shoulders moving up and down with each breath.

The councilmen jerked back slightly as if she were about to attack. She understood their fright, especially if she had been a fully trained Templar. They were deadly in a bind. As head of the knighthood, they obviously thought she had all the training she needed.

Gronis put his hands together and pressed his fingers against his lips. "Yes. Follow us."

They turned and marched into another room the size of a ware-house, if not bigger. Over fifty Anunnaki mechs stood in the center, all equipped with shoulder-mounted missile turrets and blasters as arms. They towered above everyone, their shadows stretching across the floor.

"Do you trust Sleuth in one of these?"

Eden shot Gronis a hard look. "What are you saying?"

"Enlil hasn't been king long enough to know the many passages his father created under each city, and the many weapons, tech, and mili-tary units he stored here for militia purposes. These were for backup in case we lost an invasion. We could get down here, wait it out, and send a surprise attack at the enemy in a moment's notice."

"What are you saying? We'll attack Enlil's army?" The idea was absurd. With a little over a dozen councilman, they didn't have a chance.

"No. They're getting ready to walk through a portal at Black Gap military base. We join their ranks there. When one of us has Enlil in sight, I send everything I've got at the bastard. By Anunnaki rule, I'm next in line as king. Once crowned, I stop the invasion."

"How do I know you'll stop the invasion?"

"Because as my first order as king, I'll give the throne to Sabra. She'll run Nibiru like her father, with justice and love." He scratched his chin, his eyes coming down upon Sleuth. "So I ask you again, can Sleuth pilot one of these?"

Eden looked the jerk at the entrance to the room, his eyes searching hers. Sleuth slowly shook his head, his heart not in it.

She shifted focus to his new arm. Her trust in Sleuth came down to that beautiful piece of metal hanging by his side. "Sleuth, suit up. We're heading into battle."

3 6

SHAE

Earth's Moon

Sabra dragged Shae toward the *Ascension*, pointing furiously at the starship. Shae exhaled and nodded, then he closed his eyes.

Ascension, *we need your help.*

I've lowered my bridge platform. Hurry.

Shae raced toward the ship, his long strides more hops than a run. Sabra chased him, heading toward the ship.

His stomach ached, and his lungs burned. He didn't know how much farther he could get before the lower gravity pushed too much blood into his head and he passed out.

His foot came down on a rock, and on his next jump, he twisted out of control. Landing on his side on the moon dust, he skidded. His heart about beat out of his chest, but his pulse quickly slowed.

Sabra picked him up with one hand and bounded forward. Shae's vision narrowed, and gray filled most of his sight. His body was weak, so she set him on the platform, then crouched beside him. The platform zipped upward at twice its normal speed and into the starship's bridge. It clicked when it locked in place, and a loud hiss sounded. Oxygen filled the bridge. Shae gasped for air, clutching his chest, and rolled to his side, sounding like a dying rat.

Sabra also breathed heavily, positioned on her hands and knees. Her chest heaved. She flopped onto her back with her arms out wide.

Shae's vision focused, and his energy rose. He hacked a few times, his coughs echoing off the walls. "Thank...you, Sabra." He crawled toward her but fell on his chest. He reached for her, grabbing her hand.

She stood and pulled him up as well. "You're welcome." She made sure he could stay upright and was able to balance, then walked to the executive officer's seat and sat. She leaned back against the chair and blinked several times, eyeing the ceiling. "We need to get to your daughter."

Shae flopped into the captain's chair, his face slack, his hands clammy. He dropped his head in his hands, then leaned back into his seat like Sabra. "I agree." But curtailing the invasion, training his people, needing to help his people stave off an armada, was ten times more important. He needed to wear his admiral's cap, not his father's hat, even though the idea that his daughter might be in immediate danger struck Shae like a missile blasting a starfighter apart. He cringed, pushing the feeling away. "We need to send a crew to get her."

"No time. We leave now."

"I have to lead the defense. I can't leave my post and my duties." He rubbed his temple. "Get some people down there to retrieve my daughter."

"Yes, you and me."

"Dammit, Sabra! I need to be here with the leaders of Earth."

Sabra nodded. "They're compromised." She pushed off the chair and stood, glaring down at him. "You have too much confidence in your people."

"Not all of them are compromised. We caught the bastards—Lloyds agency."

"Right now—"

"And we have this starship. It's superior to anything that's about to be thrown at us. If we take this away from our flotilla, we lose a gigantic piece of our defense." He had an obligation and responsibility to his people, and part of that was to use any tactical advantage he could.

Sabra brought her wristband to her mouth. "Jasper, this is Sabra."

"Go ahead, Sabra."

"Halt all operations and training scheduled for Admiral Lutz. We have a new priority."

"Yes, ma'am."

Shae stood. "What are you doing?"

"I'm saving your race."

"By shutting me down?"

"Precisely, but not entirely." She tapped her wristband again. "Jasper, we need Space Templar Marines and Special Ops deployed on Earth. This is not a drill. Enlil's on the ground. I repeat, Enlil's on the ground. Have all marine transports follow *Ascension's* energy signature and land where she lands."

"Yes, ma'am."

"What the hell am I missing here?" asked Shae.

"My brother is as impatient as he is evil. When Enlil sees an opening, he'll take it, and my guess is that your daughter is unknowingly helping the Blueline Project open portals at this moment. If Enlil's not on Earth with his soldiers now, he'll be planetside soon. What I need from you is permission to land on Earth and stop him."

"Why the hell would you need my permission for that?"

"We're already overstepping our boundaries a bit too much with this moon base. We're not here to advance the evolution of your species. If we do so, major consequences might affect your species. We're being as hands-off as possible. We can't jump-start a species' evolution when it's not ready."

"You want permission to fight on Earth's soil? Won't that be overstepping? Won't that interfere with whatever you're worried about?"

"Much like you asked us to help with Star Guild during the Anunnaki's' attack on your fleet and Starbase Matrona, we need permission from the leader of a species that has its best interests in mind. It's a terrible loophole, but it has to do with a race's energetic evolution."

Shae stared into her eyes. Sabra was serious; she needed a leader's permission. "We defend on two fronts, land and space. If Enlil's planetside, his armada will arrive soon."

"I wouldn't have it any other way."

Shae pressed a few buttons on the captain's chair. "Space Templar command, this is Fleet Admiral Shae Lutz. The Anunnaki armada is on its way and will arrive soon. All personnel to their stations on all ships, Aven pilots at the ready. Protect Earth. I repeat, the Anunnaki will arrive soon."

"Admiral Lutz, this is Captain Leif Montegue. Orders accepted and initiated."

Shae turned off the comm and shifted his focus to Sabra. "Yes, you have my permission." He sat, resting his hands on the armrests. "Starship *Ascension*, activate engines and lift." *Ascension* rumbled and left the ground. Shae looked at the vidscreen, where stars twinkled in the blackness.

Sabra pursed her lips. "My brother is clever. To get someone to locate the portals and open them is evil but brilliant."

"*Ascension*," said Shae. "Can you get a lock on my daughter?"

Scanning.

"Thank you."

Sabra brought her hand to her heart. "I'm sorry for the turn of events, but I didn't see this one coming."

Shae dipped his head. "*Ascension*, fly us to Earth and continue to scan."

I found her location.

"Thank you, *Ascension*. Take us there."

Ascension blasted toward Earth. *Shae, first marine transports are leaving the moon base now. They're heading in our direction.*

"Thank you."

The vidscreen split. *We have a challenge.* One side of the screen showed flashes of lights that blinked into existence, then more and more.

Large dreadnoughts, cruisers, battleships, carriers, and all the class types Shae could imagine popped into Earth's space. His chest tightened.

The Anunnaki had arrived.

EDEN

Nibiru

Eden stood in the two-story tall mech. The cockpit mirrored Star Guild mining mech cockpits, the HDC, holographic display console, attached below the cockpit window.

Strapped in, minus wearing a jumpsuit on account that no Anunnaki suit would fit her, she took a step forward and then another. The soles of her boots landed on a treadmill-like foot rail, keeping her in one place, but moving the mech down a wide city street.

Strapped inside the cockpit, her hands were wrapped around two joysticks attached to moveable arms connected to the cockpit's sidewalls—each joystick controlled shoulder-mounted weapons, cannons, and mech arm functions.

She eyed the councilmen's mechs in front of her. The mechs' feet cracked the hard asphalt, sometimes taking a chunk of the street under metallic foot and spitting it out a moment later.

She looked left. Her cockpit head turned to match her movements, the motion motors and actuators humming beautifully. Windows on the buildings she past reflected the menacing machine she piloted, its thick shoulders and arms swinging, its long strides looking all too human. Hovercars were parked on the side of the roads near sidewalks that hugged the buildings.

The displacement gyros and suspension shocks made the ride feel as if she were floating, much different from the jostling mining mechs that Star Guild used.

She pressed her hand on a button, activating her comms. "Sleuth, you managing okay?" She stepped over a young child that ran in the middle of the road, his eyes full of glee, his mom screaming after him.

"Shut up."

Eden rolled her eyes. "I'm guessing you aren't."

He didn't reply.

He did everything he could not to get inside a mech, even going as far as asking if he could find Enlil on his own. That brought eyes to Eden. She reminded the council she was a Grand Master. The council more or less forced Sleuth to comply. Gunpoint came into play. It surprised her that the Nibiru Council valued the Grand Master's position so highly, even as much as allowing a deranged lunatic to come on a mission of utmost importance.

Yet again, she trusted Sleuth's arm, not him. She couldn't help but wonder what drove Sleuth and why he was the way he was. The monks wanted her with him, perhaps so she didn't fall into the negative trap of going down the dark route of the way her mother raised her. His family had abused him, or so it seemed. Maybe the monks thought she'd rub off on him or he'd learn a thing or two. If not, at least that arm of his kept him on the positive route whether or not he wanted to. Still, why was Sleuth so important? Perhaps his genius with tech?

The commlink crackled. "ETA in seven minutes."

Gronis came over the line. "We're arriving late and will be at the back of the regiment. We make a slow, concerted effort toward the front of the line. When we're told to fall back, which we will, don't fight it. The goal is to move close enough in the regiment to get a line of sight on Enlil and end him, causing minimal collateral damage. If we don't get a good look at him, we follow through the portal.

Regardless of when you see him, I kill him. None of you take a shot. Understood?"

"Understood," came several voices.

He continued. "Once I assassinate the king, we'll be pounded by friendly fire. Do not shoot back. I repeat, do not engage. When the commanders calm the troops, they'll identify me as the killer and the new king."

Eden's eyebrows squished together. That made little sense. "What do you mean they'll king you?"

"Eden, you're not aware of our ways, so I understand your confusion," replied Gronis. "Our laws state that if the king dies by another man's hand, the killer becomes the new king."

She cleared her throat, not believing she heard his response correctly. "Can you repeat that, please?"

The councilmen rounded a street corner, moving down another wide road. A volcano drooling lava came into view, a puffy stream of smoke drifting out its mouth, graying the golden sky. As they continued to walk, street hoverlamps moved out of the way, avoiding the mechs swinging arms. A hover vehicle flying down the road sped up, then turned quickly to not get scrunched.

"Eden," said Gronis, "let me be clearer. If a man such as myself openly declares in a public forum that he wishes to be the new king, and slays the sitting king, the killer then becomes leader."

"So, you must announce you'll kill Enlil before you do so?"

"Yes. That's how Anu did it when he took over as king, rest his soul."

Her shoulders drooped, her mech mimicking her. "That takes away the element of surprise."

"I'll flip on external speakers and make my claim as new king moments before I send Enlil to his grave. He'll be more than surprised."

She shook her head, the head actuators moving along with her. "So, any Anunnaki can become king as long as they get a lucky shot off on the sitting king?"

"I do not consider being king a desirable career. It's a stressful endeavor. Once the new king is crowned, he'll be tested by the council. If the king doesn't fit proper intellectual ranges and other qualities we look for, then that king will in turn be killed. Like I said, it's not a desirable position."

"So, they could kill you after being crowned."

"No. I am more than fit. But I'll be handing my position to Sabra."

"Then, you'll be killed afterward?"

"Not unless Sabra wishes to end me. If so, I'll have no other choice than to give my life for the new queen."

Quite the strange custom. But she bit her lip, holding her tongue from asking the myriad questions forming in her mind. Nothing mattered, except to kill Enlil, and that's where she'd keep her focus.

The mechs slowed, and she followed suit, Sleuth behind her. A large facility, surrounded by high, black ebb walls taller than the mechs, glared back at them. Cannon turrets manned by soldiers were mounted on top. The same dense ebb making up the walls made up the doors leading into the installation.

Eden blew out her cheeks. "We've got a mighty predicament here. How do we get inside?"

"We're not the only sympathizers left alive," said Gronis.

A red bead of light slipped through her window and onto her stomach, the tinted cockpit windows not blocking out the laser light. She froze, her eyes widening. She went to move out of the way and her mech jostled, trying to parrot her movement.

"Eden, it's protocol. Do not move. The snipers manning the walls will only shoot if you give them a reason," instructed Gronis.

More beads of light streamed from the walls onto the mechs.

Sleuth huffed. "I don't like this, guys."

"Sleuth, you'll be fine," said Eden.

"Says you."

She eyed the top of the wall, cannons and missile turrets aimed at her. A drip of sweat made its way down her temple to her cheek, and she swallowed down her nerves. "Gronis, why isn't the door opening to let us in?"

"We've got some complications."

Her eyes darted around, looking for possible suspicious activity, like anyone attaching explosives to her mech. "Like what, may I ask?"

"We're trying to patch through to someone."

She looked up at the sky, wishing she could patch through to *Swift* or *Nyx*. They probably had no clue where Eden was, or what was taking so long. She hoped the Marines she left at the forest's edge could somehow contact the starship. If not, maybe Nyx would take *Swift* down here.

She closed her eyes. Swift, *can you hear me?*

She waited for a minute. Nothing came through.

Swift, *it's me, Eden. If you can hear me, I need you to locate and fly to Black Gap Military Installation. We need to take out a portal.*

No reply. She sighed, dropping her shoulders.

Commotion came over the soldiers on the wall, several running around, and jumping into unmanned cannon turrets.

She leaned closer to the HDC. "Gronis, why are they panicking up there?"

"I don't know."

"Shall we blast our way through the gates?"

"Negative."

She held her thumbs over the missile launcher on her joystick. "Are you sure?"

"Don't do anything stupid."

She relaxed her thumbs. "Have you spoken with your—"

The doors to the installation opened, swinging inward. A hover-jeep on the other side hovered in reverse. Sticking out of the open roof, a man with two bright sticks motioned them forward.

One by one, the mechs walked inside. Eden strode past the doorway and into the military structure. Massive warehouses and buildings filled the facility, along with stretches of wide, empty landing pads.

As the jeep continued to reverse, Eden brought her attention to the runway they were headed toward. In front of them were over twenty mechs, and in front of the mechs were military craft, vehicles, and thousands of troops.

The comm staticked, and a voice not Gronis' penetrated the speakers. "They've allowed us front line duties."

Eden, stunned, spoke into the comm, her voice disbelieving. "Are you serious?"

"It's the mech's frontline, not the infantry. We'll still be in the rear," replied Gronis.

Eden walked her mech forward and took a wide-angle like she would with a starfighter, to come around the line of mechs. She followed Gronis and his men, parking their mechs in front, and not leaving much space between them and the hovertank's backline.

"Keep your eyes peeled for Enlil," said Gronis. "Again, don't shoot. Let me do the killing."

"You know, this mech ain't half bad. I've been playing with the HDC, and fooling around with the data links," said Sleuth.

"What does that mean?" asked Eden.

"Well, I found a way to the portal development team."

"Again, I'm not following."

A pause came over the comm, and Eden scanned the bantering troops a little way off. They stood beyond the tanks and the starfighter-like craft. The infantrymen pushed, shoved, and laughed like children, as if the coming conflict on Earth would be nothing but a carnival ride. Apparently, King Anu's troops standing before her were elite trained. These men probably imagined any potential combat with a less technologically advanced army would be child's play. They would be right.

She'd been to Earth, and they had nothing to contend against the Anunnaki advanced weaponry. Enlil would decimate them rather quickly. She didn't know how well Space Templar Special Ops and Marines would fare. She imagined Enlil's father's military outnumbered the Space Templars at least five to one or more.

Sleuth came over the line again. "I can shut off the portals before they open."

"What do you mean?" asked Gronis.

Sleuth laughed. "You guys boast you have bigger craniums and that you're smarter than us Earthlings." He laughed more.

Eden clenched her jaw. "Get to your point, Sleuth."

"All right, damn." He sighed. "I can shut all power to the portals. There isn't a fail-safe either. Whoever designed the security firewalls and the wire loops sending energy to the portals didn't figure on anyone hacking into the system."

"Are you saying you can turn off this portal?" Eden's felt her insides about burst into a cheer.

"No. From the readings I'm looking at, if we turn this one off, it'll blow, taking us with it. Portals apparently need to ramp up slowly and shut down just as slowly."

"Then what's that any good use for—"

"I can turn off portals that haven't opened yet, ones that aren't activated. And from the long-ass list displaying on the screen in front of me, the only activated portal right now is this one, Black Gap."

Gronis' voice boomed through the mic, his voice jovial. "Good on you, Sleuth. I'm sorry I doubted your decision to bring him along, Grand Master Eden."

"Turn them off, Sleuth," Eden said.

"In the process." His giggles came over the comm in waves, as if each shut down caused him more pleasure than the last. "They're shutting down, one by one. I bet the techs are pissing their pants." He paused. "And what do you know, there's Enlil."

Eden lifted her chin, her eyes landing on Enlil walking between a group of parted soldiers, a comm device in his hand. He spoke into it. He'd come from a tunnel that led underground where Eden supposed the portal was located. He paced between the soldiers, yakking away.

Eden pulled up her targeting array. "I can take him out right here and now. Do you have a good read on him, Gronis?"

"I don't," he said. "We need to switch locations."

She eyed the line of mechs beside her and saw Gronis attempting to move his mech forward. The problem was the parked tanks in front of him.

"We must move the entire line," the senator groaned.

"Announce it, Gronis. Let them know you're challenging the king, and I'll take the shot. They won't know it came from me."

"That's not noble, and it may go against my case as king."

She couldn't care less. One shot and Enlil would be a mess splattered on the concrete. "I'm taking the shot."

"Negative."

Eden narrowed her eyes on the crosshairs forming around Enlil. She eased her thumb on the trigger. "He'll be dead in a matter of seconds. Let me take the shot."

"Do not. I repeat, stand down."

"What? He's right there."

"If you take that shot, ramifications accrue."

A fire burned inside Eden, and her cheeks flushed. "Dammit, let me end him here and now." She activated missiles. "I'm taking the shot, sending everything. There's no way I'll miss."

"That's a negative," roared Gronis.

Enlil nodded and spun toward the tunnel. He walked into it, the tunnel's shadow darkening him. "I have him in my direct line of fire. Let me engage, dammit."

"No."

She relaxed her thumbs from the trigger. "Shit. He's leaving my line. Can you see him? Can you engage?"

"Not yet. Move everyone, move."

She moved around Sleuth, who probably hadn't heard a damn thing because he didn't move a millimeter. Most likely, he was continuing to hack more Anunnaki netcomps.

"Hurry, people, hurry," yelled Gronis.

Enlil disappeared under the tunnel and out of view. Gronis' disappointed exhale sounded through the comm. "Move forward. We're going through the tunnel."

"How? There's no room unless you smash vehicles in front of you," said Eden.

"They'll move, or yes, they'll be smashed."

"They'll open fire on you," Eden warned.

The infantry near the tunnel's entrance moved forward. A councilman's voice came through the comms. "Enlil's ordered troop advancement. The portal is large enough and open. Earth occupation begins."

"Holy Guild," Eden said under her breath. "It's started."

"I'm about to turn on external speakers and voice my challenge to the king. If Enlil hears, it might slow things down until I can face him. Everyone, get—"

"Guys," said Sleuth, cutting Gronis off. "We have a problem. You know how I hacked their portals? Well, not a good idea. They've tracked me and locked onto my position."

Gronis yelled, "You little—"

A blast rocketed off of Sleuth's mech's upper back, and it lurched forward. Eden turned, backing away. She aimed and brought steady cannon slug fire on a missile turret. Her slugs streaked red and sliced the turret as though cutting cheese on a grater. Debris and explosions splayed outward. She quickly surveyed the top of the wall and saw more missiles launching from several turrets.

Eden twisted her mech. The infantry, and Enlil's mechs and vehicles came alive. Gronis and a few of his councilmen broke from the ranks, smashing hoverjeeps and tanks underfoot. Cannon fire riddled their thick armor, ripping pieces away.

The mechs at the back of the regiment rushed after the councilmen. Her stomach sank when a few mechs broke off from the chase and headed in her direction.

38

ALI

Pachacamac, Peru

Wind thrashed against the canvas, and Ali dug deeper into her lies. "Near Washougal, Washington by Beacon Rock." She'd heard of that place somewhere, though she couldn't recall when. It sure as hell didn't have a portal location.

The ground shook. The portal had likely opened wider. A massive boom went across the sky. Ali stepped away from the sidewall as it bent further inward from a heavy gust.

Dexter held out the recording unit. "More."

"I'm going as fast as I can." She tried to remember locations across the world as fast as possible. There was no way would Ali give him actual portal sites. "Angel's Rest, Zion, Utah."

"Okay, good. Keep going." Dexter walked to the entrance and took a glance outside, smiling when he stepped back in. "The portal is growing. It's wild, Ali."

Ali's body tightened, her eyes dropping to the ground for a moment. She eyed a rock by her feet. She bent down to pick it up.

A *phftah* sounded, and dust kicked in the air as a bullet took a chunk out of the ground in front of her. She fell back.

"I wouldn't do that if I were you." He held out his gun, the muzzle pointed at her. "Get up and resume."

"You're a bastard." She wanted to knock this guy out, or worse. "You won't get away with this."

"I already am. Now continue."

She touched a stone tablet and traced her hand to the right, touching a location. "It says Sumbaya, Lomboco, Indonesia, butterfly gardens."

He tilted his head to the side. "Where's that?"

She made it up. "An island in Indonesia. I'm sure Enlil, the all-powerful, can find it." She tapped a spot on the stone map in the ocean east of Jakarta. He couldn't eyeball exactly where she pointed, seeing that he stepped a few meters back after he pulled the trigger.

A beep sounded, and she looked up to see Dexter lifting a communit to his mouth. "This is Dexter."

Enlil's voice came over the line. "I see you have one portal opening. Good job, and I don't say that lightly. We're waiting. I'm calling in a few more regiments to enter through after we arrive. Also, my fleet has entered the Earth's system."

Dexter smirked. "Ali's naming off locations as we speak."

"Excuse me? She's listening to us?"

Dexter cleared his throat, looking uncomfortable. "Yes. But we have her friends at gunpoint. If Ali doesn't follow instructions, we kill them."

"Not good enough."

"What do you mean?"

"Killing them is fine and good but dismantle them slowly."

Dexter brought the communicator closer to his lips. "Can you explain?"

"I have to spell out everything to you humans." Enlil sighed. "Ali will be more apt to following instructions if you torture her friends, not flat out kill them with one shot. Do you get what I mean?"

Dexter shifted on his feet. "I do."

"Good. Now, get the information you already have to the sergeant and have him send the volunteers to the portal locations. I'm sending my armies across my planet to several Nibiru portal gates. Earth will soon crawl with my men."

"Yes, sir."

"And, Ali," boomed Enlil's voice. "I'll see you shortly. Heading through the portal now. Out."

"Ali, stop translating." Dexter walked toward the tent's entrance again.

Ali called out another location to piss him off. He pursed his lips and poked his head out of the tent. He yelled for the sergeant, as the wind whipped more violently. Dexter gave the locations to the sergeant, then ducked back inside. "Those better be the right locations. If not, you heard Enlil."

"Loud and clear." Ali squinted her eyes, giving him an angry look.

There was another loud boom, and Ali flinched. Sounds similar to stomping feet pounded in her ears, and a moment later, yelling that reminded her of tribal battle cries filled the air.

She closed her eyes and rubbed them, muttering to herself, "Dammit. Where are you, Space Templars?" The Anunnaki army had made its way to Earth, but the Templars hadn't. The worst scenario had just become a reality.

The wind died down, but more sounds—the whir of hover vehicles, the hum of starfighters—carried to the tent.

The tent opened, and a giant man with a red beard walked inside and stood tall, his head nearly hitting the tent's apex. He smiled at Ali, almost as though glad to see her. "If it isn't my arch-nemesis."

Ali backed away. "I didn't choose to be your enemy. You gave me that title."

He nodded. "I know. But I gotta hate someone more than everyone else, and since you tried shooting me to death, I think I have a good reason for that person to be you."

"You tried to kill me first. I was defending myself."

"I created you." He threw his hands out wide, touching tent walls. "Hell, my race created your entire species. I'd say we have free rein on who we kill and who we don't. If it weren't for my people, your race wouldn't exist."

"I've translated tablets all over the world that say otherwise."

He pushed out his lips in thought. "I don't think so."

"With Anunnaki help, Sumer scribes created Sumerian tablets with your species' words and your race's lies. You wanted humans to think your scientists created us. You had nothing to do with our creation other than manipulating our DNA to enslave us."

He shrugged. "You don't have a clue what you're talking about."

Didn't matter. "I'm not translating any more locations."

"Good, because you gave us an incorrect location. One that doesn't exist. Lomboco? I mean, really? You couldn't think of a better one than that? I thought your mixed blood would put a little more smarts in you. How many more did you lie about?"

She straightened her lips. "I didn't lie."

Enlil snapped his fingers. Dexter walked in, an Anunnaki following, carrying a kicking and thrashing Daf.

"Get your damn hands off of me, you piece of ebb." Daf sent an elbow across the Anunnaki's chest.

The Anunnaki took Daf's hit like a feather brushing across his skin. He dropped her on the floor and exited the tent. Enlil pulled out a knife attached to his utility belt. He tossed it on the ground near Dexter's feet. "Pick it up." He pulled Daf's black hair back, her chest arching, and her chin toward the tent's roof.

Dexter reached for the knife, clasping it in his hand. "I got it." He examined the weapon. It was the size of a mini-sword compared to a human-made knife.

"What are you sick and twisted pricks going to do?" Ali instinctively reached for her sheath to pull out her sword. She swiped at air.

"Give us the actual locations, Ali," said Enlil.

"I am."

Enlil flared his nostrils. "Dexter, do your thing."

"What's my thing?"

"Cut her finger off."

"No," screamed Daf, blinking rapidly and kicking awkwardly at Dexter.

Dexter held the knife out. "Are you serious?"

"I said dismantle them, didn't I?" Enlil shot a look at Ali. "It's the only way she'll cooperate."

Dexter's neck bent forward. "Are you sure?"

"For the sake of Nibiru and my people, yes."

Dexter hesitated.

Enlil crossed his arms. "Give me the knife, and I'll do it myself."

Dexter shook his head. "No. I'm fine." He stepped forward.

Daf moved, and Enlil kicked her legs out from under her. She tumbled to the ground, and he leaned a knee on her back, holding her arm out to her side. "Start with her index finger."

Ali leaped at Enlil, wrapping her arm around his neck and squeezing. He dipped his shoulder and threw Ali on her back. He pulled a double-barreled blaster from his side and pointed it at her. "Do that again, and you get a hole in your arm." He kept his eyes on Ali. "Now, Dexter cut off Daf's index finger, and if Ali doesn't cooperate still, we take off Daf's hand."

Ali stood cautiously. "All right, all right. I didn't give the right locations."

"Gee, you don't say?" Enlil winked at her.

Daf tried to wiggle out from under Enlil's pressure with no luck. "Ali, don't say a word. I'm trained as a Templar, and I can deal with the pain."

Enlil snorted. "We'll see about that. Now, Dexter cut that finger off."

Dexter swallowed and nodded. He bent down and pressed the knife against her finger.

"Fine." Ali quickly studied a location on the map. "Stonehenge, England." That seemed like an obvious portal spot, yet she still lied. She'd have to continue this show until the Space Templars arrived or until Enlil found out she'd spoken untruths again.

"More," said Enlil.

Ali was about to say the Sphinx's left paw at Giza when an eruption outside interrupted her, shaking the tent. She jolted back with a start, and Enlil immediately stood.

Another blast rocked the area, and then another. Yells and shouts, rifle fire, and what sounded like missiles launching and impacting, growled across the area.

3 9

SHAE

Entering Earth's Atmosphere

"The armada has arrived. I repeat, the armada has arrived," Shae yelled into the comm. He eyed the ships blinking into existence, forty-thousand kilometers from Earth.

Sabra leaned forward, cupping her hand over her mouth. "Get to your daughter. Our fleet can hold off Enlil's ships."

"Are you sure?"

"More than positive."

He knew they could. He just didn't like the fight not to be in his control. Shae brought up rear cams. He eyed dozens of Space Templar Marine transports on his six. "Do we have enough Marines?"

"No, but more are coming."

We're about to enter Earth's atmosphere. I'm cloaking into a cloud, said *Ascension.*

"You're what?" asked Shae.

From Earth's surface, they'll see a cloud, not me.

Shae gave a thumbs-up. "Do your thing."

The starship vibrated as it flew through Earth's atmosphere. The shaking quickly died down as *Ascension* leveled into a glide. Its engines revved, and the bridge purred like a cat. Thrusters initiated and slowed her down.

We're over Peru. I'm scanning Ali. Her sword is not in her presence.

Shae cocked his head to the side. "Where is it?"

Atemporal Mansion.

The ship hovered high above clouds, the Marine Transports hovering next to her.

She's in danger, Shae, and so are her friends. But those harming her need her, so she'll be safe for the time being.

Shae grimaced, his shoulders lifting as he straightened his posture. "Then we go save her."

Sabra put her hand up. "She needs that sword." She stood, hurrying toward the bridge's exit. "Let's go."

Shae remained seated. "Where the Guild are you going? We need to get down there and change the scenario."

"We're going to Atemporal Mansion and retrieving the sword."

Shae threw his hands up. "No, we'll retrieve my daughter." He thrust his finger at the vidscreen. "If you want to get the sword, we get it after we grab her." His chest tightened. Space Templar leader or not, Sabra shouldn't go above the fleet admiral. "*Ascension*, take us to Ali."

"*Ascension* can't descend any lower. We want the fewest number of Earthlings to know such technology exists."

Shae twisted around, staring at Sabra and demanded sharply, "Why?"

Sabra made it to the door. It opened, and she stood in the doorway. "Like I said before, we can't advance the evolution of a species, and we'll do everything in our power not to." She stood taller. "We're taking a transport to your daughter."

Shae pushed off the seat, hurrying to the exit. "We're taking two transports. You get the sword, and I get Ali."

They rushed down a corridor, Sabra shaking her head. "Two transports are fine, but I can't carry the sword without it practically burning my hand off. I'm not of the bloodline like you and Ali."

"Got it." He didn't like this—another situation out of his control, one directly involving his daughter. "Get the Marines to Ali's locale. Get her out of there."

She brought her wrist band to her mouth. "Echo One. *Ascension* is sending you drop coordinates. If Enlil's army is at the location, engage."

They rounded another corridor, rushing toward the launch bay. Shae's hand tingled, and his breathing was short and fast. He was unable to inhale without his windpipes feeling blocked. He bent over, resting his hands on his knees.

Sabra hurried to his side. "Are you okay?"

Shae flexed and relaxed his fingers a few times, then shook his hand. His heart palpated, and an image of Stan's dead body jumped to his mind, the blood pooling around him.

Shae stopped and shook his head. "Guild Dammit, Stan." He rested a hand on a corridor railing.

Sabra's hand came to his back. "You're remembering your past."

Shae cleared his throat. "It's surfacing on its own." He flinched when another image came. Shae's gun extended, and a shot exited his gun's barrel, connecting with Stan's chest. Shae grunted and grimaced, pain searing across his face. He shook his head.

"Deep breaths, Admiral." Somehow, her swirling hand touching his back calmed him, her voice doing the same. "Focus on your breathing, not on anything else. Breath in, breath out."

Shae took her advice, and breathed in when she asked, and breathed out. She continued speaking to him, her voice like magic oozing through his body, and inch by inch, easing him. He slowly stood, dipping his head, feeling better. "You get going. I'll catch up."

She wrapped her elbow around his. "I'm helping you." Sabra moved forward at a slow pace, Shae walking with her. In about ten steps, he felt stronger and wiggled his arm out of hers.

They went down the elevator and took a hover platform to the launch bay. Inside, they each made their way to an almond-shaped transport.

Shae sat, the door shutting, and the ship automatically turning on.

Welcome, Shae.

"Who's this?"

An extension of me, Ascension.

"You can be in two places at once?"

More than two, but yes, I can be in two places at once. My consciousness is expansive. Shall we get you to the mansion?

"Yes."

The launch bay door slid open and blue sky with white clouds filled the expanse beyond. The ship lifted off the tarmac and picked up speed, darting out of the bay and through a white cotton ball in the sky. The craft veered and dropped low, the green and brown terrain coming to view.

"Where's Sabra and the Marines?"

Heading to Pachacamac.

"And that's different from where we're going?" He slid his hand in his pocket, feeling the vidcom.

We're going to Lima. It's nearby.

"ETA?"

Five minutes.

It was enough time to call Helen. He tapped on the vidcom. He could see his smile from the reflection on the vidcom's screen.

"Shae?" Her face beamed at him, her lips coming to the holographic display, sending him a kiss. "You had me worried. How many times did I tell you to see the doctor?"

Shae bobbed his head up and down. "I know. I'm sorry, love. I'm just letting you know that I'm fine."

"So, the bad guys aren't coming?"

Shae's chest just about caved in. "They're here."

Her eyes became saucers, and her mouth opened. "That's not fine, Shae."

"I was talking about me. I'm fine."

"Can you come home?"

"Not yet, but soon." Shae lifted his eyes from the vidcom and eyed the transport's display. An enormous home, with two floors, long and wide, came into view. Painted in white, the home's grounds were impeccable, lavished in green grass and vibrant flowers. A rounded driveway looked perfect for a landing. This ought to scare the tarnation out of the owner. "Love, I need to go."

"Promise me you'll be safe, okay?"

He winked and blew her a kiss. "I love you."

"I love you, too."

The holoscreen blinked out, and he shoved the comm back into his pocket. The ship lowered and jostled as it touched down. The door hissed open, and a ramp extended.

"Where is Sol?"

Upstairs, the only room on the left and down a long hall. From what my sensors tell me, it's under a bed, blood on the hilt. Someone not of the bloodline carried it there. I'm guessing he didn't like the consequences.

"Got it." He rushed down the ramp, the cool air breezing around his body. He took in a deep breath, feeling Earth's fresh oxygen flow through him.

He raced across the driveway, and up steps leading to the front door. He knocked, waited, and in his impatience, opened the door.

A man walking down the stairs stopped in stride, his mouth agape when he saw Shae. His eyes dropped to Shae's holster holding two guns.

Shae put his hands up. "I mean you no harm. My daughter left something here that I am in a hurry to retrieve."

The man's lips changed from fear to a grin. He walked down the rest of the steps, extending his hand for a shake. "Alejandro Garcia. Who's your daughter?"

Shae shook his hand. "I'm Fleet Admiral Shae Lutz of the United States Navy. Ali is my daughter. She's been staying here and needs me to grab her things as soon as possible."

Alejandro gave several quick nods. "Oh, yes, yes. Her room is upstairs and—"

Shae rushed by him and pounded up the stairs. "She told me."

"I'll be right back, sir. I need to grab something myself."

Shae reached the top of the staircase and looked left down a long hallway. A door at the end marked the treasure he needed.

He hurried to the door and opened it. He dashed to the bed across from him and stooped low. Looking under, he saw the sword, blood on its hilt. Just as *Ascension* mentioned. Whoever stole it from Ali had disliked the side effect.

He snagged it in his hand and wiped the blood off on his pants. Rushing out the door and down the hall, he scrambled down the stairs, passing Alejandro. "Thank you."

He almost paused his mouth curling into a frown. Was the guy holding a gun? He went to turn to see what the man held in his hand when flashes spit off the end of a muzzle. Bullets ravaged Shae's side, and he flew backward, the sword falling out of his hands.

He tumbled down the stairs and onto the driveway, the sword landing next to him, clanging loudly. More bullets exited the weapon, some missing and sparking off the concrete, and a few more sinking in.

EDEN

Nibiru

Enemy mechs approached, and Eden twisted her unit around. Missiles shot from wall turrets and slammed into her backside, rocking her cockpit. Her head whipped back, the restraints holding the rest of her body in place. More shots hit, and Eden tensed. Eyeing her HDC, the last volleys had come from the mechs now behind her.

Eden rushed forward, taking her mech at dizzying speed toward the tunnel. Her metallic foot crunched down on the runway and then the other, chunks of cement sprinkling outward, creating huge divots.

A mass of troops ran from her, and the rest of the council's mechs and pilots in hover vehicles drove away like madmen, trying to escape their lives being stomped out of existence.

Further ahead, soldiers and vehicles headed toward the tunnel, some disappearing into its shadows. Closing in, Eden imagined the enemy wouldn't dare fire upon her in fear they could harm their own infantry or the tunnel entrance.

More solid impacts to her rear and Eden's hope went swirling down the drain. Troops parted as she ran closer. She eyed two mechs in front of her and realized they weren't councilmen and were attacking and chasing her new-found friends.

She aimed her guns for arms at them, her hand slipping off one of the control sticks as pulse weapon fire, missiles, and slugs littered her unit, nearly vibrating her brain out of her skull. The HDC beeped red, indicating major damage to her posterior armor.

She clenched her jaw and moved her feet faster. Sweat beaded down her face.

"I'll blare my challenge to the throne and call for Enlil's death again," said Gronis through the comms.

"I'm breaking apart," a voice screamed. "My mech can't take any more."

"Hang in there, Banej," called Gronis.

An explosion rocked the runway in front of Eden, fire growing in a small mushroom cloud. The mechs chasing the councilmen hesitated. One attempted to jump over the explosion, and its leg snagged on the fiery downed mech. It tripped and crashed chest-first onto the ground.

Another enemy sidestepped, and Eden aimed both her pulse blasters at the bastard and held down both control stick triggers.

A loud whir and hazy, clear translucent beams fired, taking chunks of armor from the mech's back, sending boiling armor sliding off like melted butter. The mech stumbled as if the pilot hadn't expected the massive pummeling. Eden sent missiles toward him, leaving smokey entrails in the missile's wake. The enemy twisted its torso to face Eden and, as the projectiles connected with its chest, it tilted backward. Off balance, it stepped a foot back to remain upright. Eden, in a run, lowered her shoulder and rammed him.

Lifting off its feet, the enemy mech fell awkwardly. Eden raised her mechanical knee as she barreled onward, connecting with the mech's lower torso, and sending it hard to the ground. Dust spun like a cloud as it hit, and as Eden ran by, she aimed her cannon arm at the pilot's cockpit. She let loose a pulse blast, splitting the cockpit apart in a display of fireworks.

Reaching the tunnel's entrance, she watched as Gronis' mechs entered and descended into the shadows as more shots rocketed off of her. Passing the entrance, the weapon's fire abruptly stopped. She let out a breath and took her hand off the joystick. She splayed her fingers on her chest, feeling her heart beating rapidly. "Holy Guild."

She turned on rear cams. The enemy mechs were still on her tail but slowing down as they entered the tunnel. Perhaps a ceasefire had been issued, most likely to not blow the portal gate to hell and back. With the thought of hell, Sleuth came to mind. "Sleuth, where are you?"

The comm crackled. "Behind you. Well, behind the mechs that were chasing you." His breathing came fast. "This arm is amazing. It took over and controlled everything. It's a master brain. I have to give it a name or something."

"All right. You do that." She slowed down, seeing a bright glow beyond the tunnel. She walked by soldiers that eyed her, either out of contempt or awe. She couldn't tell which. Did they want to engage but couldn't, or were they confused, not knowing who to shoot?

"Eden, I think my hack slowed them down. They zeroed in on my location, yes, but I see they're having a hard time fixing the other portal gates."

"Do you think they'll be able to unhack what you hacked?"

"Yes."

"How long do you give them?"

"Hours or days. I don't know."

She tightened her lips, her chest flexing. She didn't like the next words about to come out of her mouth. "Good job, Sleuth."

A pause. "Uh...thank you."

She almost stopped dead in her tracks. He thanked her? She shook her head. She probably imagined it. She continued at a slower pace as she came to the end of the tunnel. Passing through, she entered a colossal structure with a massive, shining portal staring back at her. It was big enough for a medium-sized ship to slip through. Troops and vehicles were walking through as if walking into a waterfall and vanishing from view.

"I challenge Enlil, king of Nibiru, to the throne." Gronis' voice echoed inside the underground installation.

More troops eyed them as they trekked forward. No one

responded. Eden didn't know the protocol when such a challenge was issued. She leaned close to the mic. "Gronis, nothing's happening."

"Because Enlil's not here."

"You think he went through the portal?"

"Guaranteed. He's as impatient for blood as a Xiberian moon-tick."

"I'm going through. When we enter Earth-side, we find some cover and run our asses to it. They'll be waiting to blow us to that Xiberian moon and back."

"No can do. I'll blare my challenge as we pass through the portal. I'll need you and the rest in front of me. I won't engage my own people, so I'll need as much protection as possible. If you engage, aim to miss." His voice lowered. "Unlike you did back there."

"They killed your councilmen."

"To die is an honor."

The light widened as she took steps toward it, watching infantry and the last of the hovertanks passing through. She marched with a few of his councilmen in front of Gronis.

She cleared her throat, not liking being a shield for a guy she barely knew. "Sleuth, come around in front of Gronis."

"I won't be his cannon fodder." His mech picked up speed. "Dammit, knock it off, arm."

Eden cracked a smile. "I'm glad it's got a mind of its own."

Sleuth moaned. "I don't like this. I'm not trained in fighting of any sort. I really think I should wait back here."

"Your arm is Space Templar trained. You'll be fine." She moved forward, the cockpit brighter from the portal's white, electric-like branches zapping off of it. Scientists watched Eden and her team's mechs, their eyes wild. One of them spoke frantically into a comm unit, probably talking with Enlil or someone else on the other side.

Eden brought her eyes forward. "Sleuth, and the rest of you guys, get ready. They know we're coming." She stepped through, and the light engulfed her. Her skin tingled as if she'd been pricked by needles. "Weapons ready. Here we go."

4 1

SHAE

Lima, Peru

Shae twisted as the pain grabbed him. Every muscle in his body spasmed. He reached for his gun as Alejandro's trigger clicks sounded across the driveway, creating a predicament Alejandro probably didn't want, an empty magazine.

Pulling out his weapon, Shae aimed. The Peruvian went to turn, but Shae littered him full of bullets. The man dropped, holding his stomach, and crawled back into the mansion, kicking the front door closed with his foot.

Shae grunted, wincing in agony as he stood. His left arm was limp by his side, blood dripping from who knows where. He dropped the gun and picked up Sol. His leg dragged behind him, blood running down his thigh.

He pulled himself into the craft, blood trailing him from the ramp to the cockpit. He sat carefully and set the sword on the co-pilot seat. "Get me into the air and to my daughter."

Affirmative.

The craft lifted, turned a hundred-and-eighty degrees and ascended. Shae swallowed, bringing a shaky hand to his stomach. He touched the blood and looked down. "Dammit." Alejandro had shot him several times.

He wanted to call Helen, but he couldn't let her see him this way. His eyelids began to feel heavy, and his energy waned. He blinked several times, doing his best to keep his eyes open.

His body shook, and he cleared his throat loudly as he tried to stay awake. For a moment, it worked, and he straightened. He sucked in a shallow breath as his core temperature cooled, and his body began shivering.

He had to make it to Ali. He looked at the clouds, his body leaning forward on its own. He jerked awake, his shivering more intense.

"Stay with me, Shae," he told himself. "You can do it."

He glanced at the sword, more to do something than anything else. He smacked his lips together and tasted blood. He knew he was in trouble, but the blood in his mouth brought him to the reality of the situation. He probably wouldn't make it.

We're almost there, Shae.

"Thank you, *Ascension.*"

The ship descended, and he eyed the brown desert terrain below. A battle raged, explosions and puffs of dirt fogging the area. He couldn't figure out who was fighting who. Was Peru involved in a civil war?

He shook his head, waking himself up. He wasn't thinking correctly. Peru didn't have hovertanks, mechs, and soldiers with advanced weaponry. The closer he got, the more he realized someone had started a civil war, and that someone was Enlil. Mechs in combat with his own?

"Hurry and get me there. As close to Ali as possible."

ETA, one minute. She's in a tent. I'll get you as close as I can.

"Again, thank you, *Ascension.* You're a lifesaver." He let out a little laugh, chugging back a cringe of pain, eyeing his bloody hand. "Well, not a lifesaver in my case. But hopefully for the rest of the world."

We'll see.

"Shae."

Startled, Shae peered at the source of the new voice. If Shae wasn't so weak, he would have jerked back in fright at Captain Stan Jenkyns staring at him.

Stan sat in the co-pilot seat, the sword in his hands. He gave Shae a grin and examined the sword as if it was the most beautiful thing he'd ever witnessed.

"You're not supposed to hold that thing, Stan."

Stan shrugged. "I'm dead. I can hold anything when I'm dead." He winked.

Shae looked at him and smiled. "I see you've healed." The captain's chest didn't have a bullet hole in it, the one caused by Shae, or blood staining his shirt. His face was a healthy shape, his skin pink, and not flaking off like the last time Shae saw him.

"The adage that time heals all is true." Stan touched his chest, continuing to hold the sword with his other hand. "I think I forgive you, Shae."

Shae's smile widened. "I'm glad to hear that."

"And you're beginning to forgive yourself."

"I feel that, too."

Stan nodded. "I see the errors of my ways. I mean, you're no angel but had I followed you through the hard trials of separating ourselves from the Anunnaki, we'd have been in a better place."

"I think so."

"It's not your fault. I don't hold you responsible. Not anymore."

"I pulled the trigger."

"Like you said, I would have killed you if I pulled the trigger first."

"Why did you go for your gun?"

Stan's brows rose. "I thought I had a chance."

"But weren't we friends?"

"That's what I thought. I betrayed our race. That's clear, but it wasn't clear to me before I died. I thought I was saving the race. We had different opinions. Mine turned out to be wrong. I'm glad I died, and I'm glad you lived."

"Thank you, Stan. I wish you would have lived. We could sit together and save humanity a second time."

"Well, we are my friend."

Shae chuckled. "I mean in reality."

Stan dipped his head. "I see." Stan frowned. "I'm a little concerned about you."

"What do you mean?" Shae looked down, his shirt now drenched in blood. "Oh, yeah. Not looking good."

"No, not at all."

"Any tips?"

"Yeah, don't die."

"Well, that's a no-brainer."

"For you, it'll be more difficult than you can imagine." He gestured with a nod to the cockpit window. "It's about time you left, Shae."

"What do you mean? Leave to where?" He brought his hand to his face and saw more blood. "I can't leave Helen on her own. I just came back to her. And my daughter needs me."

"No, you need to leave." Stan gestured at the cockpit window a second time and stared ahead.

Shae followed his gaze. The ship had landed, and weapon's fire whizzed by. A line of tents stood in front of him at the base of a hill.

The craft shuttered from a concussion blast. He faced the cabin. The door had opened, and the ramp was extended, sitting on the desert floor.

He went to get up, cringing from the tight pull in his stomach. He sat back down, resting his elbow on his knee, the other dead and hanging loosely by his side. "*Ascension*, where's Ali?"

She's in the last tent on the right. Go, Shae. She needs you.

"Okay, I can do this." He stood, groaning and took a step toward the exit.

"Shae, you're forgetting something." Stan had his arm extended, balancing the sword's blade on his palms, hilt pointed at Shae.

Shae shuffled toward him and grasped Sol. "Thank you." He smiled the best he could. "I miss you, Stan. See you someday."

"Yes, you will."

Shae limped down the ramp, each step feeling like a baseball bat hitting his stomach and razor blades tearing at his leg. He dragged himself toward the tent, using the sword as a cane. Oddly, the world around him sounded dull, the weapon blasts muffled, and Anunnaki and human alike raced around him as if he weren't there.

Maybe he looked like an old man, dying as he was, and they had pity on him. He didn't know and didn't care. Getting to Ali consumed him. Sabra said she needed the sword, so he'd do everything he could to get it to her.

Another step and he was halfway there. A sharp stab sank into his ribs, then another. He dropped, the dusty ground caking his face, the sword falling by his side. That pity nonsense turned out wrong.

His chest burning, he tried to call Ali's name, but nothing came out. His vision fading, he reached out, grasping for a tent that was too far away. "Ali." A whisper exited. He yelled her name a third time, his voice louder, though he didn't know how loud. He lifted his head. Someone approached. It was as if he watched through a blurred, hazy window, and he couldn't make out the person's features.

A hand touched his back, and a soft female voice spoke into his ear.

4 2

ALI

Pachacamac, Peru

The earth shook, and Ali almost lost her balance. The tables holding the stone maps buckled. The Sumerian tablets fell into each other and onto the ground.

Enlil marched to the tent's exit. "What in the Nibiru moon is going on?" He stepped out of the tent, the other Anunnaki accompanying him.

"I challenge Enlil for the crown," a voice echoed across the air.

More explosions and the world bounced in place. Ali went to move, then froze. Dexter had set the knife on the ground and pointed his gun at Daf, who slowly pushed herself to a standing position. Ali watched his trigger finger and lowered her stance. She shifted her feet and dug in, then pushed off and rushed Dexter.

She dove for his hips, wrapping her arms around him. The gun went off and he fell back, tumbling to the dirt with Ali on top of him. She wrestled for the gun, then planted a foot and leaped, landing a knee on his wrist.

He yelped in pain, a few of his carpel bones either broken or heavily bruised. The gun spun out of his hand, and she snagged it off the ground. She stood and walked around Dexter with the weapon aimed at him. She took a side glance at Daf to see if she'd been hit. Luckily, the shot had gone wide, and a hole showed through the tent.

"Don't move, Dexter." Keeping the gun pointed at his chest, she walked over and pushed open the canvas entrance. A pulse blast hit the ground a ways from her, and soil slapped across her chest and face. She spat out dust and wiped her hand across her cheek and mouth. She crouched, eyeing the mess outside.

"Stay down, Ali," said Daf, crouching behind her, staring at Dexter, who held his wrist, squeezing his eyes shut and clenching his jaw in pain.

"Look at all those Templar ships," whispered Ali in awe, her voice breathy.

Templar craft dotted the hills, and dozens more sat across the desolate field in front of them. All almond-shaped, the ships glowed silver, switching to gold, then back to silver. Hundreds of Space Templar Marines, their camouflaging fatigues matching the ground they crawled or ran upon, were in the midst of engaging the growing Anunnaki Army. Shield wielding Templars stood in the front line, blocking Anunnaki fire.

Looking up, Ali spotted more Templar ships coming in for a landing. Her heart lightened, and relief pulsed through her veins. The saviors had arrived.

Taking a glance to her left, hovertanks, mechs, hoverjeeps, soldiers, and everything Enlil could dream of, fought back. Ali scrunched her brows. As expected, the Anunnaki were fighting the Templars, but something stuck out to Ali as more than peculiar. "Are the Anunnaki also fighting themselves?"

Several mechs were battling it out, one blaring a challenge over its external speakers. Anunnaki troops surrounded them, sending volleys and shredding their armor. Hovertanks raked powerful pulse weapons, melting the mech's armor. They chased each other like a game of cat and mouse. Ali's jumbled mind quickly came together with the weight of the situation. Enlil battled on two fronts.

"I've no idea what's going on over there, but if it's bad for them, it's good for us," said Daf.

A moan carried across the combat zone close by. Ali looked around, and her eyes locked on someone crawling toward her. She pointed. "CJ." He was five meters away if that. Ali dashed to him, sliding to her knees. "Are you okay?"

He rolled to his back, his face gnarled in agony. "Do I look okay?" Blood and dirt covered his clothes, Dexter's men having had their way with him. "My buddies took out Dexter's boys." He grimaced at his next breath, trying to smile, his eyes upon hers. "Aren't you just my little ray of sunshine?"

Daf ran to his side. "Medic. Medic." Several slugs skidded across the ground, and she jumped back.

"Help me pull him over there." Ali thumbed over her shoulder at the beginning of the tent line, the one place fighting wasn't taking place.

She grabbed his arms, hesitating when she heard her name. She shook her head. She was hearing things. She and Daf pulled CJ out of the battlefield. She paused when she heard her name again.

She searched the area and her hand flung to her mouth, a knot instantly forming in her throat. Her heart skipped a beat, and she ran as fast as she could to her father lying on the ground, covered in blood.

She crouched next to him, her lower jaw trembling. "Dad?"

He looked up, blinking his eyes as if doing his best to keep them open. "Ali, is that you?"

She choked on her next words and nodded as the tears welled. She stood, her entire body tightening, "Medic. I need a medic."

She felt a tug on her lower pant leg. She went to her knees, her hand on Shae's back. "Dad, we're getting you a medic." She knew it didn't matter. He'd been riddled with too many wounds.

"I brought...your...sword." He coughed. "I can't see...you." He raised his hand, and she wrapped her hand in his.

"Dad, please..."

"It's okay."

"No, it's not." She raised her chin. "Medic. Guild dammit. Medic!"

"Don't worry. Everything is…" he dropped his head, his chin hitting the ground.

She lowered herself and picked up his head. "Dad." She gazed around, tears streaming down her face. "Medic!" No one heard her. The battle raged on, fallen soldiers on both sides, medics racing across the field and pulling injured soldiers out of harm's way, Shielders in front protecting them.

"I love you. Tell your…mom…too." His eyes closed and his body relaxed. A lengthy breath exited his lungs.

"No." Ali shook him. He didn't wake. She shook him again, then made a fist and pounded his back. "Come back. Don't you leave me and mom. You selfish bastard. Why did you volunteer for this? Mom was more important. They didn't need you. You…" She flopped on him, sobbing.

An explosion picked up the earth near her, pummeling her with smoke and debris. She didn't budge and wrapped her arms around her favorite person, crying.

Daf came to her. "Ali." She paused when she saw who Ali held. "Oh, my Guild. Let's get the admiral over by CJ."

Ali shook her head. "No, he's dead. He's…dead."

Weapons fire peppered the ground, throwing more dust and soil on top of her. Her soul empty, her mind numb, she didn't care what the hell hit her or how many times.

Daf grasped her arm. Ali pushed back. Daf grabbed Ali around her ribs. "I know this is hard, but you have to get out of here. Enlil's advancing."

The bastard's name lifted her head in a start. She'd almost forgotten about him, the man who had just driven a stake in her heart. "Enlil," she yelled. She stood, pushing Daf off of her. She twisted, her eyes narrowed. Her breath seethed in and out. Pointing Sol at the coming army, she sent out a scream and curled her fingers tighter around the hilt. Lightning quick flashes of plasma exited the blade's tip, slicing through several oncoming Anunnaki troops. The bolts hit their marks, and several Anunnaki fell as dead as Enlil's heart.

"Enlil, fight me, you piece of ebb!" She squeezed the hilt again. More plasma bolts shot across the mass of enemy soldiers.

Her eyes widened when she saw Enlil, and like a madwoman, she ran in his direction.

43

EDEN

Pachacamac, Peru

The armor on Eden's mech dripped off like slime. The machine's ability to continue to function, blocking shot after shot in front of Senator Gronis, amazed her.

Around Eden, hovertanks and mechs sent all they had at her and the councilmen. Only a handful of the councilmen still survived. Heaps of smokey metallic mounds were scattered across the desert terrain, reminders of what was left of the councilmen who died.

The Space Templars moved back slowly, the Anunnaki outnumbering them five to one, at least. Smoke billowed everywhere, and she could see dead Anunnaki soldiers littering the ground.

She searched for Enlil as they circled, her head whipping back at another direct hit. A few more hits rocked her back and forth, then a lone beep sounded in her cockpit. An instant later, the HDC shut off. She held her breath as her mech toppled forward. She instinctively put her hands out in front of her, the restraining belts pulling her toward the back of the cockpit. She sucked in a sharp breath. Her nerves spiked, and her blood turned cold. "Oh, no."

The ground rose toward her, and she braced for impact. The glass shattered but held when it hit, a thousand cracks and crooked lines inundating the windshield. She hung from the belts, swinging back and forth. The next moment, quiet filled her cockpit. She unstrapped as quickly as she could, falling and twisting. She landed feet first on the windowpane and felt the glass crunch beneath her boots.

Her mom's voice flashed in her mind, insulting her, telling her she better die if she wanted any semblance of the Templars to remain intact. "You have no right to lead, Eden. No right at all." Her mother's voice picked up, screaming in a terrifying shrill. "You couldn't help me, you worthless brat, so what makes you think you can help the Space Templars?" Laughter reverberated off of Eden's inner skull.

Her heartbeat rose, and she slapped the cockpit hatch button. "Not anymore, mom. You have no authority over me, and you're no longer welcome in my head or in my space." She clenched her jaw. "I'll prove you wrong." The hatch unlocked, and she kicked it open to the nearly deafening sounds of war.

"Enlil, you coward, I challenge you to the throne," came Gronis' voice over his external comms.

She rushed out of the cockpit and into the midst of battle. The wind outside swirled around her, black clouds forming overhead as if they were Earth's disapproving stare glaring upon the conflict.

She twisted her wrist and activated her shield. Crouching low, she eyed the area. Enlil's war machine advanced forward. Behind her, Sleuth's arm maneuvered his mech like a genius, absorbing hits where thick armor remained, his mech dancing around like Sleuth had been born in one of these and had mastered the mighty beast.

She didn't need to see him to know he pissed and moaned inside, hating every second, complaining at every pounding he took.

She ran toward a hovertank. A soldier manned a turret up top, and she leaped at him. With the Sight flowing through her core, she extended her non-shield hand. Every emotion she could conjure exploded out her fingertips. A scream rushed up her gut and out her mouth, carrying it faster. Energy surrounded the soldier, picked him up, and tossed him over the side.

Landing on the tank, she climbed into the turret. She looked over the edge. The soldier she had thrown moved to get up. Eden initiated the Sight, picked him up, and slammed him against the next tank. He slumped unconscious.

She grasped the turret's pulse weapon handles and aimed the cannon on the tank. Pulling the trigger, a loud zap slapped the air. The tip of the cannon barrel cracked off, and red heat melted it more, twisting and gnarling the barrel.

She moved the turret, sending blasts at another tank. It hit, jostling the tank back and forth, melting the side armor like hot cheese. The soldier mounted on the top quickly turned the turret he sat in and took aim.

Good.

Eden jumped off, landing on the ground, and ran from the coming impact. The turret she previously stood upon blasted apart, and fire jumped out the top of the tank, taking it out of commission.

Moving at a fast past, she jumped toward a large indentation in the ground and twirled in the air. Another pulse shot came at her just as she brought her shield around. Connecting hard, it pushed her back. She fell with a hard thud, and rolled into the large divot in the ground, staying low, her back aching from the bad landing.

"Enlil, fight me, you piece of ebb," said a voice that thundered across the combat field, as if all sound ceased when the voice roared.

Eden's eyes went wide when she saw Ali, Sol in hand with fire blazing around its blade. Ali marched forward, Daf behind her. Ali's eyes were wild as if she was hunting prey.

Enlil stood only twenty meters from her. He spun on his heels, blaster in hand and took aim. Ali didn't stop or take cover. Eden dashed from the make-shift foxhole, her hand pointed at Enlil. She sucked in a deep breath, her insides tingling, and let out a yell. She pulled the energy around Enlil and he flew off his feet, landing hard on his back.

Ali rushed closer, and Enlil pushed to a standing position. A crunch sounded behind Eden and she lost her balance and tripped, the earth shaking around her. She tumbled to her back and looked up. A mech bounded over her, its foot sinking into the terrain mere meters from her position.

It was Gronis' mech. She rolled out of the way as Gronis' voice boomed the same challenge in a menacing tone as he rushed toward Enlil.

Eden raised her arm again, extending it toward Enlil just as he brought up his blaster and took a shot at Ali. She blocked it with her sword, deflecting the bullet into her shoulder. Ali spun off her feet, tumbling across the ground. Eden shoved the Sight forward, taking Enlil to his back a second time.

Eden dug in and shoved off, running fast, her legs taking her to Gronis' mech. She grabbed for her sidearm, Enlil less than ten meters away.

"Eden, do not engage. I repeat, do not engage. The Anunnaki are now cooperating," said Gronis, the speakers seemingly twice as loud as before. "I'm challenging the king. It's the only way."

She ignored him, because screw Anunnaki customs. Enlil had to die for the sake of the planet he was invading. If it had to be by her hands, so be it.

The sound of actuators took her eyes off Enlil and to Gronis' mech. Gronis shifted the mech's torso, pointing cannons in her direction. He fired. Eden jumped and flipped, her shield pointed at Gronis. The blast sunk into the ground in front of her, the concussion ripping dirt, roots, and rocks. She let out a grunt as earth smacked against her, the force fast and heavy. She flailed her arms and slid across the ground. She tried to exhale as her diaphragm spasmed, the wind knocked out of her.

Up ahead, cannon fire sent Gronis' mech to the side, the mech taking the last it could. It dropped and smashed troops, undoubtedly killing them on contact.

Eden went to move, but pain engulfed her. She winced, seeing she landed on a sharp chunk of armor left by a tank or a mech. The armor had cut deep into her side, blood reddening the metal.

44

ENLIL

Pachacamac, Peru

"Damn you, Templar."

Shoved off his feet for a second time, Enlil stood, blaster still in hand. A smile creased his face. Moments ago, he took out his rival, Ali.

He brought his eyes to the woman, his lips curling into a frown. His shot didn't kill her or maim her. He had aimed for her heart. He rarely missed. But today wasn't his day. "You're a relentless little mixed race, aren't you?" He wanted to shoot out the small portion of Anunnaki blood that snaked through her veins.

Across the way, Ali stood. She held her shoulder, and from this distance, Enlil could tell she had nothing more than a flesh wound. He'd change that. He leveled his blaster.

Several plasma bolts zipped by him, nearly taking off his nose. Startled, he shot wide of Ali. He jumped back as another blast grazed the ground at his feet. He dashed behind a blown out hoverjeep.

"I challenge you to the throne, Enlil," came a voice.

His body went rigid. Gronis. He peeked around the jeep and saw a mech's cockpit hatch open. Gronis approached him, blood oozing down his forehead. He walked as if drunk, potentially dealing with a concussion.

Enlil's brows rose, rage growing in him. The guy should be dead, strewn in pieces on the battlefield. He paused, his eyes darting around. His troops, his military vehicles, and all fire had ceased, including the Space Templars'. His soldiers slowly walked toward the jeep he hid behind, their weapons down.

"What's the meaning of this?" he spat.

"I challenge you to the throne." Gronis continued to approach, barely able to walk, clearly out of his mind. "You must accept."

Enlil laughed. "I accept."

"Then come out, you coward."

This would be the easiest kill in the history of a king to a challenger. How dare a man, let alone a councilman, impede keeping Nibiru safe and alive?

Enlil lifted his blaster, stepped out from behind the jeep and took a shot. Gronis lifted his weapon a moment too late and blood splattered from his chest. Gronis dropped like his fallen mech.

A whirling sound came at Enlil, like a fan blade moving quickly. He looked to see Ali's arm extended in his direction. He swallowed hard when he saw the sword spinning at him. An instant later, his ribs cracked as the sword sliced through his chest.

He dropped his weapon and fell to the desert floor, the sword sticking deep in the ground, pinning him. He wrapped his hand around the hilt to pull the sword from him, then yelped when it electrocuted and burned his skin.

He let his arms lay wide, his back arched. "Well, brother." He winked at the black clouds hanging above and grinned. "You got your wish." He'd meet his family on the other side and beat the crap out of his brother if he could.

He huffed and cringed, each breath was like scraping a knife against his lungs. He never had an heir or anyone to groom to assure white powder gold continued unabated in the Nibiru atmosphere, and that slavery remained in place throughout the galaxy in the form of mine workers and mine societies.

He failed his people. He failed everything. "Death, take me swiftly."

He slipped lower on the blade, blood streaking across it. He moaned, a sharp pain moving up and down his spine. He screamed at the sky. "Take me, dammit."

Footsteps came near. Ali grabbed the hilt. Her lips pursed, she spit in his face. "Your time on Earth ends now."

4 5

ALI

Pachacamac, Peru

Ali kicked Enlil's blaster away from him, her chest heaving. She wanted to chop the snake's head off, crippling his army for what they did to her father, for what they attempted to do to Earth's people.

With her fingers gripping Sol's hilt, she pulled the sword out, and Enlil screamed. His hands came to his chest. He looked at the blood on his hands, his eyes like saucers. He reached for his other blaster holstered at his hip.

Ali slammed her boot into his hand before his fingers met his gun's grip. He pulled his hand back to his chest, a few fingers bent in the wrong direction.

She unholstered his weapon and lifted her eyes to the growing crowd, Anunnaki and Templar alike. She didn't have time to think about how strange two armies, both wanting to kill each other moments ago, now abruptly took pause to assemble at the challenge between Enlil and some other guy.

And she didn't care. She turned away, face slack, tears beginning to form again. She spun again quickly, her muscles flexed, and pointed the gun at Enlil. She brought her eyes to his. "You took my dad. He was all my mom had. He was everything to me." Her tears dripped on Enlil. "Why? He was a good man."

"Admiral Shae Lutz was a noble adversary." Enlil blinked as if doing his best to stay conscious. "You should be happy he's dead. There's honor in that."

"Why did you come here? You couldn't just leave us alone?" She wanted answers. She didn't know why, but perhaps it'd give her more reason to kill him. "You just kill to kill?" She balled up her fist, her finger pushing through the trigger guard.

"I did what I had to do for my people." He coughed, wincing. "And your father did the same. My people will die without me. I put part of that blame on you and on your father. There's a sick hate that I have for you, Ali, more so now than ever."

"Hate." Ali nodded. She lowered to her knees and pressed the muzzle against his head.

"Do it, Ali. Kill me. Take my pain away."

She pulled back, the word hate repeating in her mind. Hate. Hate. Hate. She slowly shook her head. Her dad wouldn't kill because of hate. He'd kill to protect. He'd kill to preserve goodness. He'd kill in defense of his family and in defense of his own people. But never for hate.

She closed her eyes, the love of her dad overcoming whatever she had for this piece of ebb lying on the ground next to her. She stepped back, another tear dripping on Enlil, this time on his cheek. "This is for my father."

He nodded, closing his eyes, and turned his head to the side. "Do your best."

She turned and walked by Daf, who stood, her head down at the man who tried to take Earth. Ali walked by an Anunnaki soldier, his face expressionless and covered in dirt, his height twice hers. His eyes were innocent, like a teenage soldier who hadn't experienced life long enough to have fear or judgment of the situation at hand.

Striding past, the Templar dipped his head. His eyes beamed wisdom that bore years of war and combat. Reading his eyes would be like reading a history book.

She halted in front of him and handed the Templar the blaster. She bit her bottom lip, doing her best to stop her quivering chin. He held pain in his eyes, mirroring hers as if he could feel the loss of her father as much as she.

She continued forward, noticing Sabra pulling a man into a standing position. It was the man Enlil shot, the one who threatened Enlil's throne. His chest now concaved and blood-drenched, the challenger to Enlil's kingship was somehow alive. He carried a gun and limped, his arm around Sabra's shoulders as he made his way toward Enlil.

Ali walked and walked, finally making it to Shae. She sat next to him, legs crossed. She looked up to see CJ carted off into a craft. He gave Ali a thumbs up before the door shut.

She took Shae's hand in hers and lowered her head. The sound of a blaster whirred, and a cheer engulfed the battleground. She flinched at Enlil's death, but only a flinch. She brought Shae's hand to her heart, rocking back and forth. "Thank you for finding me. Being with you was the best time of my life. I'll never forget what you meant to me, how you filled my heart and gave me life again. I love you so much."

She furrowed her brow. Was his chest moving? She looked closer. He breathed, though it was barely noticeable. She stood, screaming, "Medic."

A woman broke from the crowd surrounding Enlil's execution and sped toward her, more medics in tow. The woman, wearing a helmet and slick jumper suit, crouched by Shae's side. She pulled a wand from her utility belt and scanned him. Worry in her eyes, she glanced at Ali. "He's holding on but doesn't have long."

Ali watched, her fingers splayed on her chest, as they slapped Shae on a hover gurney. They hurried toward a ship, and up its ramp and out of view. Ali took a step forward, then dropped to the ground when the ship lifted and flew toward the clouds.

Why didn't she accompany her dad? She looked at the ground, her mind numb. She didn't know how long she'd been there before Sabra helped her up. Eden, with a bandaged side accompanied her, and Daf walked with them.

"My dad," Ali mumbled.

"He's in the best hands the galaxy's got," replied Daf. They walked toward a ship, each step Ali took dull and heavy.

Ali didn't know when, but Sabra had ordered the Anunnaki to leave through the portal. They did. The man who challenged Enlil, sending a plasma blast through Enlil's skull, named Sabra the new Nibiru queen. He then faded away, death taking him.

Ali sat in the ship, curled up, her knees pulled into her chest, her mind on her father. Daf spoke to her, rubbing her back, but she couldn't make out what Daf or anyone said. Her mind was a cloudy mess, caught between black and white, that saw and heard nothing but gray.

They flew her to a military installation. The rest of the night blinked in and out, fading between thoughts and reality. Upon landing at the installation, the plane taxied into a hangar. Sabra handed her Shae's vidcom, and told her a Space Templar found it on the battlefield. "Is my father alive?"

"They're working on it. He's moving between this reality and the one beyond." Sabra touched her shoulder, then left the plane.

Ali walked down the steps, exiting the plane as well. She leaned against a wall, a light flickering above her, buzzing. "Make it, dad. Please." She slid to her rear. She couldn't wait any longer. She pulled the vidcom out of her pocket, pressed on it, and called her mother.

Helen answered, her holographic image hopping above the comm. Her smile faded into dread. "Oh, no. What is it, Ali?"

"Dad." She cupped her mouth with one hand, tears streaming without end. "I don't know if he'll make it."

Helen held down a frown, her strength to hold a smile, her courage to keep her composure for her daughter, more than Ali had in a thousand lifetimes. "Where is he?"

"I don't know. The Templars are working on him."

She spoke, her voice cracking. "Your father and I knew he may not live through this. I feared for both of you." Her eyes welled, and she put up a finger. "Hold on."

She left the vidcom and came back moments later, holding a piece of paper. "This is for you, Ali. It's a letter from your father. He wrote me one and you one, just in case. When you get here, it's yours to read if you can. But hold strong. If I know your father, he's stubborn. Death won't take him easily."

"Read the letter now, Mom."

Helen paused, then nodded. She unfolded the letter. "Dear Alison, my daughter, the apple of my eye…"

Ali didn't hear the rest. Her eyes closed as her father's smiling face came to mind, as well as the memories of him helping her read as a child, bucking hay, play fighting with her dolls, and letting her be the kid she wanted to be.

As a kid, when she thought she'd lost him for the rest of her life, he miraculously came back. Few were that lucky, and as her mother ended the letter, Ali smiled. "Pray for a miracle."

Helen touched her heart. "He's right here in both our hearts. He'll come home."

Ali placed her hand on her own heart, hoping her mother spoke the truth. But she hadn't seen him, the amount of blood loss, his body ravaged with bullets. She took a long, deep breath. "I'll see you soon, Mom."

"Yes, you will."

She turned off the vidcom, eyeing the plane parked across from her. Daf's boot steps clanged across the structure. She halted in front of Ali. "CJ made it. He's in a healing chamber right now. Dexter's behind Templar bars. And Sabra and the Space Templars destroyed all portal links." She sat next to Ali.

Ali leaned her head against Daf's shoulder. "Thank you for everything."

"I'm here for you."

"I know."

"I'll be here for you as long as you need me."

She wrapped her arm around Daf, hugging her. "Thank you."

"You're my best friend, Ali. That's what best friends do."

Ali nodded, feeling the weight of her head heavy against Daf's shoulder. She went to say something, but sleep took hold. She dreamt of her dad, her as a child, running around the field like they used to, playing games she had no names for.

EDEN

Earth Orbit

Eden lay on her back in *Swift*'s viewing room, staring out the sky-view glass ceiling. She stared at Earth, its white clouds, its blue oceans, and a continent known as North America stared back at her.

Her side hurt, but it was nothing the Suficell Pods hadn't already helped tenfold. She let out a deep breath, her heart still pumping hard from the hell she'd been through, and the responsibility she had in front of her.

Oddly, she didn't hold apprehension. Her nerves didn't tingle as much as they used to when she thought of leading a massive Space Templar organization. Nor did her mom haunt her mind, her last words to her mother still firmly planted in her brain. They had somehow catapulted Sonya out of her life. At least for now.

"About time you came to see me." Eden turned her head, the door to the viewing room sliding open. Nyx and Jantu stepped inside.

Nyx rolled her eyes. "You felt us. Well, aren't you Miss Amazing?" She cracked a smile.

"Her Sight is getting better," said Jantu.

They sat next to her, and Eden moved into a sitting position. "I couldn't keep them alive." Her heart sank at her words. She eyed the wall, shaking her head. "I watched them die."

Jantu put his hands together at his chest. "Skye and Enki are both in a dimension where you need not worry about them."

Eden nodded. "I don't doubt that." She cleared her throat. "How's the state of the fleet?"

"No change," answered Nyx. "We didn't as much as throw a rock at the Anunnaki armada. They jumped in and soon after, jumped out of Earth's system. Almost too uneventful, if you ask me."

Jantu leaned to the side. "As queen, Sabra stopped the invasion. She did so only minutes after being named queen in the land of Peru."

"The country of Peru," corrected Eden.

Jantu nodded. "Also, the monks designated us your secondhand helpers."

Eden screwed up her nose and furrowed her brow. "And what's that exactly?"

Jantu raised his hand. "I'm your secretary."

"And I'll be helping train you in the Sight every stupid day until you're at my level, and then you see the monks in Bali again," complained Nyx.

"I see."

"And the monks gave you a bodyguard," said Jantu.

Eden's eyebrows lifted. "Grand Masters have a security detail?"

Nyx lowered her eyes, picking at the floor. "No, but this isn't like any bodyguard we'd recommend. It's to advance you, to keep you on your toes, and to help you get over some trauma."

Eden palmed her forehead. She couldn't help but laugh.

"Yes," answered Jantu. "It's Sleuth."

Eden shrugged, letting out a gush of air. She tried to get mad, but either the numbness from war had hold or the idea of him didn't faze her as much. "Well, I guess we grew together...a little."

Nyx stood. "I'd say a lot." She reached for Eden's hand.

Eden let her help her up. "What do you mean?"

"He's different, and it's not because of that cool-looking arm. He didn't moan, curse, or throw a tantrum when we told him his new position. He accepted it, and none of us caught what we usually catch when we Sight Sleuth."

"What do you usually catch?"

"His past memories torching his mind. He'd been abused his entire childhood. But now it's as if he's calmed and as if he matured after Enlil died. Not by much, mind you, but with Sleuth, a minor improvement is a major improvement."

Jantu moved to stand and headed toward the door. "It's time to go."

"Where are we going?" asked Eden.

"To the President of the United States. Your first diplomatic mission awaits." He stopped in stride, smiling. "You ready for this, Eden?"

An image of Skye smiling at her came to mind. He gave her a wink and a nod. She grinned and cupped her hands like Skye used to do. Her heart felt light, her mind holding less weight. "Yes. I'm ready."

ALI

Unknown

Daf stood in front of Ali, her hands on her hips. Ali looked at the Starjumper waiting to take Daf to planet Aurora. She eyed Ali. "It's no problem at all. I can help on your farm. I can do what you need until you don't need me anymore. My family is safe and fine. Plus, they've seen enough of my face."

"You won't need to. My dad's going to make it." Relief washed over her, hearing her words out loud.

It had been a day, and Ali stood in another hangar. They flew her to the United States but didn't specify what state or what base. She wanted to see her dad more than anything, to be by his side. She wasn't allowed. Initial reports claimed Shae significantly improved in just a few short hours, Space Templar technology doing its work. Templar doctors conducted critical surgery and other methods on Shae, and any distraction wouldn't be in Ali's best interest. Or Shae's. Hence, she'd be updated, but not allowed to hold his hand.

An American soldier walked by, pushing a twelve-foot tall Anunnaki that lay on a long table. He wheeled the dead man toward the back of the hangar. Pressing a button, they buzzed him in. He disappeared behind doors that automatically locked when they shut.

Ali dipped her head toward the doors. "You'll let them experiment on a dead ET?"

"They won't find anything other than bigger organs."

"And what happened to the Blueline Project?"

"Not our business. We'd love to dismantle them, but we've already stepped too much into human's crap if you know what I mean."

"So, you're going to let them continue?"

"They'll grow, cause issues, then die down like agencies do. But, in the meantime, Sabra explained to me that without a way to open the portals, the Blueline Project will have to screw with something else on your planet. The Anunnaki portal openings won't be one of them."

Ali rubbed her face, trying to get the sleep out of her eyes. "Well, that's good." She'd slept maybe an hour on Daf before someone woke her to guide her onto a plane for a flight to this undisclosed hangar. She hadn't slept since. "The United States government didn't get any Anunnaki or Templar technology, did they?"

Daf shrugged. "I don't know. That's not in my wheelhouse. Sabra only gave me a small bit of information. I'm just a grunt."

"You're more than that."

"I know." Daf grinned. "I'm pretty damn awesome, aren't I?"

Ali threw a gentle jab at Daf's shoulder. "Meh. I wouldn't go that far."

Daf giggled. "So, one more chance. Let me help you on the farm."

"We can handle it."

"Are you sure?"

Ali gave her thumbs up. "I got it. You get to your family. I'm not going to take you away from them. But when will I ever see you again?"

"I'm coming back one of these days."

"Let's hope in peace and not to defend my planet."

"With Sabra as the Anunnaki queen, I think you'll have some outer Earth peace for a while."

"Good." Ali pulled Daf into a hug. "I'll miss you all over again."

"Yeah, me too." Daf hugged her tighter. "Take care, all right?"

Ali nodded, pulling away. She grabbed a piece of paper out of her pocket. "They gave this to me en route here. Tell them I decline but thanks for thinking of me."

Daf eyed the paper. "The Space Templars tried to recruit you again?"

"Yes, as a captain. Even going as far as drawing out a recruiting letter on paper instead of on a holopad."

"Where's Sol?"

"In Templar hands. Tell Starship *Tranquil* I'll always remember her, and that someday, someone of the bloodline more worthy than me will fly her."

"Will do. But more worthy ain't gonna happen." Daf gave her one last hug and twisted around. She walked to the Starjumper, waving goodbye. "See you, Chief."

Ali chuckled. She'd almost forgotten her old rank as a mech miner on planet Eos. She waved back. "See you, lacky."

She watched Daf enter the ship. The hangar doors opened, and outside, rain drenched the surrounding forest landscape.

The Starjumper lifted off and flew into the overcast, gray sky. "Bye Daf." She stared for a while until the doors shut. She sighed. "I hope I see you again."

She dug into her back pocket and pulled out the vidcom. Turning it on, she called Helen. Her mom popped on the screen, her inner glow filling Ali's heart. "Mom, they tell me I'll be home in a few hours."

4 8

EDEN

The Whitehouse, Washington, D.C.

A day after Enlil died, Eden sat in the oval office, Grand Master duties already at hand.

Harry S. Truman sat at his desk in front of three windows at the office's south end. An empty shot glass sat to his side on the desktop. He caught Eden glimpsing it. He looked at the shot glass himself. He grinned. "Just one a day, ma'am. It keeps my juices going."

He wore a navy-colored suit, and a red, white, and blue checkered tie. The thin-rimmed, round glasses fit his face well, rounding the rest of his features. He had gray hair parted to the side. He didn't hold as many wrinkles as she thought a leader of a country would.

That made her feel better. Perhaps leading a sizeable group, such as the Space Templars, wouldn't be as difficult as she imagined.

She sat on one of two sofas in the room, a table between. Looking over her shoulder, her eyes passed Sleuth and several monks who stood behind her.

Sweeping her eyes back to Truman, she caught sight of a long clock next to the Oval Office's northeast door. An oval carpet lightened the room. The presidential seal was monochromatically designed on the carpet through varying depths of the cut pile.

Truman cupped his hands, resting them on his desk. He leaned forward. "You brought some interesting bodyguards with you."

"The perks of being a Grand Master."

The Balinese monks, wearing orange robes, their faces expressionless, insisted on Sleuth being on her security detail. Something in him had changed after the battle in Peru, but not everything. A sense of loyalty, for some odd reason, now imbued him. His mind, though, was still a mesmerizing mess, the opposite of what Nyx and Jantu mentioned. But the monks explained she and Sleuth could work on their similar past issues together. Yes, the monks had interesting customs, but hopefully effective.

"You assure us we won't have another invasion like this?" A hopeful gleam sparkled in Truman's eyes.

"With me as Grand Master, I assure you. With the Nibiru king dead, a leader within the Space Templars' ranks became the new Nibiru queen. She runs the planet now."

He sighed. "Okay, and your assurance is all and well, but there's still something we ask to protect ourselves from future... potential...invasions."

"I'm sorry, Mr. President. We'll protect you if such a situation arises again, but we cannot give you technology." She paused, turning her head toward a monk, and then back to Truman. "The material you commandeered from the battle wreckage no longer remains in your custody."

Truman flinched and sat up straighter. "What do you mean?"

"We took it back."

He scrunched his brow, then softened when the phone rang. He put his finger up. "Excuse me." He answered it. "Thank you, Susan. Yes, patch him through." He leaned back in his chair, tapping his finger on the desk. "Well, if it isn't President Rivero. What can I do for you?"

Truman nodded, his lips fading into a straight line. "Jose, I apologize. I—" He nodded again. "Yes, we had some military exercises in Peru." He grimaced. "No, the locals didn't see ten-foot-tall men or ships flying into space. If so, that wasn't us, and we don't know where they'd get such an idea."

He let out a sigh. "Jose, you'll have to take that up with your last president, Manuel. He allowed this exercise, and it's not our fault you won the election, and out of spite he didn't inform the incoming administration."

Truman frowned. "Oh, you took it up with him. And he's stating he knows nothing about it?" He hesitated and eyed Eden. "Listen, Jose. Let me get back to you and sort this all out. It's a big misunderstanding." He lowered closer to the phone's cradle. "Yeah. Okay. Yes. I understand. I have important business here in the office. Yeah. I have to go. Jose, yes, got to go." He hung up the phone, rolling his eyes. "Apparently, there was some situation down in Peru." He winked.

"Other than the technology we can't give you what else would you like to request from us?"

"Yes, ma'am." He put his hands back behind his head, breathing loudly. "We have a problem with the Russians. They're getting a little ahead of themselves if you know what I mean."

Eden stood. "Thank you, Mr. President. If there's nothing else, it's time for us to go."

He stood at once. "Hear me out."

"Before I leave for my swearing-in on planet Aurora, I'll give you something in exchange for helping a friend." She pulled a vidcom from her pocket and set it on his desk. "Take that apart, study it, reverse engineer it, and you might figure out a better way of chatting with someone on something that doesn't require a long cord attached to an ugly contraption."

"The contraption's called a phone."

"Yes, the phone. What I gave you will do you one better than a phone."

Truman shrugged. "Thank you." He picked up the vidcom and held it in both hands. "I've played with one of these before, but you Templars never let me keep one." He cleared his throat. "Okay, and who's this friend of yours, and how can I help this person?"

4 9

ALI

Lowell, Michigan

TWO WEEKS LATER

Ali sat across from her mom at the dining table. The morning sun shone through the kitchen window, highlighting the checkered linoleum floor. A week after Shae finally came home, they quietly chomped on his favorite morning desert, cinnamon buns.

Without Shae working the farm, and with Helen's brother taking on a job requiring him to move out of town, it was just Helen and Ali for the moment. Shae rehabilitated in bed upstairs, his body healing from the trauma that would have killed most others.

"Time to learn how to farm," said Ali over a mouthful of food.

Helen took another bite. "I can show you some things. My brother could have stuck around and shown you everything."

"It's not his fault. He couldn't turn that job down."

"For his sister, he could have." Helen stared off through the window. "We've got no money left."

Ali stopped eating. "What do you mean?"

"We've been having problems with the farm for quite some time. After you and your dad came back, he helped, but not enough."

"Why didn't you tell me this before?"

"I didn't want to bother you. In the meantime, I can't fix up the tractor. I can't hire help. We're out of money."

"We'll figure it out."

Helen drooped. "We have a month of cash left upstairs. That's for food and bills, and then we're clear broke."

"I'll get a job."

"We'll need to sell the farm, Ali. It's getting too hard for me. Before your father returned from being gone for over twenty years, I had someone interested. Plus, being a farmer isn't a career for you. You deserve to do what you love, and I know farming isn't a passion of yours."

"Wanting to be a farmer or not, you love this place, Mom. We'll work on the farm and make enough money to hire good hands. And a tractor."

"Farmers don't take nicely to women doing business."

"Well, they'll have to."

There was a knock on the door, and Ali paused. No one came around their house, and with the neighbor harvesting, which Ali should do now even without a tractor, she doubted it was them.

Ali walked to the door. Opening it, a man and a woman stood before her, caps on their heads, and pulled down over their faces. They wore blue post office outfits.

"Howdy, ma'am," said a man with a heavy southern accent. He handed her a clipboard with a pen and paper attached. "Courtesy of Harry S. Truman."

"Courtesy of Ha—" A truck pulled up, towing a brand new tractor. Another truck was right behind it, with two new Ford coupes on a long trailer.

"The tractor, the truck towing the Fords, and the Fords are yours." He pointed behind Ali, toward the back door past the kitchen and dining room. "We also took the time to install a few more things in your backyard."

Ali cocked her head to the side. "What?"

"Look, ma'am."

Ali marched toward the back door. What was going on? Her mom sat at the dining table, her mouth ajar.

"Who are they, Ali?"

"I don't know." Ali hurried past her to the door. She looked out the window, her eyes widening. "What are those?" She turned the knob and pushed open the door. There stood two large wooden structures. They stuck out like sore thumbs. How did they get there? They hadn't been there yesterday.

She heard footsteps behind her, too heavy to be her mom. Turning, the two delivery people came through the kitchen, walking toward her. They pulled off their caps, and Ali gasped. "Daf? CJ?"

CJ giggled. "You guessed 'er, Chester."

Daf raised her arms in a hug. "Hey, pretty lady."

Ali froze. "What the heck are you two doing here?"

"I said I'd be here for you," said Daf, taking Ali into a hug. "And I meant it. Plus, CJ over here likes you."

Ali backed away and eyed CJ. "Okay, seriously. What are you doing here, and what's with all these new toys you brought with you?"

"Since you won't join the Templars and hang out with me, I decided to join you." Daf twirled a strand of her black hair. "We've been watching you and know you need help. So we're making this farm a new Templar training ground."

Ali put her hands on her hips. "What?" She tipped her head toward the wooden structures. "We have to get those out of here."

CJ walked past Ali and down the back steps to the yard. "But those are beautiful. It's harmless down here. Grand Master Eden Gaines told us we'd be fine with it."

"Too big. Make smaller ones. We might have some permit issues with them, too." Ali put her hands up. "Okay, let me get this straight. You'll train on my land?"

Daf nodded. "We'll farm on your land, training our intern agriculturalists here on the most beautiful planet in the galaxy. We aren't training troops here. That would be hard to hide. In exchange for you allowing this, Ali—and I'll make you allow this—you'll have the best and most productive—"

"I'll be the salesman." CJ pointed to his chest.

"When will you bring your farmers for training? Heck, the U.S. government will see your craft, and so will the neighbors."

"We made a deal with your government. And we have ways for your neighbors not to see us, plus we'll only be coming and going like every three months, each time with new interns. It won't be that big of a deal," said Daf.

Ali twisted around to see her mom's face tight in a smile. "Ali doesn't get to decide. I do. You both are most welcome here, along with however many interns that would like to help with the farm."

Ali pointed to the two houses. "But get those out of here."

"Where are we going to live?" asked CJ.

Ali looked around, a bit confused. "What do you mean?"

Daf kicked at the ground playfully. "Well, we're hoping to live here for a while, then go back and forth between our duties on Aurora and your farm."

"You'll live with me?"

CJ bobbed his head up and down. "Yep. If you let us."

Ali eyed them both, not believing her ears. "And those vehicles out front are really mine and mom's?"

CJ nodded. "Yep."

"Wow." Her face brightened. "I mean, wow." She brought them both into a hug. "If you can till the land, and make us money to survive, then you're more than welcome here."

"You forgot the because we're friends part, too, Ali," said Daf.

"That too. But make those structures smaller."

CJ crossed his arms. "Will do. But first, in order to complete this agreement, we've got to go to dinner, then dessert."

Ali pointed at him and then at her chest. "Just you and me?"

"Yes, it's…uh…in the contract."

Ali lifted her brows, looking him up and down. "Nice try."

CJ looked at Daf, his face twisting into a playful frown.

"Try again later," said Helen, standing next to Ali. "She'll change her mind."

"Oh, my Guild." Ali backed up, unable to stop shaking her head and not believing what just occurred. "I'm at a loss of words. You're really going to help mom and me?"

CJ lifted his chin, looking at the sky. He puffed his chest out and raised his voice. "We're Space Templars. We're the most loyal bunch of whackos you'll ever meet. And we have your back through thick and thin. Once a Templar, always a Templar. We help the most vulnerable, those who can't defend themselves, and make way for peace in the gala—"

"That's great. But you're still not getting dinner with me."

He slapped his hands together. "One of these days."

Ali grinned. "Well, maybe." She pulled CJ and Daf into another hug. Letting go, she asked, "When do the interns arrive?"

Daf thumbed over her shoulder. Ali jerked back, her hand coming to her mouth. "You're kidding me." Men and women were fanning out into her field.

"They start today, my friend," Daf told her. "Nothing better than the here and now." She smiled. "Look behind you."

Ali did. She didn't know whether to jump up and down in happiness or droop. Sol gleamed back at her. Its blade was thrust in the ground, the sword case in a small man's hand. A Bawn. "Thun?"

"We were all set, ready to defend Earth when the Anunnaki Armada retreated. We didn't get to fight, Ali." Thun's lips turned down.

"Come here." Ali motioned for a hug.

Thun grinned from ear to ear, running like a child happy to see his mom. He grabbed hold of her waist and squeezed his arms around her. She held him tight. "It's great to see you, but why is Sol back in my presence?"

Daf crossed her arms. "It's yours until you die, Ali. And…"

"And what?"

"Apparently there's this cousin, two steps removed, from Sabra. He's starting to cause some political upheaval in the galaxy. He's not too happy there's a female Anunnaki leader, and he's pissed that we're halting slave activity worlds."

"What does that have to do with me and Sol?"

Thun stepped back, looking up at her. "Well, just in case, we have Starship *Tranquil* parked nearby."

"Parked where?"

"At the bottom of Lake Michigan," said CJ. "If it ever comes to that, we hope you—"

Ali threw up her hands, cutting him off. She rolled her eyes. "It's just one thing after another with those Anunnaki."

SHAE

Lowell, Michigan

Shae leaned on his crutches and lifted a hand to touch the window. Cool against his skin, he attempted to open it. He grunted, his body too weak. Saying hello to his friends in the backyard below would have to wait.

He chuckled. Thun hugging Ali, and Daf, CJ, and Helen by her side, life couldn't be better. More Templars walked toward them from the wheat field. From watching the interaction below, he could tell they were here to help.

The Space Templars never ceased to amaze him.

He lowered to a seat on the bed, his body aching less than yesterday. Each day presented a step closer to a healed body. Riddled with so many bullets, he doubted he would have lived had he been taken to a local hospital.

The Templars worked on him for hours, used devices, gadgets, and gizmos he'd never witnessed before. And in a day, they claimed him healed enough to survive. Three days later, after several more tests and treatments, they gave him the all-clear. They shuttled him home from the moon base.

A week later, he could walk around. He dared not try to make it down the stairs and potentially falling. Reversing the Templars' healing work didn't seem like a smart idea.

A painting of a white rose, a gift from Devon Gray who was also known as Robert Rose, hung on the wall. Before Shae left the moon, Devon came for a visit, his mentor Naveya by his side. "I made this for you."

"Thank you." With shaky hands, Shae held it. "Why the rose?"

Naveya, her aura brighter than the last time Shae met her, chimed in. "The ivory rose represents perfection. No matter what happens in life, it's always for your personal growth. There is perfection in that."

Devon touched his chest. "And for me, it's love. You're the reason everyone I know is alive. Back on Starbase Matrona, you led us to safety. For that, we all love you."

"Thank you."

After a lengthy visit, they went on their way. Naveya kissed Shae's forehead. Devon shook his weak hand. And now Shae sat here, in his home, surrounded by love. The painting, the Templars outside, and his wife and daughter.

He brought his hand to his Space Templar necklace. It hung around his neck, and he squeezed the pendant.

His eyes shut as if on their own accord. In his mind, he lifted into the air, across green terrain, to a massive body of water. "Lake Michigan," he said to himself.

Submerging into the water, he sunk into the depths of the lake. Sun rays beamed through, highlighting yellow perch, lake trout, and largemouth bass. Sinking deeper, the light faded into darkness and finally, to black.

After several minutes, he halted. A light turned on, and then another, and another, until an enormous starship brightened. A starship next to it blinked on as well, both shimmering in brilliant silvers and golds.

Both ships spoke in unison. *Hello, Fleet Admiral Shae Lutz.*

"*Ascension*, it's nice to see you again." He shifted his focus to Starship *Tranquil*. "And great to see you too. But why are you here?"

To observe you more easily.

"But why?"

You're family. And we don't leave family.

Shae felt another reason. "You're not telling me everything."

Tranquil and *Ascension* illuminated more.

Humanity has a lot of pitfalls ahead. And all I can say to you is that if you need us again, we're here to protect and serve. And we have many waiting on the moon base to keep humanity safe from outside sources.

"But what about helping the Space Templars?"

They will be fine.

Shae put his hands together at his chest as if in prayer. "Thank you." His eyes shot open, and he again sat on his bed, staring at Robert Rose's painting. He pushed up on his crutches and leaned forward. Touching the glass window and grunting a second time, he pushed the window open.

Everyone looked up. Ali and Helen smiled.

"What are you doing, dad?"

"Enjoying life, I guess." He grinned. "Helen, are you going to ask our fine friends and family for dinner?"

She tilted her head to the side. "I thought you knew me better. Because I already have, my love. I already have."

THE END

AUTHOR NOTES - BRANDON ELLIS

JULY 18, 2020

Thank you for reading the last book of the Star Guild Saga. I spent a long time on this series, and I hope you enjoyed it. I loved every aspect of it. And, before I go, let me tell you a small bit about the backstory of the Star Guild Saga.

The main characters of this series, Petty Office Ali Johnson, and Fleet Admiral Shae Lutz, were named after my cousins. Both are brother and sister in real life.

When first rewriting this series, I was at a rustic resort in central Oregon. My cousins, who grew up next door to me, who nowadays I don't see much anymore, came to visit me at the resort. They were fascinated that I wrote books for a living. They asked question after question, and I finally said, "Well, what if I named two main characters in one of my books after you two? In fact, how about the two main characters in the book I'm currently rewriting now?"

"What? No way, that would be rad!" said Ali.

"I'm for it," responded Shae.

I had a motive, though. They mentioned they both don't read much, and that they "should." I winked and said, "When I'm done, I'll send you both signed copies. They're essentially 'you' in the book, so you'll have to read the series."

High-fives and hugs. They loved the idea.

Here's the thing: Ali, in this series, is—like I said—Ali, my cousin. This main character has my cousin's personality. She's a no-crap, no-bull type of individual. You either tell the truth or she'll steamroll over you to find that truth, and if she finds that you're lying, she'll give you a tongue-full.

That's Ali. She's strong-willed, bull-headed, and blunt. But she fights for what's right. All the time. For example, in eighth grade, she heard that our forest (we grew up on the edge of a large forest) was going to be cut down and replaced with homes. Not if Ali had anything to do with it.

She recruited me, and our mom's banded together and created a petition for Ali and I to run. Ali didn't want our childhood forest, the place we spent many days running through, exploring, making wildlife friends, to become a concrete playground surrounded by large homes.

So, we went from door to door, gathering signatures, explaining what our city council wanted to do. And we stopped the development. It wasn't until after we graduated high school that the city indeed chopped down that gorgeous forest and replaced it with homes and streets. Mine and Ali's response is another story.

I digress...

Ali was one of the best athletes in the state where we grew up (Oregon). We're the same age, and I remember in third grade she played on my all-boys basketball team, her being the only girl in the league. She dominated. The next year, the coaches in the league decided that they didn't want her in the league and told our coach that she'd have to play in the girl's league. It was a big ordeal, and my dad and her dad argued and argued with the league's coaches, but eventually my dad and uncle lost.

Ali was kicked out of the boy's league and they moved her to the all girl's league. I kid you not, she averaged forty-points a game. Through the years, she won awards in basketball, softball, and when she took up bike racing, she became the best in Oregon in her age group. Literally, #1 on her bike's front plate, which meant best in the state.

We were a sports family, so I played all the way up to college, winning awards as well; all-league basketball and all-state baseball. But Ali was something special, always the top of her league in just about every statistical category. Eventually, she was placed on the all-USA team in softball, and she was heavily recruited by colleges for basketball. She was a gymnast as well, so she had bulging legs and toned arms, and was always the fastest, strongest, and most aggressive athlete in the game.

Pregnant at age nineteen put it all to a halt, but now she has three wonderful kids that take her no-crap attitude and her all-star sports approach to being a mom to heart. She raised them well and happy. And yes, her kids were/are tops of their leagues in all the sports they played/play.

And then my cousin, Shae...The brother I never had. A couple of years older than me, he grew up next door with my cousin, Ali. Same mom. Same dad. We saw each other every day. He taught me how to play baseball and basketball. Again, my family is a sport's family. So that's what we knew.

Shae was and is a leader in everything he did and does; on the basketball team, baseball team, golf team, and now in his career. He has the "help everyone" personality and the knight in shining armor attitude. When I was a kid, he stood up to anyone who tried to bully me, and saved me from drowning when I was a youngster. Not once. But twice. You'd think I'd learn to swim before I jumped in, eh?

Growing up, I was a skinny, scrawny kid, so I was picked on a lot, made fun of, and it finally came to the point that when someone would try to fight me on the way home from school (happened all the time...I grew up in what you'd consider a suburban ghetto town), I'd say, "Do you know Shae Lutz?" Their eyes would widen since he was the most popular kid in our town. "He's my cousin. He'll beat you up if he knows you're being mean to me." They'd then leave me alone. However, one time an older boy didn't care and said he'd beat up my cousin, too. When he approached closer, I said, "Okay, I'll tell him you said that." The kid put his hands up and backed away. "Don't tell him. I'm just kidding," he cried out.

Eventually, Shae taught me how to tackle and wrestle. He taught me how to stick up for myself and as time went on, people didn't mess with me anymore. Shae, to this day, is one of the biggest-hearted individuals in the world. He'll take the shirt off his back for you, which, to me, makes Shae the Fleet Admiral of our family. Everyone's face lights when his name is uttered by a family member.

Who am I in this book? Captain Eden Gaines. Yeah, I made myself a woman. She's got my personality and my style. My weird thoughts, and my spiritual type of attitude.

And Koda? Well, he's a dog, of all things. Yes, I have my friend's dog in this series and I transformed him into a human. Koda, the dog, passed away a few years back, and was a hero to my friend. My friend asked me if I could make a hero out of Koda in one of my books in memory of him. And that's what I did.

Now you know a piece of this story's past.

And, at this moment in life, it's still lockdown and COVID is still "out there," so I'm stuck in Bali (the best place to be stuck at during a time like this). I'm on the beach typing to you right now. The waves are crashing, the sun is beating down, and I hear my nine-year-old daughter in the background on the phone with her best friend. My partner, Lotus, just laughed at something my daughter said. Life is good. It always is through the good times and the bad. In all of it, we learn.

Much love to you and yours. Thank you very much for reading.
Brandon Ellis

Facebook Reader's Group:
www.facebook.com/groups/EllisIsland/
Website:
www.brandonelliswrites.com

CONNECT WITH BRANDON

Enjoy the book? Then take a gander at Brandon's Facebook Group where you can help him and the rest of his rag-tag team of readers decide on pertinent information in the next books in this series or any other series he's writing... https://www.facebook.com/groups/EllisIsland/

His Facebook crew are fun, engaged readers, and can think of an alien race name for his books in a minute flat. There, you can read early chapter drafts for books Brandon is working on, join his ARC Team and read finished books before they are released, and much more. Again, here is the link: https://www.facebook.com/groups/EllisIsland/

And, join Brandon's Sci-Fi rebellion as well by subscribing to his newsletter. Brandon's a sucker for ancient alien information (is it real, or fake?), writing about ancient archeological sites that will blow your mind, and mixing in SciFi as well in just about every email he sends to you. Grab his free bestselling book, Starfighter: Freedom Star Book 1 (https://dl.bookfunnel.com/utmbp42qyd), to hop on his list. He doesn't spam, so sit back and enjoy the entertaining ride.

And of course, please check out Brandon's website to stay up to date with new releases.

https://brandonelliswrites.com/

BOOKS BY BRANDON ELLIS

You can find a complete list of Brandon's books on his website here:

https://brandonelliswrites.com/books/
Or at Amazon here:

https://www.amazon.com/kindle-dbs/entity/author/B00BLVIYNW

9 781649 710703